Discovering Her Delight

A Harwell Heirs Legacy Romance

Harwell Heirs Book 5

Regina Kammer

Viridium Press

Published by Regina Kammer and Viridium Press, Friday Harbor, Washington
ISBN-13: (paperback) 978-1-953496-01-0
ISBN-10: (paperback) 1-953496-01-6
ISBN-13: (ebook) 978-1-953496-00-3
ISBN-10: (ebook) 1-953496-00-8

The Harwell Heirs

Victorian aristocracy has very strict rules concerning marital connections and familial obligations. But the Harwell heirs—Helena, Sophia, and Arthur—discover love doesn't always follow the rules. Scandalous affairs force these scions of society to choose between duty and desire, deference and destiny.

Book 1: *The Pleasure Device*

Book 2: *Disobedience By Design*

Book 3: *Where Destiny Plays*

Harwell Heirs Legacy Romances

Travel beyond England's shores for these stories featuring beloved secondary characters from the first three books of the series. The Legacy novels delve into the romances of the friends, family, and intimates of the extended Harwell family.

Book 4: *A Delicate Seduction*

Book 5: *Discovering Her Delight*

Book 6: *Their Noble Deceit*

Dedication

To my mother.

Chapter One

London, England, July 1880

Kiss me kiss me kiss me.

Beatrice Smythe stood on tiptoe in the Elgin Room of the British Museum, pretending to study the ancient marble slabs, hoping her companion would steal a kiss. William Peel, however, remained absorbed in describing the battle scene depicted in the magnificent Greek frieze, his russet brown eyes flashing excitement for the story. His height set him precisely at the same level of the sculpted bodies of athletic nudes, while Beatrice had to stretch just a bit to see the figures.

Her precarious position placed her lips almost in perfect alignment with William's mouth, but not quite close enough to kiss.

He glanced at her, a crease deepening between his brows. "The Lapiths were unaware the Centaurs were unused to drinking wine—"

Beatrice rose higher on her toes. William's lips were now mere inches away.

He returned his attention to the sculpture. "So they were taken quite by surprise when, at the wedding feast—"

Marriage. Ugh.

"—of the Lapith king Pirithous, a Centaur tried to abduct the bride"—he flicked his gaze in Beatrice's direction—"wanting to take her as his own—"

William stopped, his ivory cheeks coloring a lovely shade of pink.

Her heart pounded in her ears, her chest constricted under her corset. Just one more inch and her yearning mouth would press against his—

"And the battle ensued." Did his voice hold a tremble? "The Centaurs were defeated."

William's gaze fell to her lips, now quivering from want, and his eyes widened, probably from realization of what she expected him to do. His stare proved a beat too long for rashness to prevail.

The echo of footfalls sent William retreating and Beatrice to almost lose her balance if it had not been for his heroic grasp of her elbow. She glanced behind her. A man arm-in-arm with a woman entered the gallery. Not too far behind the couple, Beatrice's chaperon, the Countess of Banbury, followed.

At least Lady Banbury had given them a chance. Or rather, had given Beatrice a chance to be alone with the object of her affection. But propriety demanded a chaperon at least *look* like she was doing her expected duty, especially when others were present.

"Lord Elgin removed these slabs from the Athenian Parthenon?" Beatrice felt compelled to show their sudden audience that she was not attempting to seduce her companion. "And dragged them all the way to England?"

"Yes." William's voice held a gravelly cast.

"And the sculptures date from when precisely?" From her own studies, Beatrice knew full well how old the sculptures were.

William cleared his throat, looking somewhat dazed. "The fifth century before Christ."

"How interesting that the story of the Centaurs and Lapiths is so much older than the sculptures themselves."

"Yes." William stared at his palm still cupping her elbow. The blush returned. His hand dropped to his side.

Beatrice smiled politely as heat rose in her cheeks. "Homer, correct?"

The loud swoosh of too much silk followed by the strong odor of French perfume meant Lady Banbury had decided to take her rôle of chaperon a bit more seriously.

"Are you two discussing Greek mythology again?" She smiled at Beatrice before hiding her expression behind her fan. "Why, in my day, a girl was content to paint or make a pretty needlepoint pillow."

Most certainly Lady Banbury had done no such thing in her girlhood. At least not by choice.

"Mr. Peel and I have only a summer to learn all we can together, Lady Banbury. Then I'm off to Girton, and he to Cambridge."

"I wish women could attend our lectures." A wistfulness imbued William's voice. "I really don't see why you cannot."

Lady Banbury gave William's arm a gentle swat of her fan. "Too much of a distraction for the young gentlemen, I should think."

Goodness. Did Lady Banbury just wink at her?

"I rather imagine having the young ladies in attendance would be motivation for the men to do well." The corners of William's mouth turned upward. "Miss Smythe is quite the scholar. She would put many of the male students to shame."

Now Beatrice's cheeks really did burn. "Thank you, William," she said softly.

The other couple finished their casual perusal of the marbles and left. Only they three remained in the Elgin Room.

Lady Banbury let out a grunt of sorts. "I need to sit. Ease these old bones of mine."

The countess was probably not much older than Mama or Papa. Still, she sighed as if she were a weary crone.

William offered a bent arm to Lady Banbury. "Shall I escort you to a bench, my lady?"

She waved her fan with a skilled flick of her wrist. "No, no, Mr. Peel. I know of a perfect spot. Just return Miss Smythe to me when you are ready."

Which meant Beatrice could have William all to herself.

"My lady?" William was clearly as astonished as Beatrice by the implication.

"Yes, yes, please go on." Lady Banbury waved her fan again. "I simply do not have the stamina to keep following you young people about. Every week a different museum, and still Miss Smythe remains unscathed. I cannot fathom what possible disrepute you might subject the young lady to here in the British Museum."

Beatrice caught William's eye with a devilish smile. *Maybe just a kiss?* He paled before looking askance. No. William would never dishonor her.

But she could not promise to not do the same.

WILLIAM SQUELCHED HIS utter enthusiasm at Lady Banbury's directive.

It was perfect. Too perfect.

He and Miss Smythe would have the whole British Museum to themselves.

Well, not really. There would be other museum-goers, like the two who'd just left the Elgin Room. But he and Miss Smythe—his Beatrice—would be able to walk through the galleries without a care. Why, they'd been given permission from the countess herself.

Like the gentleman Papa expected him to be, William escorted Lady Banbury to a bench against a wall in a nearby gallery.

"Thank you, young man. Now, I won't breathe a word of this to Beatrice's father." Lady Banbury fanned herself. "Take all the time you need, Mr. Peel."

More permission. Unbelievable.

He drew in a deep breath, fortifying himself as he returned to the Elgin Room. Miss Smythe was giving him that smile she'd been giving of late, innocence tinged with a sort of seductiveness.

His pulse picked up its pace. She obviously wanted to kiss him, had been wanting to kiss him these last few weeks during their museum adventures. And he so desperately wanted to kiss her, as well. But the moment had to be exactly right, and a furtive peck in these hallowed halls did not seem to be the optimum opportunity.

"Where would you like to go next, Miss Smythe?"

"How about the Roman Empire by way of the Egyptian galleries?"

Miss Smythe's angelic voice slid over him like warm water in a bath…which led to the unexpected thought of being nude and wet in her presence, which then startled his prick to action. Luckily, he'd bound his privates under his drawers so no evidence of his desire would be apparent.

Miss Smythe was a delight to be savored, not a prize to conquer and discard when another came along.

He checked himself. That was absolutely not what had happened between him and Lavinia—*no*, he should not think of Lavinia as *Lavinia*, but rather as Lady Foxley-Graham. It would be disastrous should he ever slip up and call the lady by her Christian name.

"That path through the galleries sounds marvelous, Miss Smythe." William held out his arm.

She looped her hand around the crook of his elbow. "William," she said quietly, "I insist you call me Beatrice. We are friends, and are allowed familiarities."

Familiarities. Once again his cock stirred. Would ancient Rome be enough of a distraction?

"Of course, Beatrice."

Arm-in-arm, they glided along the floor as if dancing, artifacts from ancient cultures floating past in a blur of history while William's attention seemed to be preoccupied with the present. Beatrice, however, had an unquenchable fascination for antique objects. The polished stone of massive sculptures, the intricate detail of a tiny porcelain scarab, the life-like quality of an encaustic Fayyum mummy portrait—each held equal interest.

Her intellectual curiosity and knowledge of history were, he had to admit, somewhat arousing.

"This portrait is so exquisite. One could imagine her in the flesh, don't you think?"

Flesh? Oh, the encaustic portrait. "Yes, it is rather good, isn't it? Well preserved. The woman is quite beautiful."

"I suppose she is."

Mortification descended. "As are you, Beatrice," he blurted.

She laughed. "Thank you, William."

He should apologize. She was more than just beautiful. She was brilliant, and she should be assured he knew that.

"Shall we go visit the Romans now?" Beatrice secured his arm with hers and began leading the way.

The Greco-Roman rooms seemed to be more popular, or perhaps more people chose to visit the museum in the late afternoon. The third exhibition gallery led to a staircase to a basement room. Perhaps there would be privacy there.

His spirits sunk the moment they arrived at the bottom step and discovered they were not the only intrepid museum-goers. However, Beatrice's enthusiasm for the display of mosaics was heartening. She pulled him toward a fragment of a mosaic floor showing a woman on horseback.

She studied the tesserae, moving her head as if following the line of marble pieces that made up the arcs of the horse's tail and the woman's flowing cloak. For an image made with tiny square tiles there were a lot of swirls and curves.

"'Atala'?" she said, reading the stone inscription. "Oh, Atalanta. There's a bit cut off at the edge." She squeezed his arm. "What is your assessment?"

That he was lucky to know a beautiful young woman who could read Greek? "My assessment? How do you mean?"

"Year, place, meaning. That sort of thing."

William studied the fragment. "It's an emblema, a scene from a larger floor. The bit on the right that's cut off implies whoever took it from the ground had no idea how to read Greek. The black border indicates the whole floor was probably made up of lots of individual scenes as this."

"I wish they had preserved the entire floor."

"I suppose somewhere there is a mosaic floor with bits cut out."

"And where do you think it's from?"

William eyed her. "You know all the answers to these questions, don't you?"

A smile slithered across her lips. "I do find all this fascinating. I try to challenge myself with analyzing artifacts, then I read the guidebook to see how well I've done."

Marvelous. "And what is *your* assessment? Of course, if you already know the answer I will tell you that is cheating."

"The workmanship, the size of the tesserae, and the use of many colors all point to an original location of a wealthy villa. However, the awkward execution of some of the details, like the horse's head, imply a villa on the outskirts of the empire, not near Rome. And a late date."

William fished the catalog from his jacket pocket and thumbed through, finding the page for the Roman gallery. "You're quite correct. Excavated at Halicarnassus in Turkey and from the fourth century AD." He put the catalog away. "How did you know? You said you've not traveled much."

"I haven't. I've seen similar objects at some of the grand homes my family has visited. I listened to all the stories from the collectors, then read all the books I could get my hands on. And I've read all of Professor Stanfield's lectures in classical archaeology."

The professor was a noted scholar of the Hadrianic era and one of the proponents of archaeology as a course of study at Cambridge. "From Lent Term?"

"And Easter Term. Papa was able to garner copies from Professor Stanfield himself."

The curiosity and intellect of the Miss Smythes of the world were precisely why Cambridge would not let young women attend lectures. The men would walk out in despondent envy.

"And if you could travel, where would you want to go most?"

Another squeeze of his arm, this time accompanied by a tiny sigh. "Italy, of course. Then Greece. And the Turkish coast where there are the ruins of so many ancient Greek cities."

"Have you seen much of our own Roman ruins?"

"No. I can't wait until I reach my majority. Then I'll have the freedom and money to hire companions to accompany me as I explore Roman Britain."

"And Italy?"

Beatrice grinned. "Everywhere."

William inhaled courage. "And will you invite your husband on such journeys?"

She colored and glanced away. "I'm not getting married."

His heart slumped. "Oh? I thought the daughters of earls were expected to marry."

Beatrice met his gaze, her gray-green eyes intense under a stern brow. "My father has no such expectations. He knows if I marry I would become the property of my husband. I would never be able to see the world that way."

"Not all husbands would be so cruel."

"The ones wanting to marry daughters of earls would be."

She was probably right.

"And I don't want to entice the wrong sort with my title, which is why I style myself Miss Smythe, not Lady Beatrice."

William attempted a smile. "Well, you're probably too clever for most men anyway."

"Not all of them." Another squeeze. "You like inscriptions, don't you?"

He nodded.

"Look there." She pointed to a mosaic of a wreath surrounding Greek script. "I would love to hear you read me every word."

He would do anything she asked of him.

* * * * *

BEATRICE LEANED HER HEAD against William's shoulder as he read the Greek inscription to her.

"Health, Life, Joy, Peace, Good Cheer, Hope."

Each utterance sounded like the words to a poem. A poem that described the life she wanted to live…

With him.

Her heart skipped a beat, then crashed to her stomach. Could one be in love and not be married? More precisely, could a woman be with the man she loved without condemnation and expectation of marriage?

Because she had no intention of marrying anyone, ever.

"That's a pleasant sentiment, don't you think?"

William's query brought her back to the present. "I suppose." She straightened. "I mean, yes." She gave him a smile. "Yes, it is."

He led her back up the stairs through the now almost empty Egyptian galleries. Beatrice dared once again to lean her head on his upper arm while they stopped before a sarcophagus. William did not flinch. In fact, it seemed he pressed his arm against her ever so slightly.

A man from the museum approached them then, saying the museum would be closing and that "an aged woman was looking for them." Lady Banbury had apparently been dozing when the museum official had discovered her, and she'd asked after her charges.

The three left the museum, Lady Banbury walking at a respectable distance behind. William kept his arm looped around Beatrice's, thrilling her.

He stopped at the curb where cabs waited. "Shall we finish our study of the British Museum next week? There's so much left to see."

"Yes, please." She did not want their summer excursions to ever end. "And then there's the South Kensington Museum. Let's do that the following week."

William thinned his lips. "I regret to say two weeks hence will have to be our final outing. My father insists our family return to Lincolnshire. He wants to take a hunting holiday before I'm off to Cambridge. He enjoys camping out."

"Camping out?" The notion sounded romantic. "Do you do that sort of thing often?"

"Every year for my birthday. And whenever Papa wants the peace of nature."

"Is it your birthday?"

William stood a little taller. "I'll be nineteen next month."

"Then I will buy you a slice of cake at the refreshment room in the South Kensington Museum. I hear it's quite lovely. And Lady Banbury does enjoy having her tea."

"She does." His smirk was adorable. "And thank you, Beatrice. I do love cake." He glanced at her with a sheepish expression. "Perhaps this autumn we could find some way to meet up while we are both at university? Attend a lecture together?" Wistfulness lingered on his suggestion.

"Visit a museum together?" she said.

He grinned. "Yes. Definitely."

Lady Banbury cleared her throat.

"William, I must return my chaperon to the comfort of her home. Shall we meet in front of the British Museum next week at our usual time?"

His face lit up as he leaned forward. She wanted to present her cheek for him to kiss. Instead, he lifted her hand to his lips and pressed a kiss there.

Anything. She'd take anything he'd give her.

CHAPTER TWO

Girton College, England, November 1880

"The tutor's questions were dreadfully difficult, didn't you think, Beatrice?"

For Beatrice, history was an exciting avocation rather than grueling drudgery, and certainly not as tortuous as some of her sister students thought. Still, pride was not a virtue, as Papa always said.

"Yes, Mildred, today's lesson certainly was a challenge." Beatrice offered a sympathetic smile as she opened her umbrella.

Mildred wrapped her arm around Beatrice's waist as they strolled across the green of the courtyard shielded from the light rain. "How do you remember all those dates?" she asked quietly.

"I think making little note cards with important information helps. You know, like names and dates of emperors. That sort of thing."

"Yes." Mildred sighed. "I suppose I could try that."

"Oh, and I highly encourage attending Miss Simons's lectures in classical studies. She truly makes history come alive by play-acting. She even wore a beard when discussing the emperor Hadrian."

"That sounds diverting." Mildred's tone conveyed she wasn't altogether convinced.

Beatrice gave her friend a gentle squeeze. Mildred was cleverer than she gave herself credit. But she was not always as disciplined in her studies as she could be. Her head was too often in the clouds.

"Do you have special plans for when you go home after term ends?" Beatrice asked.

"My family hosts an annual Twelfth Night ball. My sisters and I create magical costumes with fantastical headdresses and masks so no one knows who we are."

"How marvelous." Knowing Mildred, the costumes would be magnificent. "I've never heard of a Twelfth Night masquerade."

"I do believe it is ours alone. And you, what are you planning?"

"Spending time with my sisters. It will be the last time we are together giddy and carefree. Olivia, my eldest sister, is engaged to be married."

"Oh! When is the wedding?"

"Next summer." So poor Olivia still had a bit of time before the end of her freedom.

"You don't sound pleased, Bea."

"Do I not?"

Mildred pursed her lips. "You do not. I know you disdain marriage for yourself, but others find it an amenable institution."

Beatrice turned to her friend. "A married woman can own nothing. Not property, not a business, not even her own clothes. Her husband owns everything."

"That's why some women have marriage settlement agreements."

"Legal arrangements only available to the wealthy. Poor women often avoid marriage altogether." Beatrice shook her head. "And what few voting rights women have are only allotted to unmarried women because politicians think husbands should own our votes, as well."

Mildred shrugged. "Despite all that, if I knew a fine young man, I might consider the possibility."

"But wouldn't you rather just remain *very* good friends with the young man?"

"Very good friends—how do you mean?" Mildred's gasp a moment later signaled she understood very well what Beatrice meant. "Beatrice!"

"As an unmarried woman, I intend to own a house filled with finds from my archaeological expeditions."

"And men." A sly smile curled the corners of Mildred's mouth.

"If I discover interesting men on my expeditions, so be it."

They both giggled.

Inwardly Beatrice sighed. Only one man had ever sparked her interest. And maddeningly, although William was geographically quite close, they rarely saw each other.

"Oh." Mildred's squeak stopped Beatrice's musings. "I see Miss Dobbins. She's helping me with my Latin." Mildred pecked Beatrice on the cheek. "I must fly, Bea. I'll see you later?"

"Yes. At dinner." Beatrice stood still for a moment in the courtyard, the bite of cold air on her cheeks, the scurrying of students to avoid the rain all around.

William. The mere thought of him made her heart skip a beat.

They'd met several times at the beginning of the term, continuing their friendship by visiting the Cambridge University museums—but with groups of friends or other students. And just like as it had been in London, he never kissed her, despite her desperately wanting him to. Being with William was simultaneously maddening and glorious.

Beatrice gripped her notebook more tightly and headed toward the red brick dormitory.

She thought of him every day, during every lecture, while studying, while eating every meal.

While alone in her bed at night.

She'd learned how to pleasure herself after that fateful night in June when she'd danced with William for the first time. Mama had apparently thought Beatrice's subsequent distractedness and forgetfulness warranted medical attention.

At the office of a very eccentric doctor, an assistant used a device to help Beatrice achieve the "hysterical paroxysm," a moment of profound pleasure Beatrice could never have imagined. She'd left more energetic and emboldened, feelings that persisted during her summer outings with William.

In a subsequent visit, the doctor's assistant had taught Beatrice how to relieve physical frustrations by her own hand. Hand stimulation was as effective as the machine, and just as pleasurable.

When thoughts of William plagued her, Beatrice discovered that her hand was indeed quite effective.

She shook out her umbrella, then took the stairs to her room two by two, practically slamming into Mabel, her neighbor from across the corridor.

"You seemed determined to be somewhere," Mabel said.

Beatrice sighed. "I've a headache. I need a lie-down before dinner. I'm determined to be in my bed, I suppose."

Mabel's expression melted into one of concern. "Oh, sweetie." She patted Beatrice on the shoulder. "I'll see you at dinner, then."

Beatrice fled to her room and quietly locked the door, leaning against it for a moment. If only she could impart the knowledge of self-pleasuring to her friends. Doing so would be like a form of women's solidarity, of women's empowerment and independence.

Well, except when Beatrice pleasured herself, all she could think about was a man, which didn't seem like a particularly independent preoccupation.

After undressing to her underthings, she crawled into bed. She opened her legs and slipped her hand through the slit in her drawers. Her middle finger slid between the cleft of her sex.

She was plump and wet like she always was when she thought about William. A stroke of the little nubbin elicited a wondrous jolt of excitement that pushed her into otherworldly delight. Another stroke provoked a warm tingling. The third stroke sent her into a relaxed state where fantasy took over.

Always the same memory-turned-fantasy played in her head. She and William waltzing at the Raeburn ball as he controlled the turn of their bodies through the crowd, gliding her along the parquet floor until they were outside, alone on the terrace, his hold on her growing tighter, more demanding. Releasing her right hand to entwine her in both his arms, tilting his head, leaning forward, taking her in a kiss, his lips melding between hers, their bodies pressing together.

They then merged in an ethereal union, his breath becoming her breath, his heart beating the same rhythm as hers, their moans of pleasure in perfect harmony. Every sound, every sensation built to a crescendo, until all at once, for one precious moment, Beatrice became one with William, her William, grasping at the moment, wanting it to linger one second longer…

Beatrice stared at the dark oak beams of the ceiling as she slowed her breaths in the aftermath of climax.

Would it be anything like that when she and William became lovers?

If that ever happened. She would have to find a way to get him to kiss her first. He always got a tad nervous when she got too close to him.

Oh, William…

If she were ever to marry he would definitely be the one—

Egads! Where on earth did that thought come from? She was certain she was in love with him, but she could not compromise on her dreams. She'd convince him to be her very special friend. He could even live with her in her house. But marriage? No. Absolutely not.

She rolled out of bed. She'd read for a while, a distraction for her poor beleaguered heart before dressing for dinner.

Cambridge University, England, November 1880

WILLIAM STARED AT THE blackboard in the lecture hall, the legal terms written in chalk like unintelligible words muddled further by the drone of the professor until nothing made sense.

What was his Beatrice doing at that moment? Wearing a tight dress, just a touch of provocative scent, a string of pearls drawing attention to the low cut of her neckline…

A cough from the student next to him brought him back to the lecture hall, and the professor ending his lecture with "Good afternoon, gentlemen."

Blast it all. How long had he been daydreaming? And had anyone noticed?

William huffed in self-annoyance as he gathered his notebook and pencils and slid them into his satchel. Such moments had been getting more frequent of late.

Perhaps because it had been too long since he'd last seen Beatrice. Two weeks ago, was it? At the Fitzwilliam Museum. And no solid plans see her again.

They had mutually decided against corresponding too often, a ruse to deflect any suspicion about their relationship. Although, as they had seen each other once a week during summer, every member of his family and probably every member of hers, plus anyone close to their families knew they were courting.

But were they?

Courtship ended in marriage, did it not? And Beatrice did not want to get married. To anyone.

A nudge at his left reawakened him to the emptying lecture hall.

"Will, didn't expect to see you at a lecture on the law." Jerrod, a fellow freshman in archaeology, leaned across the row of seats in front of William.

"My father said if I were not going to read law, then I should at least avail myself of the lectures. He's a solicitor."

Jerrod chuckled.

"What're you doing here?"

"Similar. Except it's my uncle who's the solicitor." Jerrod waved at a passing student. "Care to join Linus and myself for a cup of tea?"

William shifted as if to get up. *Blast.* As always happened when he thought of Beatrice he was incredibly hard. Luckily since he'd figured out how last summer, he always bound his cock against his body so no one knew he was practically constantly in a state of arousal.

"Thanks. But you go on." William stuck his hand in his satchel and pretended to look for something. "I'll see you at the Antiquarian Society meeting tonight?"

"Wouldn't miss it." Jerrod doffed his hat before skipping away.

William continued to fuss with his bag as he listened to Jerrod's waning footfalls. A quick glance around affirmed he was quite alone.

He had to make quick work of himself. But his room was a mile away.

A *bang* startled him to attention. A mustachioed man had entered from a side door and proceeded to gather papers left by the professor.

So tossing himself off in the lecture theater was certainly not an option. He'd have to wait until he got to his rooms.

Outside, a light rain was made gloomier by a distinct chill in the air. He'd left his umbrella back in his rooms, which meant his academical gown would get soaked. William turned up his collar and trudged along Tennis Court Road, passing Fitzwilliam Street—

At the end of which was the Fitzwilliam Museum. Just the thought of the museum reminded him of Beatrice—and how hard his prick was. Maybe he could find a corner in the usually quiet library there.

He turned down the street and fished through his satchel. Somewhere he had a ticket signed by his tutor allowing him access to the library.

Blast. He'd probably left it in his rooms next to his umbrella.

Well, there was the sculpture gallery in the basement. Lots of nooks and crannies to hide in, and since it was November, not many students trying to cram for examinations.

William dashed up the steps through the imposing Corinthian columns. He shook off his gown under the classical portico modeled after Hadrian's temple to all the gods. Maybe the gods would be on his side that afternoon. He strolled casually through the picture galleries to the back, to the stairs leading to the basement. Once downstairs, he proceeded to walk with purpose, as if he were an undergraduate in want of scholarly edification and not an adolescent in need of jerking off.

He sauntered through the dimly lit sculpture gallery, passing busts of emperors and figures of gods. Even though he was the only visitor on the entire floor, guilt vexed him. There was something rather seedy about the act when done in semi-public.

Hell, there was something seedy about doing it at all, really. Most men and boys would deny they ever performed the act in keeping with what their vicars told them was right.

But if tossing oneself off was not right in the eyes of the Church, why would God himself have designed man to take so much pleasure from it?

William found a spot on the north side, away from the stairs, in the shadow of a dusty Grecian urn donated by some chap named Bunsby. His heart pounded as he unbuttoned the flies of his trousers and drawers and pulled up his shirt. He loosened the binding cloth that held his cock against his body. His erection broke free of its confines, bobbing, exhorting him to just get on with it.

He grabbed the stiff stander and tugged, a twinge of relief fluttering low in his belly, building toward ecstasy with every pull.

William knew what it was like to be inside a woman, to feel her body squeeze him with want and need, the swell of her breasts pressing against him with every orgiastic arc of her spine. He had been initiated into the act by the best, Lady Foxley-Graham, now married and very dedicated to her husband, the Earl of Petersham.

It did not matter. William had no desire for the lady now. He wanted to experience his Beatrice squeezing him, pressing into him, hear her moans of pleasure, her murmurs of gratitude.

As Beatrice was a virgin, everything she felt would be new, and he would be the man to take her to that plane of rapture, to be the first to witness her succumbing to pleasures she had never known.

He closed his eyes and saw Beatrice's beautiful face, her lips puckered as they sometimes were when she was deep in thought. A blush dusting her cheeks. He wanted nothing more than to kiss her then, to dip his tongue into her mouth, tantalize her a moment later to say there were other places a man might kiss a woman.

God, to watch her lose herself under his ministrations, to feel her writhe because of his pleasuring…

A bolt of lust surged through him, awakening him to the reality of the sculpture gallery. He grabbed his handkerchief, wrapping the fine linen around the crown of his cock as he spent his seed, stifling grunts of release with his other hand.

He exhaled a sigh, then arranged his flaccid member under his binding and restored his clothes to rights. A deep breath steadied him for the walk back to his rooms.

Tossing oneself off in darkened corners was no way to live one's life.

Was there no hope for him and his Beatrice?

CHAPTER THREE

Harwell Hall, Lincolnshire, January 1881

Beatrice surveyed the grand ballroom at Harwell Hall. While elegant dinners had been hosted over the years, the expansive space was decorated for what was purportedly the first Twelfth Night ball ever held at the ancient estate.

Light from lamps and candles glittered off silver and crystal—and the jewels of those in attendance. The event was not hosted by the Marquess and Marchioness of Richmond who actually resided at Harwell Hall. No. The event was instead hosted by their son, the Earl of Petersham and his new bride.

The new Countess of Petersham—Lavinia—just happened to be a very good friend of Papa's. Many years ago, when the countess had been known as Lady Foxley-Graham, she had worked with Papa on women's rights legislation in Parliament. With this connection, Papa had garnered an invitation for their entire family to the Harwell Hall Twelfth Night extravaganza.

And it just so happened that the Peel family were neighbors to Harwell Hall. Mr. Geoffrey Peel—William's father—and Lord Petersham were very good friends and business partners.

During the last few days at the rambling manse, Beatrice had been spending time with Lavinia, her sister-in-law Mrs. Phillips, and her niece-in-law the Countess of St. Albans. Two infant boys were related somehow. All four of Beatrice's sisters especially delighted in playing with the babies.

And while getting to know everyone in so intimate a setting had passed the time quickly, a restlessness had agitated Beatrice. She had absolutely no privacy as she shared her room with her younger sister Isabella. She simply could not perform her usual task of self-release. And fantasies of seeing William tormented her to no end.

Beatrice shifted on her feet. All of the countryside of Lincolnshire seemed to be there. But still no William.

The Countess of St. Albans approached with a polite smile. "Miss Smythe, you look positively radiant tonight."

If anyone looked positively radiant, it was the countess. She was spectacularly beautiful in her olive-green gown, a string of emerald beads around her neck glittering in the dim gaslight.

"Thank you, my lady."

"Please, call me Helena, even in company. We are contemporaries, and I consider you a friend, Beatrice."

"Yes, of course, Helena. I've enjoyed getting to know you these last few days."

Helena had a very close relationship with William, it turned out. Because their mothers were friends and their fathers were business partners, Helena and William were as close as brother and sister.

Helena slipped her hand in Beatrice's. "He'll be here soon, don't fret so."

Heat rose in Beatrice's face. "Does it show so dreadfully much?"

"Only to those who know you."

A commotion at the entrance to the hall drew their attention. Lord Petersham was boisterously greeting a very tall mustachioed man, a man with features that seemed familiar.

Mr. Peel. Which meant—

"Look, there's William." Helena squeezed Beatrice's hand. "Let's secure him for our own before one of these other lovely ladies in attendance does so."

They scurried as quickly as they could across the crowded ballroom. William saw them and waved.

"Helena," he greeted as he grasped her hands and kissed her cheeks.

"William, I'm glad you finally arrived." Helena gestured to Beatrice. "You remember Miss Smythe, do you not?"

William grinned as his gaze swept over her from head to toe. He took Beatrice's hand and bowed over it. "I could never forget Miss Smythe."

A flush burned Beatrice's neck and face. The hum of the ballroom was drowned by the slamming of her heartbeat in her ears. "Mr. Peel, it has been too long since our last outing."

Helena took William's arm, then looped her other arm around Beatrice's. She led them away from the crowd. "William," she began, "I insist you dance with me tonight. And there are other young ladies here as well. Perhaps one or two of them."

The words sliced like a knife into Beatrice's chest.

"Yes, dearest Helena. I will save you a dance. And perhaps one or two for our neighbors."

Dearest? He called her dearest?

"I only say this to remind you that you should not spend every minute with Miss Smythe. While this is not a ball during the Season, and therefore has a touch of informality, this does not mean you can act without propriety. Have a concern for Miss Smythe's reputation."

William leaned over Helena. "And when can I dance with Miss Smythe, countess?"

Helena stepped back, releasing them. "It seems a new dance is about to start. I would say now is a very good time."

* * * * *

William had dreamed of this moment ever since Papa had told him the Earl of Ryburgh's family had been invited to the Harwell ball.

But he hadn't been able to properly imagine how utterly beautiful Beatrice would look.

She was stunning in a tight dress of the palest ice blue, the fabric sleek and shiny in the glow of the chandeliers. She wore pearls like he'd imagined, but the low-cut neckline of her gown was fringed with white fur. Her tight sleeves fell below her elbow where her white kidskin gloves continued down her slender arms. Only a man who was her intimate would know her gray eyes did not match the blue of her dress, but instead had a greenish tinge.

Still, as he took her in his arms for the waltz, it was difficult to focus just on those eyes, when before him was a vision.

"Beatrice, you look lovely tonight."

"Thank you, William."

The muscles of her back relaxed into his hand.

He dared tell her his thoughts. "I've missed you so."

A blush colored her full cheeks.

"I've missed our visits to museums. I've missed our talks. I've missed being with you."

A tear glittered at the corner of her right eye.

"Darling," he whispered. "Have I said something horrid?"

"No." She released him for only the moment it took for her to wipe the tear with her gloved hand. "Your words are too perfect. I've missed you so very much, as well."

"I thought since Cambridge and Girton were close, we would see each other more often. I was unprepared for the deluge of work university life entailed."

"As was I."

"But we're here now. Together."

That brought a smile, a glorious smile that brightened her lovely visage.

He wanted her all to himself. "Is it too cold to venture outside?"

"Perhaps if you lent me your coat?"

Despite the exhortation thrumming in his chest, he waited until the waltz finished. Then he offered his arm, and with that smile that melted his heart, Beatrice looped her arm in his and they headed for the Great Courtyard.

She shuddered as winter's chill descended the instant they were outside. He stripped off his coat and draped it across her shoulders, the cold air biting through his waistcoat, linen shirt, and woolen undershirt.

He took her arm, the warmth of both their bodies mingling, and they strolled to a quiet corner of the courtyard. Despite the January weather, others strolled and chatted in the courtyard. And when one group or couple left, another took its place.

So much for being alone with his Beatrice. Whatever plans he had were thwarted by the very notion they would be seen.

At least he should tell her he wanted to kiss her, shouldn't he?

But wasn't it enough to just be with her? His heart no longer ached for want of her. His body calmed in her presence.

Besides, a kiss would not be prudent. Helena had insinuated as much.

As THEY STROLLED AROUND the courtyard the flames from torches offered a romantic light, a soft glow perfect for lovers. Beatrice squeezed William's muscular arm. When they'd danced she'd noticed his chest was a little thicker than what she remembered from last summer.

"Are you active in sport at Cambridge?"

"What? Oh. I suppose. I've been taking punts out on the river. I find the physical exertion relaxes me."

"I think it's given you a fine figure."

William stopped and turned to her. "Really?"

"Really." She reached up and rested her hands on his shoulders, then lifted herself on her toes.

His mouth parted.

She licked her lips and leaned a hairsbreadth closer.

William sucked in a mouthful of air and stepped back. "Darling, we shouldn't." He glanced around. "There are too many people. Someone might see."

Every couple in the courtyard was completely absorbed in their own conversation.

"Like Helena said, I must have a care for your reputation."

"Yes, of course." *Damn her reputation.*

"Please know that I would love to kiss you, Beatrice, but, but…propriety…"

Damn propriety. Still, now was not the time to argue. "I understand, darling."

They strolled in silence until they were on the side of the courtyard opposite the French doors leading into the ballroom.

"The family apartments are here, are they not?" Beatrice indicated the stone wall along which they walked. "I mean on the first floor."

"Yes," said William. "Is that where you're staying?"

"We're in rooms on the north side." Beatrice had to get her bearings. "Isn't there another courtyard?"

William stopped. "The family's private courtyard."

"Do you know the way?"

"Oh, Bea," he said with a sigh, "you know I do. You know I would take you there in a heartbeat." He gazed at her, his lips quivering. "But I think we've already been outside too long. We should return to the ballroom."

She shivered. "Yes, William." Anything to spare damage to her reputation.

They strolled arm-in-arm to the threshold of the ballroom. There William removed his jacket from her shoulders, then once again took her arm and led her into the space where couples continued to dance.

And her frustrations continued to seethe.

* * * * *

LAVINIA—*Lady Petersham*—greeted William and Beatrice when they entered the ballroom. William's body, surprisingly, no longer reacted to the lady's presence.

"Mr. Peel, so lovely to see you," she said. "Cambridge has been treating you well."

"Thank you, Lady Foxley—pardon me, Lady Petersham."

Lavinia laughed softly. "When one has lived with one name for decades, many people find it difficult to change." She nodded to Beatrice. "Miss Smythe, you look simply divine tonight."

Beatrice blushed and curtsied. "Thank you, my lady. As do you."

"If you don't mind, Beatrice, my husband would like to introduce William to a colleague." Lavinia searched the hall. "Ah, I see your father is with the gentleman instead." She turned a smile to William. "I would like to escort you to the gentleman in question, William." Then to Beatrice. "You don't mind? Helena is just over there. She'll find you a dance partner."

Beatrice offered a wistful glance before trotting off to Helena. William's heart broke the moment they separated.

"Beatrice is a wonderful girl, William," Lavinia said as she took his arm. "This meeting should only take a moment of your time. Then you should dance with Helena—"

"Or you?"

"Or me, or any other woman before you dance with Beatrice again."

He sighed. He just wanted to be with Beatrice. Why were there so many rules?

Lavinia led him to a corner of the ballroom where it seemed all the middle-aged men had gathered while attempting to appear interested in the party. Papa beamed the moment he espied William.

"Ah, thank you, Lavinia, for finding my son." He bowed to the countess before she took her leave. "William," Papa said as he pressed a hand to his shoulder, "I would like to introduce you to Mr. Alistair Tubney, a man with a great deal of money."

William smiled and shook the man's hand. Papa had a great deal of money. What was the fuss?

"Young William Peel, an honor and a pleasure to meet you," enthused Mr. Tubney. "I am a collector of antiquities and a financier. When I was your age, my aspiration was to be an archaeologist, but I lacked the talent. However, I can use my talent with money to fund archaeological expeditions."

That had William's full attention. "Oh?"

"For my next enterprise, I have engaged Professor Albin Stanfield."

A shiver ran up William's spine. "The foremost scholar of Hadrianic antiquities, sir?"

"The very same, my boy."

William exchanged glances with Papa, whose constrained smile showed he was trying to hide his glee.

Mr. Tubney cleared his throat. "He is here, tonight, if you care to discuss the matter with him. Although I do understand there are a great many distractions for a young man at a dance."

Professor Stanfield was at Harwell Hall? "If you please, sir, I would love to talk with him."

"Very good. He has ensconced himself with a quiet glass of brandy in Lord Petersham's private library." Mr. Tubney grasped Papa's and William's arms. "Come, let's descend upon him and cause a bit of a tumult."

BEATRICE SHUFFLED HER FEET as she stood on the fringes of the ballroom with Helena and her husband Nicholas, the Earl of St. Albans. Restlessness roiled within. The one dance with William had not been enough to relieve her agitation.

"Arthur has outdone himself with this ball," remarked the earl.

"Indeed, Nicky," agreed Helena. "Everyone seems so happy. Even Grandmama and Grandpapa."

"Lord and Lady Richmond are just happy to see their sprawling mansion filled with life again."

"True." Helena's smile was tinged with memories and understanding.

Beatrice shifted her weight. Perhaps a bit too dramatically. Or maybe she had exhaled too loudly.

"Beatrice?" Helena pursed her lips. "Oh, you should be dancing, shouldn't you be?" She turned to her husband. "Nicky?"

The earl held up his still full champagne glass. "I'll take the next one."

Helena surveyed the room until she spotted someone. She nodded upward and gave a discreet wave.

The Earl of Petersham sauntered over. He raised a brow the moment he spied Beatrice.

There was a time last summer when it seemed Lady Richmond had wanted Beatrice as a bride for Lord Petersham. The match would have been wrong for so many reasons, first and foremost being Lord Petersham had been very much in love with Lady Foxley-Graham.

For her part, Beatrice had wanted nothing to do with a man who was thirty years her elder, and, well, after she'd met William, a man who was not William.

However, she did have a fondness for Lord Petersham as he was the one who introduced her to William.

"Uncle Arthur," said Helena, "Miss Smythe has lost her dance partner. Be a good host, if you please?"

Lord Petersham shook his head almost imperceptibly. "Miss Smythe, it appears your dance partner has left to discuss archaeology in my library with a professor."

What? "Oh? And who might that be."

"A Professor Stanfield."

Beatrice tried to hold her emotions in check. Apparently not very well.

Lord Petersham leaned in. "You will not leave Harwell Hall without meeting Professor Stanfield. Trust me." He held out his arm.

She'd rather be in the library discussing archaeology, but politeness dictated she dance with Lord Petersham. She took his arm and they began to waltz.

Waltzing meant she had to pay mind to the man. He was handsome for someone as old as her father. And a skilled dancer. He exuded an attractive charm that gave her a sense of ease in his arms. As well as a sense of daring.

"My lord, is there somewhere we can go for a breath of fresh air? Somewhere that is not the Great Courtyard teeming with party guests?"

He seemed startled. One corner of his mouth lifted. "I believe so, Miss Smythe."

When the dance finished, he took her by the arm and led her across the Great Courtyard and through a passageway on the opposite side. They exited onto a sparsely lit and empty courtyard, the bite of winter and a sense of disquietude sending a shiver down her spine.

"This is the family's private courtyard, is it not?"

"Yes. My apartments are across the way." He pointed to a dull light shining through diamond paned windows.

Panic gripped her for one moment before dissipating. Lord Petersham was not the sort to try to lure her into some indiscretion.

Rather she was the one with indiscreet intentions.

"I suspected you had something to ask of me, Miss Smythe."

She did. She just had no idea how to proceed.

"I suggest you just out with it."

She sucked in air. "I want you to kiss me," she blurted.

A profound silence descended, followed by a heavy sigh.

"Kiss you? Miss Smythe, you do realize I am a married man?"

"And I think I was considered as a wife for you at one point."

He grumbled. "Miss Smythe…"

"And you can tell Lady Petersham if she asks that you had kissed me last summer."

He shook his head. "I do not lie to Lady Petersham."

"Oh. I suppose you wouldn't." They seemed too much in love.

"Why are you asking this of me?"

"There's so much drama, so much expectation. I just want to get it over with."

"Get it—" Lord Petersham glanced away with pinched lips. "Miss Smythe, I hardly think this is an appropriate request."

She sighed. "I suppose it was foolish of me to ask."

And then his arms were around her, his face so close, too close, his mouth on hers, stifling her gasp of surprise. She wanted to have had more warning, more *something*. He was…prickly, his lips cold and hard. It was strange. Not erotic at all. And she really needed to breathe.

Beatrice pushed at his chest and he stepped back, releasing his hold on her.

She huffed mouthfuls of air. "Lord Petersham…I…that was…" She gathered her senses. "That was not at all what I imagined."

"Because I was not whom you had been imagining." He chuckled softly. "Miss Smythe, if I may be so bold as to offer advice?"

"Of course, my lord."

"Getting things over with is not always the best tack. Some things require far more thought. And when you do finally kiss your intended young man, it will seem like your first kiss. You'll see that this was nothing more than a poor demonstration of what to possibly be prepared for."

"Yes, my lord."

"Now, I think you could use a brandy. I most definitely could use one. I keep a fine vintage in my library. Where I do believe the man you should be with right now is discussing archaeology."

Good God. Would William know what she had just done?

Lord Petersham wrapped Beatrice's limp arm around his rather rigid one and led her to his library.

Aₙ EXPEDITION? TO TURKEY? And they wanted him along?

William could scarcely believe his ears.

Mr. Tubney was financing an archaeological expedition to Ottoman Turkey to be led by Professor Stanfield, and, astoundingly, William's name had come up in conversation as "a bright student" who would be an asset for such an undertaking.

Other names had been mentioned as well, of course. But Professor Stanfield had been so impressed with William's questions during his lectures on classical archaeology last term that he had hand-picked him for the endeavor.

William's head spun. It wasn't quite a dream come true, because he hadn't even dared dream it. He gulped a little too much of his brandy in his enthusiasm, and now his head spun a little more.

Papa patted him on the back. "I'm proud of you, son."

"We depart just after the end of Lent Term," said Professor Stanfield. "You have plenty of time to acquire necessary supplies." He surveyed William. "I recommend a wide brimmed hat for a red-haired, fair-skinned young man such as yourself."

A hat, along with workman's clothes, and tools… "What sort of tools should I bring?"

Professor Stanfield grinned. "I'll send you a list, my boy. You should be able to gather what you need in Cambridge, or"—he glanced at Papa—"in London."

Another gulp of liquor and William was finished with his brandy.

"I thought we might find everyone in the library." Uncle Arthur's voice was jovial as he came through the door.

With Beatrice following right behind.

William's already excited heart began to pound even more.

Uncle Arthur went to the liquor cabinet and poured out two brandies. He handed one to Beatrice.

Shocking. Although no one else in the room seemed to mind.

"Geoff," Uncle Arthur said to Papa, "pardon our intrusion. I found Miss Smythe looking for her dance partner, so brought her here." He winked at William before turning to Beatrice. "Miss Smythe, I think you already know Mr. Geoffrey Peel, William's father?"

Beatrice smiled politely. "Yes. Good evening, Mr. Peel." She took a sip of her brandy.

"Stanfield, Tubney"—Uncle Arthur bobbed his chin at the two men—"may I present Miss Beatrice Smythe. Miss Smythe, may I present Professor Albin Stanfield of Cambridge, and Mr. Alistair Tubney, a banker by trade."

Mr. Tubney bowed his head. "Miss Smythe, a pleasure."

"Beatrice Smythe?" said Professor Stanfield. "I know the Earl of Ryburgh has a daughter named Beatrice. Lady Beatrice Smythe. She's a student at Girton."

Uncle Arthur chortled. "Yes, this is she, the very same young lady."

Beatrice straightened, perhaps with a bit of pride. "I have chosen to disregard my honorific and employ the common epithet, professor."

"Then you are Lord Ryburgh's daughter?" Professor Stanfield said with great surprise.

"I am." Beatrice nodded. "My father disdains titles, despite feeling he must keep his own as he is a peer in the House of Lords. I think he would prefer to be called Mr. Smythe and be in the House of Commons."

All chuckled at Beatrice's quip. She glanced at William. He grinned back at her.

"Radicals are a very interesting breed, are they not?" commented Mr. Tubney.

Professor Stanfield studied Beatrice. "I suppose you hold some of your father's Radical views, then. Votes for women and such."

Beatrice did not bat an eye. "Not all women will choose to be married. Who will speak for them in Parliament, if they do not have husbands to rely upon?"

"Indeed." Papa snickered behind his glass.

"Besides," Beatrice continued, "not all husbands and wives see eye to eye. I know my mother and father have heated discussions about a great many issues. A married woman should vote as she chooses, not as her husband deems."

Papa's face scrinched up as it always did when he tried not to laugh.

"Sounds like she's been talking to your wife, Petersham," said Mr. Tubney.

"While Lavinia is indeed a family friend, I believe Miss Smythe's observations are her own."

"Most excellent," pronounced Professor Stanfield.

A tiny crinkle formed between her eyebrows. "I beg your pardon, professor?"

"Oh, my dear girl, how rude of me. Let me explain. My wife and I had dinner not too long ago with your Miss Simons." He glanced at all in the room. "Miss Simons is the lecturer in classical studies at Girton." He beamed at Beatrice. "And Lady Beatrice Smythe here is her most valued student."

A blush colored her cheeks, the rosiness making Beatrice even more beautiful, if such a thing were possible.

"Lady Beatrice—pardon, I mean Miss Smythe," the professor continued, "if I may be so bold as to present a proposition. If it sounds interesting to you, I will have to seek more proper permissions from your father."

All eyes turned to Beatrice, who did not flinch at the attention. "Yes, Professor?"

"I would love for you to join me on my archaeological expedition to Turkey where we will be exploring remains which I hope to confirm date from the Hadrianic era. I understand you've taken an interest in Roman antiquities? We leave in April after Lent Term, but I'm afraid we will still be abroad during Easter Term. Does this sound at all like anything you'd be interested in?"

The blush faded to pallor momentarily before returning. "You are asking me to accompany you on an expedition?" She sounded as if she could not believe her ears.

"Yes, Miss Smythe," the professor said with a smirk.

William's heart raced at the prospect of spending so much time with her in a foreign land, away from family and friends.

"I think I would quite like that." A smile spread across her lips. "I mean, I would be honored." Her glance in William's direction set his cheeks to burning. "Will Mr. Peel be joining us?"

"Mr. Peel will be one of our scholars on Greek and Latin epigraphy."

Beatrice's radiance provoked even more heat.

"Lord Ryburgh is here tonight, gentlemen," Uncle Arthur said. "Shall we discuss this with him now?"

All in the room agreed. A servant was called, then dispatched to find Beatrice's father.

William just wanted to jump for joy. Going abroad with Beatrice—his Beatrice? Of course there would be quite a bit of work to do. But then there would be times when they could sit in a tent and talk and talk and talk and—

His cock reminded him the possibilities were endless.

CHAPTER FOUR

The Mediterranean Sea, April 1881

"And how do you two know each other?"

Clarissa Trent looked up from her sketchpad at the sound of Mrs. Stanfield's query. The professor's wife had paused during her stroll along the deck of the *Le Smyrne* to address Beatrice and Mr. Peel, startling the two as they made a quiet study of the Turkish language.

And most likely continued a study of each other.

As Miss Smythe's chaperon, Clarissa watched the young lady like a hawk. During their journey from London by train and now a French packet ship, she realized the poor girl was utterly besotted with William Peel, and young Mr. Peel was very clearly desperately in love with Miss Smythe.

A sea breeze fluttered the brim of Beatrice's hat. "My father knows a woman who is married to William's father's business partner."

William let out a snort. "Except she wasn't married to my father's business partner at the time." A flush colored his already sun-stained cheeks. "But they were in love with each other."

Clarissa chuckled to herself. Well, there was a story behind all that elucidation, wasn't there?

Beatrice ignored William's intrusion. "And when everyone discovered that William and I both had a keen interest in archaeology, they introduced us to each other at a ball."

"That sounds lovely," said Mrs. Stanfield. "And did the two of you dance at this ball?"

Now it was Beatrice's turn to blush. "Yes. William is an excellent dance partner."

Both smiled bashfully from what was obviously a pleasant memory. Luckily for them, Mrs. Stanfield had decided to move along to where Clarissa lay stretched out on a chaise longue in the shade of the upper deck. To her left Cornelia Acker, the wife of Mr. Spencer Acker, a Cambridge lecturer and ancient coin specialist, had decided the afternoon was a fine time to enjoy an exuberant snooze.

Mrs. Stanfield glanced at Clarissa's sketchpad. "Oh, my dear, you have such a skill with your pencil." She glanced over at Beatrice and William. "Such a remarkable likeness of our two young scholars."

"Thank you, Mrs. Stanfield."

"Please, call me Althea. We've been on this journey for a week, and we'll be digging in the ground for several more. I insist we ladies cultivate a society of mutual support. There will be times when we will only be able to rely upon each other and not the men."

Clarissa, Miss Smythe, Mrs. Acker, and Althea were each women still in their prime. Which meant dealing with issues of monthly courses, the unwanted male gaze on a site filled with male laborers, and, in Mrs. Acker's particular case, maintaining her health during her pregnancy.

"Of course, Althea. And you must call me Clarissa." She glanced over at the snoring Mrs. Acker. "Cornelia will probably insist upon first names as well."

Althea laughed. She took the chaise on the other side of Mrs. Acker and pulled a book from her pocket. "Fine weather for reading, is it not?"

"Yes, it is." Clarissa glanced at her sketch of Miss Smythe and Mr. Peel before returning her attention to the living subjects.

Miss Smythe had, so far, acted the perfect lady during the journey. Clarissa was a little surprised as she had been told her charge was willful and needed to be properly chaperoned at all times. Apparently, her father's Radical politics—and, it seemed, past chaperons—had given Miss Smythe the perception that a woman should be trusted on her own. To be sure, this was a goal for the future of all womankind—but the reality was that not all men were ready for such a notion. And as such, a young woman needed to be protected from such men.

Not that William Peel was much of a threat. In fact, he was no threat at all. Rather it was Miss Smythe who would most likely put herself and her reputation in danger.

And therein lay the challenge, and why the Earl of Ryburgh had hired Clarissa in the first place. He knew his daughter was precocious, and while her knowledge and intelligence made her a credit to the expedition, her independence—which Lord Ryburgh fully acknowledged was his own doing—might be her downfall.

Luckily, Miss Smythe believed Clarissa was there simply as chaperon. She had no idea Clarissa was being paid to be a protector, mother hen, confidant, and anything else a young girl of nineteen might need.

And no one knew Clarissa had other talents that would make her a valued member of an archaeological expedition to Turkey.

Still, an overnight stay in Paris and the steamship's ports of call had not proved to be temptations to Miss Smythe, giving Clarissa opportunity to sketch or read.

But would Miss Smythe continue this subdued behavior once they had established camp?

Clarissa supposed she would find out soon enough.

Sevilen Tapinak archaeological site near the coast of the Sea of Marmara, Turkey

BEATRICE SLID A HANDKERCHIEF under her wide-brimmed hat to wipe the sweat from her brow. The Anatolian sun was seemingly hotter than the one in England. And it was only spring. Goodness only knew what heat the Turks had to endure during the summer.

Mama had overseen assembling her wardrobe of comfortable clothing, including loose-fitting, lightweight dresses, plus aprons to protect from the dust. Her undergarments were less restrictive, such as corsets devoid of boning with support only via stitching. For workday attire, Mama had eschewed petticoats in favor of loose "bloomer" trousers with an overskirt. These miraculous garments enabled Beatrice to climb the ladders in and out of the excavation pits with ease. Interestingly enough, since the Turkish women who maintained their campsite wore a similar style of dress, Beatrice fit right in—at the campsite, though, not in the trenches.

When Beatrice first attempted to climb into one of the excavation trenches, the local workmen had balked, staring at her, refusing to move or do any work. A few had clambered out of the pit, shaking their heads and wandering away a great distance. Apparently the workmen had protested to Professor Stanfield via the interpreter, stating they did not want her digging in the pit with them. The professor had then explained this to her not in an admonishing tone, but with a sort of resignation. So now Beatrice had to content herself with sorting and cataloging bits of marble and pottery in the open-air artifact tent alongside Miss Trent. Luckily Miss Trent was a very good storyteller, passing the time by recounting Greek mythology in her clever and unique way.

Still the Turkish workmen continued to eye Beatrice with suspicion. She and Miss Trent were the only unmarried women on the campaign, and the only ones on display, as it were. The professor's wife, Mrs. Stanfield, made her rounds daily to admire the progress of the excavation, but acted as her husband's secretary and so was often in his tent preparing correspondence and reports. Mrs. Acker mostly kept to herself, her pregnancy making her queasy half the day.

Beatrice gazed out at the shrubby, weedy plain strewn with blocks of ancient marble, the result of earthquakes and invaders toppling the site's eponymous Beloved Temple. In the middle of it all, one man stood out, his ease and confidence at odds with his inexperience in archaeological expeditions.

William was a wondrous sight to behold in his rolled-up shirtsleeves and unbuttoned waistcoat. He spoke with Professor Stanfield, gesturing at the ground, pointing along the horizon, the professor nodding with a thoughtful expression. They spoke a moment longer, then turned and began walking toward the artifact tent.

Excitement bristled along Beatrice's scalp, bringing on the same sort of agitation she'd experienced last summer before she'd visited the doctor. But as moments alone on an expedition were fleeting and few and far between, frustration had grown. She'd shared hotel rooms and sleeping berths and now a tent with Miss Trent. Beatrice had tried to pleasure herself one night, but the sounds of Miss Trent's slumberous sighs and snorts had been something of a distraction.

Professor Stanfield and William approached. William offered a brief smile to Beatrice before putting on a more scholarly mien. She couldn't take her eyes off him. His casual dishevelment was provocative, his masculine attributes now in clear focus. His shirt was unbuttoned at the collar, revealing a hint of a smooth chest. Fine fair hair covered his bare forearms. When he removed his woven hat, his ginger hair glinted with copper and gold in the sunlight. An errant strand skimmed his forehead. Beatrice restrained herself from tucking it back into place.

"Miss Trent," began the professor, "I understand you are a skilled artist?"

A slight blush colored Miss Trent's normally rather stoic face. "I would say I can make a fairly accurate depiction of an object."

"Oh, but you're superb!" William exclaimed.

Miss Trent seemed quite taken aback. "Thank you, Mr. Peel."

"Well, whatever you think of your own skills," said the professor, "I need someone to walk with me on this plain as I imagine the temple that once stood here. Sort of like taking dictation, but with the imagination."

"Sketching out your ideas?"

"Yes, then we'll go over them and create a likely scenario of where the temple stood and what it looked like. From there we can start some of the finer excavations. Our hope is for a spectacular find of column bases or a mosaic floor to help solidify the notion that a temple did indeed stand here."

"All right." As Miss Trent went to grab her notebook, she glanced sidelong at Beatrice, then at William.

"I would love for Miss Smythe and Mr. Peel to join us," said Professor Stanfield. "I'm sure you'll both have insightful observations."

"Thank you, Professor," said William.

Beatrice smiled politely so as not to seem too enthusiastic. "I would love to hear your hypotheses, Professor."

William held out his arm. "Come, Miss Smythe. Let's see what Professor Stanfield has been speculating."

Finally, after her initial muck-up in the trench, Beatrice would be included in research beyond the artifact tent.

William tucked Beatrice's arm around his as they headed out to the temple site.

"Beatrice," he murmured in case anyone could overhear. "It's been utterly maddening to not, well, simply be with you."

Beatrice's radiant but demure expression was all he wanted to see. That she felt the same way was a balm to his soul.

"I'm enjoying my work, William," she said quietly. "But I do miss being able to discuss history and everything else with you."

His heart doubled in size at her words. Her looped arm relaxed around his. She was so close, her presence heightening spring's heat by several degrees. Moments like this made him wish so damn much they were more than mere friends, that they were already intimate. He needed to draw her more closely, to touch her, to forget the world in her presence.

Instead, he had to maintain a veneer of formality.

Alongside Professor Stanfield and Miss Trent, they climbed to the top of the rocky mound overlooking the site. Before them was a plain overgrown with weeds and grass, the ground strewn with hillocks that, upon further reflection, added somewhat of a regularity to the whole layout.

With hands on hips, Professor Stanfield surveyed the landscape. "I will now present my history lecture." He smiled at William and Beatrice. "You two need to learn something while you're here."

William merely nodded while Beatrice stared wide-eyed.

"In the fifteenth century, an Italian merchant and antiquarian traveled through this part of Anatolia. Cyriacus of Ancona, as he was called, saw and recorded the temple of Hadrian at the site of Cyzicus just west of here. He described it as having thirty-one standing columns." The professor gestured as if before them stood such a temple. "But over the years the temple had been used as a marble quarry. First by the Byzantines and then by the Ottomans, until in our present century, the temple columns no longer exist."

William lowered his brim against the sun. So that's how once magnificent buildings simply disappeared.

"Cyriacus, our Italian traveler, continued his travels west to where we are now. He spoke with locals who recounted a legend of a temple to a youth that rivaled the temple of Hadrian at Cyzicus. However, Cyriacus only recorded a mound here"—the professor indicated the ground upon which they stood—"with a few pieces of marble covered in weeds. He speculated that this site had been quarried first, before Cyzicus."

"And that's why there is no trace of a temple?" asked Beatrice.

"An excellent speculation." Professor Stanfield nodded. "But our patron, Mehmet Alim Pasha, who owns this land, has another theory."

The pasha had not yet joined them at the site, and Professor Stanfield had been eager to make his acquaintance beyond their correspondence. William was more curious as to what type of man he was: intellectually curious, or a bureaucrat with an ulterior motive?

"A local legend has persisted over the centuries of a temple here to a youth—in Turkish they say *çocuk*. Mehmet Pasha wanted to ascertain whether or not the legend was merely a story or possibly historical fact. He hired local men to dig some preliminary trenches." The professor pointed to the trenches on the far side of the site. "Besides those bits of pottery and marble that Miss Smythe and Miss Trent are cataloging, he has found indications of a road. The pasha thinks there *is* a temple here, buried much deeper than one might think. This land is wild and overgrown, and there have been earthquakes over the centuries. The site is remote and has never been used for agriculture, or has not been used as such for over a millennium."

Beatrice nudged loose a rock underfoot. "So the columns and roof collapsed with earthquakes, and everything was buried by dirt?"

"And our job is to attempt to establish a possible perimeter of the temple?" asked William.

"Yes," said the professor. "And then Mehmet Pasha will direct his men where to begin the more delicate excavations."

From behind her dark sun spectacles, Miss Trent scanned the landscape. The professor had provided each member of the expedition with such spectacles. Shielding the sun glinting off rocks and dust was beginning to look like a good idea. William would try to remember to carry the spectacles whenever he was in the field.

"By the way, His Excellency apologizes for his absence," said the professor. "He has written that we should continue with our work while he is handling some urgent bureaucratic problems, and that he will join us presently."

"Where do you think this temple was exactly, Professor Stanfield?" asked William.

The professor glanced between him and Beatrice. "I was hoping my students would want to suggest some theories before I revealed my own."

Beatrice's eyes widened. As a female student, she was never allowed the opportunity to participate in such tutorials with male professors. She straightened to speak.

"As we were climbing this mound," she began, "I noticed a little hill on the far side of the site."

Professor Stanfield began to grin.

"So I immediately thought that the little hill might be the porch of the temple, where the columns and pediment fell. This plateau where we are now standing is situated behind the temple."

William remembered the facade of the Fitzwilliam Museum. If it ever fell in an unlikely earthquake, the front would be a pile of columns, the middle sagging. Like the very landscape before them.

"A little closer to us is where the cella—the interior of the temple was located," continued Beatrice. "You can tell by the impression or dip in the mound, which implies the enclosing columns or walls are underneath those surrounding mounds."

Good heavens. Beatrice was simply brilliant.

Professor Stanfield turned to him. "And what is your assessment, Mr. Peel?"

He had nothing to add. "I concur with Miss Smythe."

The professor clapped his hands. "I knew I had chosen the best students for this expedition." He nodded. "I came to the very same conclusion as Miss Smythe."

Beatrice tried unsuccessfully to hide her satisfaction.

"And now, Miss Trent, I do believe you and I have some visual dictation to commence."

Once again Miss Trent glanced in William and Beatrice's direction.

"I'm certain our young scholars will behave," said the professor before waving Miss Trent toward the assumed front of the temple.

Leaving William alone with his Beatrice.

William leaned over. The scent of lilac mingled with dust, teasing his nostrils. "You are extraordinarily perceptive, do you know that?"

She glanced up at him, beaming. "I do. And I thank you, Mr. Peel, for acknowledging that." Her tone held some resignation, though.

"You're not feeling appreciated, are you?"

Beatrice sighed heavily. "I'm feeling rather cloistered, really. I'm not allowed near the excavations, and I'm relegated to sorting artifacts someone else has deemed important."

"What would you rather do?"

"To sift through the layers of the earth discovering items hidden from view for two thousand years."

"Ah." Beatrice was capable and deserved to be involved more deeply in the expedition. "Professor Stanfield is treating you as he would any male student—"

"You mean he's treating me like he treats you."

"Yes, I do mean that. So I think the problem lies not with the professor but with some restriction imposed by the pasha. Perhaps Professor Stanfield can speak with him about allowing you more freedom."

"Perhaps."

"Darling, you've just been praised for your intelligence. Surely the professor knows he should be using your skills."

She blinked and gave him the queerest look.

"Beatrice, why are you staring at me so?"

* * * * *

A BASHFUL SMILE TUGGED at the corners of her mouth. "I love it when you call me darling."

The color rose in William's cheeks. "I suppose I did just say that." He gazed into her eyes. "And I mean it."

Her smile widened. "While Professor Stanfield and Miss Trent are performing their survey of the assumed porch of the temple, perhaps it might be illuminating to view the area from the other side." She pointed to the area just behind them overgrown with bushes and weeds.

William stood with hands on hips, making a display of looking at the mound where they stood, then beyond it, then all around it. He began to walk to where Beatrice had indicated, then motioned for her to follow.

So in the event anyone was actually watching them, they would think the two were merely performing academical duties.

The other side of the mound was thick with tall bushes, suggesting that, indeed, the soil was deeper there. But also providing a screen for a furtive moment in a clandestine love affair.

William ducked behind the tallest bush, pulling Beatrice with him. She glanced around. They were alone. They could see no one from where they stood—and no one could see them.

Her heart thrummed. She'd been a proper young lady during their journey so far, never even daring to hold William's hand. She could barely contain her grin.

William could barely contain a grin either.

She wrapped her hands around his neck, then lifted herself on her toes, flicking the tip of her tongue across her lips in anticipation.

He bent his head over her, angling just so to accommodate the brims of their hats. His breath hung humid in their intimate space for only a moment before he touched his lips to hers.

Her senses exploded at the warmth, the wetness, the intimacy. She pressed into him, wanting more. Then gasped when William drew away too quickly.

She looked up at him, meeting his gaze, still stunned at the new sensation. A kiss so very, very different from the one imparted by Lord Petersham so many months ago.

His brow furrowed as if he were worried he had hurt her. "Beatrice?"

"Please."

A smile played upon his lips the moment before he kissed her again, this time longer, deeper, his tongue encouraging her to open for him.

It was extraordinary. It was magnificent. It was heaven.

Mouth pressed against mouth, tongue entwined with tongue. She moved her hands to his chest, palming his glorious pectorals, before encircling his neck once again to let him pull her more closely against him, never breaking from their luscious kiss. Hands on her bottom, he held her steady as he rocked his hips against her in a most deliciously lewd manner.

She could do this forever.

But William parted from her, panting, then unwrapped her arms from his neck. With both hands on her shoulders, he urged her to stand with heels firmly on the ground.

"William?" Her tone was plaintive. "Don't you want to kiss me anymore?"

He took her hands in his, kissing them briefly before tenderly rubbing her palms with his thumbs. A tiny whimper escaped her throat.

"Darling Beatrice, I have wanted to kiss you for ages."

"As I have you."

He glanced over his shoulder, then just beyond hers.

"William," she said quietly, "we are very much alone."

He continued to rub her palms, the sensation sending tingles to unexpected places. "I would hate to lose myself in your embrace and be surprised when someone came upon us."

She sighed in concurrence. "Yes, I suppose that might happen." She could very easily become lost in his embrace.

He beamed, his brown eyes twinkling before he sobered. "Surely if someone discovers us kissing, we would have to become engaged. And I know you don't want that."

"No, I don't." But if she had to be engaged to someone, William would be her first choice.

He kissed her hand. "I'd like to see you alone more often. How can we effect that? It seems your Miss Trent is always hovering."

"She is. I even wonder sometimes if she sleeps with one eye open."

"And she is probably wondering where you are at this very moment."

Beatrice sighed. Their tryst was at an end for the time being. "You're right. We should return to a place where we can be seen."

William pulled her to him, his mouth once again on hers. She melted in his arms, reveling in his embrace, his touch sparking sensual need deep in her core.

She'd have to find a way to pleasure herself that night.

He drew back with lingering pecks until he relented and leaned the brim of his hat against hers. "Ready to rejoin the world?"

"Reluctantly."

He looped her arm around his and led her back down the hill to the dip which was the supposed middle of the collapsed temple. At the front of the temple, Professor Stanfield and Miss Trent were deep in discussion as they ambled around the site. While Miss Trent paused to take notes, the professor espied William and Beatrice and waved.

"We shouldn't be standing so close together," William whispered, releasing his hold.

"I think you're being overly cautious," she whispered back.

"Mr. Peel, Miss Smythe," Professor Stanfield called out. "Come see Miss Trent's marvelous sketches."

Miss Trent offered a weak smile as she handed her notebook to the professor. She whipped off her hat to mop her brow with a handkerchief, revealing her sagging and disheveled chignon.

"I don't think they noticed we were gone," whispered Beatrice as they approached the professor and Miss Trent.

"Look at this." Professor Stanfield held out Miss Trent's sketchbook.

Even as a quick sketch, Miss Trent's efforts were gallery-worthy. She had expertly fleshed out what the professor had described.

"This is magnificent, Miss Trent."

"Thank you, Mr. Peel." Miss Trent was still puffing a little from her exertions. She found a marble block with an elegantly carved albeit weather-worn anthemion and perched herself upon it.

The professor began to expound upon the drawing and how it matched his archaeological vision. While William nodded, enrapt, Beatrice was distracted by William.

If that was what a kiss could be, then what else might two people do together?

If only there were some way to be alone with him so she could find out.

BEATRICE STARED AT THE shadowed tent wall as she lay on her side in her bed. The kiss from that afternoon still lingered on her lips. William's touch on her back, her waist, her hips still seared into her flesh. She desperately wanted to pleasure herself. The tent was dark enough, so Miss Trent would not see her. But she would probably still hear the sounds of rustling sheets and perhaps a squeak of the metal bed frame.

Or perhaps not, as the silence of the middle of the night held disconcerting sounds of nature. Like the present sound not unlike the growl of an angry animal which sent a shiver to shirr across Beatrice's scalp. They were not told to expect wild animals. But perhaps a wild dog had found the camp and was looking for food.

She listened intently. *Gadzooks*. The sound was coming from inside the tent.

Beatrice lifted herself up on an elbow and glanced around in the dark. The noise was definitely coming from the other side of the tent. She held her breath, remaining still as she concentrated on the noise.

Good gracious. Miss Trent was *snoring*.

Which meant she was sound asleep.

And Beatrice had one chance.

Despite the loud rumbling, she slipped out of her cot and through the mosquito netting as silently as possible. She put on her dressing gown and her boots without stockings all the while keeping a close ear on Miss Trent.

The poor woman had been dragged around all day by Professor Stanfield. Of course she was exhausted.

From the doorway of her tent, Beatrice looked both ways then slipped outside. There was enough light from the moon and stars to illuminate the way to William's tent. She trod carefully, hoping her movements would not alert or waken anyone.

At the entrance to William's tent, Beatrice once again looked around, then opened the flap and entered.

As she'd never been inside before, she let her eyes adjust to the setting, taking in the desk and its chair, the chest of drawers, the bed where William slept.

She approached slowly for fear of waking him too suddenly, as he might cry out for help. His breaths fell in rhythmic swells. In, out, in, out. She followed the rhythm, letting it fill her, seduce her. Perhaps she could climb into his bed, wrap her arms around him, and wake him in her comfortable embrace.

Still standing, she took off her boots.

He stirred, stretching under his coverlet with a soft moan that resounded in her core. Never had she heard such an intimate sound. The thrill of it aroused her.

"William," she whispered.

His breathing faltered.

"William."

He stirred again, then jolted upright, the suddenness sending her stumbling backward.

"Beatrice? Is that you?" he whispered as well.

"Yes, darling." She knelt at the side of his bed and reached for his hand.

He intertwined their fingers. "How on earth did you get in here? I mean, how did you elude Miss Trent?"

"She was exhausted from today."

He let out a soft chuckle. "I suppose the professor had her traipsing after him like a puppy." He touched a finger to her cheek and drew a line to her mouth. "And now you're here. With me. What shall I do with you?"

"You should kiss me."

"I suppose I should."

He reached, groping a bit before cupping her cheeks, finding her in the dark. He bent over, his lips seeking then meeting hers. His kiss was tentative until his hands, his arms, his mouth established where she was before him.

William lifted her onto the mattress, on top of him, their bodies crushing together. Yet it was not close enough. Between her legs her sex swelled. She pressed her hips into his.

He rolled until he was on top of her, trailing kisses down her neck, fingers fumbling to open her dressing gown and unbutton the placket of her nightgown to lay more kisses along the hollow of her collarbone to her shoulder. He tugged the neckline of her nightgown aside, baring her shoulder, pressing his mouth there, the wet heat of him thrilling her. She arched for him, wanting him to continue the assault of pleasure further down, to the tops of her breasts and beyond. She speared her fingers through his hair, holding his head as he did her bidding.

William, William, oh William. At that moment all sense flew from her conscience. She would let him do anything to her. She opened her legs as far as the nightgown would allow, a bulge under his nightshirt pressing against her swollen sex.

He pulled back, his breathing labored. "Darling, this is madness. We cannot continue."

She bit her lower lip. "Why not?"

He rested his forehead against hers. "I don't think I would trust me right now if I were you."

"I don't care."

"Your father would kill me."

Papa was a kitten. He wouldn't hurt anyone.

"He would force us to get married." He kissed her forehead. "And I support your decision to remain an independent woman."

"Independence means being able to take a lover."

He grinned against her cheek. "Not until you're twenty-one. Can you wait that long?"

She could. For him. "Perhaps. Unless I find someone more willing than you," she teased.

"Oh, I am willing, love," he said with a chortle. "I fear I am just too honorable."

Compelled to test that assertion, Beatrice tugged up her nightgown, exposing her naked sex, and spread her thighs as wide as the mattress, taunting William by rocking her hips. He matched her movements, rubbing his fabric-bound swollen cock against her slowly at first, increasing his thrusts as he kissed her nipples through the linen of her nightgown. The climb to ecstasy began, this time a little differently, more intense, the pressure against her pleasure spot warm and thick, William's panting breaths in her ear enveloping her into a cocoon of sensual oblivion taking her to the precipice.

She bucked up against him as she came, pressing into him as if to perpetuate the glorious feeling. "William," she panted as she wrapped her legs around his hips. "I want more."

"Beatrice, love, I simply cannot."

"You mean you *will* not."

"All right, I will not." He pecked her lips. "I most certainly can but won't. Besides, at any moment your Miss Trent might awaken and start searching loudly for you."

She sighed.

His mouth stretched into a grin against her cheek. "It appears you are thwarted."

"And your honor assured."

He pulled her close, his heartbeat thrumming in her ear. "Darling, there will be a time and place to continue this. I confess I do not want to wait until you are twenty-one. But we should wait until we are guaranteed a modicum of privacy and plenty of time for the experience."

"Is it worth the wait?"

"I—" He hesitated. "Oh, darling, yes. Yes, it is." He kissed her temple. "Now let me hold you one more minute before propriety forces me to send you back to your tent."

Beatrice held him tightly with arms and legs, wishing the moment could last forever.

CHAPTER FIVE

From atop his chestnut Karacabey horse, Mehmet Alim Pasha surveyed the change in his land since the arrival of the British archaeological team. White tents dotted the golden plain. Dark-haired workmen labored, while men dressed in finer attire and wearing wide-brimmed hats conferred with each other.

And, unexpectedly, a woman—no, two women, conferred alongside the men, seemingly discussing correspondence.

No wonder he had received reports of immorality from the workmen. But, as he had suspected, the women were clearly working and not contributing to anyone's corruption.

He urged his horse Borysthenes toward the excavation, his small entourage trailing behind.

A clean-shaven middle-aged man with an athletic build and a jovial countenance espied him and came forward with a wave.

"His Excellency Mehmet Pasha, I presume?"

Mehmet suppressed a grin. The English were so terribly polite. He halted Borysthenes and dismounted, a servant quickly taking his reins. "I am Mehmet Alim Pasha."

"Excellency." The professor gave a bow.

"And you are Professor Albin Stanfield, I presume?"

"The very same."

Mehmet stuck out his hand. After a brief look of shock, Stanfield grabbed his hand and gave it a hearty shake.

He gestured to the field with the tents. "Shall I give you a tour, Excellency?"

"Please, simply call me Mehmet. I would love a tour of what secrets my land holds."

"Very good. If you will call me Albin. Follow me."

So this was the man with whom Mehmet had corresponded over the course of a couple of years. Professor Albin Stanfield was a noted scholar of antiquities from the era of the Roman Empire during the reign of the Emperor Hadrian. By studying aesthetics of design and forms of construction, he would surely be able to determine if the temple on Mehmet's land had been built during the Hadrianic era.

If, indeed, there was a temple on Mehmet's land. That would have to be established first.

Regardless, Professor Stanfield—Albin—had thought Mehmet's proposition that the temple could possibly have been dedicated to the emperor's lover, the youth Antinous, to be worthy of study.

They passed an excavation pit where Mehmet's hired local men chipped away at the dirt with hand tools. Nearby was a tent with open sides, inside which were tables strewn with bits of broken pottery and marble. Two women sat at the table scrutinizing each object and writing in notebooks.

Mehmet entered the tent and picked up a piece of marble, a portion of a carved acanthus leaf discernible on one corner. "What a marvelous discovery."

One of the women looked up, her golden-brown eyes flashing in his direction. She stood abruptly, her plump lips parting as she saw him, realization of who he probably was dusting her high cheekbones a lovely shade of pink. Her countenance was classical, strong like Athena, beautiful like Helen.

This woman's beauty could certainly drive a man to immoral thoughts, which was one of the complaints he'd received from the laborers at the site. However, she was wearing a dusty apron, had her hair properly covered under her wide-brimmed hat, and did look to be working quite diligently.

The beautiful woman hissed to the other woman to stand, and she did. This other woman regarded him with suspicion. She too was beautiful beyond belief, her unmarred ivory skin indicating she had not witnessed much of life. Perhaps she was the professor's daughter.

Which meant the other woman might be his wife.

No. She was too young to be mother of an adolescent. Or perhaps that was just wishful thinking on Mehmet's part.

Albin slid himself between Mehmet and the lovely woman. "Er, I, er, thought, Excellency, I mean, Mehmet, perhaps you should visit with the excavation crew to encourage them."

Mehmet raised an eyebrow in the beautiful woman's direction, eliciting a blush. "I think instead I would like to know what these lovely ladies are working on."

The professor gestured at the brown-eyed beauty. "This is Miss Clarissa Trent. She is a tutor at Girton College in classical studies. Girton is an institute of higher education for young women near Cambridge. Miss Trent, this is Mehmet Pasha, the owner of the land upon which we work."

Mehmet bowed his head. "A pleasure to meet you, Miss Trent."

She curtsied. "Thank you, Excellency."

"And this," the professor continued, gesturing to the young girl, "is Miss Beatrice Smythe. She is currently attending Girton College, studying classics with an interest in archaeology."

Ah, so not the professor's daughter. Hence, most likely, the presence of Miss Trent was as the young lady's chaperon. "A pleasure to meet you, Miss Smythe."

Miss Smythe shot a look in Miss Trent's direction, who nodded. Miss Smythe curtsied. "A pleasure to meet you, Excellency."

Mehmet turned to the professor. "Now, Albin, tell me about the treasures my land holds." Besides the sublime treasure named Miss Trent.

A WAVE OF SERENITY had energized William since his night with Beatrice. Of course he had masturbated after she had left him, but his rapturous culmination had been imbued with her lingering presence.

He had never felt so utterly satisfied in his life. His experience with Lavinia had been wonderful, to be sure, but it had lacked a certain emotional resonance.

Because he was passionately in love with Beatrice. And she in love with him.

He sighed in contentment as he studied the drawings and maps strewn on the table before him. Just a day before, the morass of information had seemed daunting, too much to organize and interpret. But the night's events had given him a confidence he'd not had before. Now he could envision the landscape as a thriving town on the outskirts of the Roman Empire. Miss Trent's drawings and the topographic maps merged to become a living story, like a theatrical performance.

He had ignored the Turkish bureaucrat who had arrived a few minutes ago. Professor Stanfield had said such men would visit from time to time. This particular bureaucrat had been expected the day before. Of course, traveling about the countryside on horseback possibly added to unforeseen delays.

However, the professor had expected the bureaucrat to want to examine the drawings and the maps, hence William's study of them. But the man was spending quite a bit of time at the artifact tent.

Where Miss Trent and Beatrice were.

Unease settled in the pit of William's stomach. He gathered up the maps and drawings and secured them in their leather portfolio and weighed that down with a rock in case a breeze should pick up.

He strolled over to the open-air artifact tent, purposely keeping his steps steady and even, repressing the urge to run to the side of his Beatrice.

"Ah, William," Professor Stanfield said enthusiastically. "Come meet Mehmet Pasha."

A tall man, wearing a frock coat, unbuttoned to reveal Western-style trousers and shirt plus a finely embroidered waistcoat, smiled at William, stretching his trimmed beard. This pasha was handsome—too handsome really. And young. Younger than William had imagined him to be. Perhaps thirty.

The professor put his arm around William's shoulders. "Mehmet, I would like to introduce Mr. William Peel, a student of classical archaeology at St. John's College, Cambridge. One of our finest students in epigraphy."

The pasha's green eyes flashed in approbation.

"William, this is Mehmet Pasha. He owns these lands."

"So not an Ottoman bureaucrat?" William blurted.

"No." The pasha chuckled. "Rather it is I who has to navigate our rather overly bureaucratic government. I have been working with our Ministry of Education to finalize the legal arrangements. Unfortunately, I am as yet unable to fully join your encampment as I still have some details to settle."

William's face burned. "My lord, I apologize for my rude outburst. It is a pleasure to meet you."

"The pleasure is mine, Mr. Peel." He turned to Beatrice. "I believe I was just about to be informed of the treasures of the past." He smiled sweetly to her.

Too sweetly. Beatrice blushed. Was she falling under his seductive spell?

William came around to Beatrice's side, putting space between her and the handsome pasha. "Miss Smythe, I understand you discovered what you think are bits of a frieze, did you not?"

"Oh! Yes, I did." While Beatrice laid out the marble chunks, William watched the pasha from the corner of his eye.

However, the pasha was surreptitiously watching Miss Trent. He seemed to have moved slightly closer to her as well, now that William had given him the opportunity. And Miss Trent did not seem to mind.

That the pasha had taken a keen interest in Miss Trent rather than in his Beatrice eased the pang of jealousy in his chest.

The professor began helping Beatrice, and together they arranged several pieces of marble with various motifs typical of classical architecture. A section of egg-and-dart was placed above a thinner and longer fragment with a beaded motif. Above both were several smaller fragments containing portions of palmette and anthemion decoration.

The pasha simply stared, spellbound and contemplating.

William took the quiet moment as opportunity to brush his fingers against Beatrice's. She squeezed his hand for a wonderful fleeting second.

"Where were these found?" asked the pasha.

"Near one of the excavation trenches. We haven't yet begun any exploration of the mound where you believe the temple to be."

The pasha picked up one of the fragments with the egg-and-dart motif. "Such a decoration would be in a cornice or architrave above the columns of a temple, correct?"

"Yes," agreed Professor Stanfield, "as an ornamental molding running in the space between the columns and the pediment."

The pasha ran a finger over the dart carved between the two raised egg-like forms. "This particular form of the dart, this deeply-carved lancet form, was used during the Hadrianic period."

"I noticed that as well, Mehmet." Professor Stanfield beamed.

"Excellent." The pasha nodded with a satisfied smile. He glanced at the professor. "Do your students know for what we are searching?"

"A temple?" said Beatrice.

"Very good, Miss Smythe." The pasha's smile was beginning to seem more fatherly and less seductive. "But whose temple?"

"Professor Stanfield said it was a temple to a youth," said William.

"And," began Beatrice, "there was a local legend, but nothing was found."

"The remote location from the larger site of Cyzicus suggests perhaps a pilgrimage site," said Miss Trent.

"I see I am surrounded by scholars," said the pasha with a grin. "My speculation is that this temple, should we find it, was dedicated to Antinous."

"The youth beloved by Hadrian?" All eyes focused on Miss Trent. She blushed.

The pasha chuckled. "Perhaps you are surprised I know this history," he said.

Miss Trent blushed again. "As Antinous was born in what is now Turkey, I suppose he is a part of Turkish history." She glanced at William and Beatrice then back at the pasha with an odd expression.

"Ah." The pasha seemed to comprehend some code that had passed between them. He turned to the professor. "I will leave the lectures on the life of Hadrian to Albin and Miss Trent."

Professor Stanfield cleared his throat.

Was there something salacious about Hadrian that William had never read about?

From the depths of a pit came frenzied yelling in Turkish. The pasha and the professor hurried over, William, Beatrice, and Miss Trent at their heels. Words flowed excitedly between the workman and the pasha. The workman raised his hand up, and the professor got down on his knees and took what the man offered.

"It's a coin, definitely Roman," Professor Stanfield exclaimed. He brushed the coin and examined it. "Yes…yes." He looked at all present. "A bearded man is on the obverse, so it may very well be from the age of Hadrian."

The workman and the pasha exchanged more words.

"Yazid tells me there are more," said the pasha. He beamed at the professor. "This is quite a fortuitous find, is it not?"

"Oh, very good, very good."

"Should we dig them out?" asked Beatrice.

"No," said the professor, "not yet." He waved at Miss Trent. "I would like Miss Trent to draw the coins *in situ*."

"Ah, Miss Trent," said the pasha with admiration, "you are an artist?"

"I am."

While Miss Trent retrieved her notebook and pencil, the pasha ordered the workmen out of the pit. He escorted her to the pit and watched as she descended down the rope-and-board ladder.

"I will keep you company as you draw, Miss Trent. I have a profound interest in the arts."

The pasha's presence would ensure the men did not balk at a woman in the pit, as they had with Beatrice.

"A cache of hidden coins," sighed Beatrice. "How exciting."

"It is, Miss Smythe," said Professor Stanfield. "Our excavations are bearing fruit." He took William aside. "Watch Miss Trent for a moment, please, while I get Acker. He's our coin expert. But I also want someone to keep an eye on Miss Trent."

"While she's with the handsome pasha?"

The professor chuckled. "I feel a responsibility to our women, I suppose."

As did William. "I will do as you ask, Professor. But I think it best I keep Miss Smythe company in the shelter of the tent. I can watch Miss Trent from there."

Professor Stanfield nodded and left to find Mr. Acker.

William took the opportunity to once again squeeze Beatrice's hand, eliciting a muted sigh.

* * * * *

CLARISSA WELCOMED THE COOL air of the excavation trench. The arrival of the charismatic and exceptionally handsome Mehmet Pasha made the humid warmth of spring suddenly more heated. And of course the day a handsome man came to visit was the day she'd decided to forgo a corset, relying solely on the light support of a corset cover. Perhaps the pasha would not notice her scandalous state of undress.

He crouched down, his hands folded. "I will confess, Miss Trent, one reason I wanted to visit is that I had heard grumblings about the presence of women in this expedition."

"Oh?" What a day to not wear a corset.

"Our culture is still very segregated between men and women. Turkish men are not used to seeing women performing tasks associated with men, such as descending into excavation pits."

He spoke English with the accent of one who had been educated in England, most likely Oxford. However, unlike any Englishman she knew, his lilt held a distinctive seductive quality.

"Well, Excellency, you may tell the men who grumble that we women are now relegated to performing tedious tasks more appropriate for our sex."

"I hardly think drawing is tedious."

Clarissa laughed softly. "I was thinking more the sorting and cataloging. Not as heroic and masculine as exploring treasures in a pit."

"Pasha Mehmet?"

Mr. Acker's inaccurate use of the Turkish honorific was a reflection of his utter neglect in attempting to learn anything about a culture other than his own revered England.

"I am Mehmet Pasha, yes."

Clarissa looked up from her drawing pad to catch a glimpse of the annoyance that flashed across the handsome visage of the dashing Turk.

"And whom do I have the pleasure of addressing?"

Mr. Acker held out his hand. "I am Spencer Acker, a lecturer at Cambridge. Very pleased to meet you."

"The pleasure is mine."

"Among other areas of study, I specialize in ancient coinage." Mr. Acker climbed down the ladder. "I'm here to take notes while Miss Trent draws the coins. I like to see for myself how the find is situated, you see. Then Miss Trent's drawing will be a reminder to the image in my head."

The pasha sat cross-legged on the ground at the edge of the pit. "I hear some expeditions have photographers for this very purpose."

Mr. Acker grunted as he retrieved his notebook from his jacket pocket. "Yes, nowadays this is very fashionable. Stanfield had apparently engaged such a man, but at the last moment he decided to go to America. We received a letter from him after we had arrived and set up camp."

"So Miss Trent was not brought along for the purposes of sketching?"

Clarissa smiled politely. "No. I was hired as a companion for Miss Smythe."

"And you just happen to have a classical education?"

"I do believe Miss Smythe's father knew my credentials and specifically chose me for my usefulness." She glanced at Mehmet Pasha, his unwavering gaze catching her off guard, bringing heat to her face again. "You may further explain to your disgruntled menfolk that sometimes women must step in when men fail to do their duty."

The pasha chuckled. "Men everywhere know this, Miss Trent. We simply do not like to be reminded of it."

"I dare say, it is lucky Miss Trent was among us," Mr. Acker said while scribbling in his notebook. "She's been a wonderful help."

"Do you enjoy being the expedition's sudden artist, Miss Trent?"

"I do not mind, really. But it means sometimes I have to leave Miss Smythe unsupervised. This is possibly another source of your men's grumblings."

"Indeed." The pasha sat in silence for a moment, his gaze burning through her hat to heat the back of her skull. "If you like, I may be able to find a local man for such a task as photography."

"You have such modern amenities in your country?"

The pasha exhaled with seeming irritation at Mr. Acker's question. "We do. We even have such men who speak English passing well."

"Well, that's jolly. My Turkish is barely understandable, I fear. Such a complicated language."

"Yet such a beautiful language," said Clarissa.

"Do you know Turkish, Miss Trent?"

"I love to listen to the cadence and rhythm," she said, deflecting. "And I am studying it with Mrs. Acker."

"My wife has a notion to be able to speak to the local women about their handicrafts. She often talks about how the language seems more natural for you, Miss Trent."

"Thank you, Mr. Acker."

"May I take a closer look for a moment?"

As Clarissa stepped aside to let Mr. Acker see the cache, she took the opportunity to catch another glimpse of the pasha. Once again he was staring at her with great interest.

And while she imagined his interest to have a sensual caste, it seemed more limned with intellectual curiosity.

"Thank you, Miss Trent." Mr. Acker studied the coins embedded in the dirt. "I'm wondering if the coins were placed here purposely. See how they are stacked and not strewn about higgledy-piggledy? Their placement seems deliberate."

"Yes, I see what you mean. I will attempt to convey that in the drawing."

"Oh, yes, please do."

"What might this indicate?" The pasha directed the question to Clarissa rather than Mr. Acker.

"Several possibilities. That the coins were not accidentally lost, that they may have been buried for hiding."

"Or buried in some sort of ritualistic fashion," added Mr. Acker. "Like an offering to the gods."

Clarissa pointed her pencil to the rocks and dirt surrounding the little cache. "So your men will need to be careful when excavating further, my lord."

"I will see to it."

Mr. Acker scribbled furiously. "Speaking of Mrs. Acker, will you be joining Cornelia for tea later, Miss Trent?"

"I shall. I do hope Mrs. Stanfield is there. She's very pleasant."

"Are these the only women in the camp?" asked the pasha. "Two wives and two unmarried women?"

"Yes, Excellency," said Clarissa.

"Must seem rather strange to you, my lord pasha," said Mr. Acker. "I suspect you have a harem of sorts."

There was a beat of silence before the pasha said coolly, "The harem in my palace is not what you think."

"Is it not where your wives live?"

Clarissa cringed inwardly at Mr. Acker's boorishness.

"The harem is where my mother and my unmarried sisters live," the pasha said with a touch of indignation. "It is not what the English think."

Mr. Acker scowled. "So your wife does not live there?"

"I am not married."

Clarissa wiped her brow from renewed heat. Certainly not from the pasha's revelation.

"I am surprised you are not married, my lord."

"You must have assumed I have many wives. It seems Occidentals always think we Muslims have many wives."

Mr. Acker laughed. "One wife is plenty for me, I dare say." He grunted. "But Cornelia is a good wife. She's taken to camping in the out-of-doors quite bravely."

The pasha shifted his position. "And you, Miss Trent, are you braving the out-of-doors as well?"

"To be honest, I've always romanticized this sort of life. I've always wanted to be involved in an archaeological expedition."

"So the romance has not yet faded for you?" There was that seductiveness to his voice again.

"No. I am still enthralled with working in the dirt and sleeping in tents." She looked up at the pasha who grinned down at her.

"Then you would not be at all interested in an invitation to stay at my palace? Where I have bedrooms shielded from the elements, beds with soft mattresses, and the luxury of a Turkish bath?"

She had no need of such things, but that was not to say she did not desire them.

"A Turkish bath, you say?" said Mr. Acker.

"Yes, a proper hamam."

"Where the genders are segregated, Excellency?" she asked. *Oh my*. Where did that come from? She was teasing him. She was flirting with him. And she felt good about it.

"Yes, Miss Trent. Where a woman's modesty is protected from the gaze of unwanted men."

But what if the man's gaze was wanted?

Oh lord, why the hell was Mr. Acker still there?

To protect her from herself.

Clarissa drew in a deep breath. "Such a luxury would not be unwanted, Excellency, especially by women who do not usually live as camp followers."

The pasha laughed a hearty laugh. "Then please, indulge me." He grinned. "At least for the women of the expedition."

"Wonderful," exclaimed Mr. Acker as he snapped shut his notebook. "I will tell my wife. She will be exceptionally pleased." He turned to Clarissa. "I believe I have all I need, Miss Trent."

Mr. Acker proceeded to climb up the ladder. At the top he took a deep breath. "Wonderful country you have here, my lord."

Then he turned and left.

If Mr. Acker was supposed to chaperon her in the presence of the pasha, apparently he had no knowledge of the fact.

"I believe I am finished as well." Clarissa slid a piece of tissue paper in her notebook so her drawing would not smudge. With notebook and pencil in one hand, she climbed up the ladder.

The pasha stood, waiting for her as she took her last step, his arms outstretched as if expecting to help her.

She did not *need* help. But perhaps she wanted help.

Clarissa stumbled, surprised at her own clumsiness, despite it being feigned.

As hoped for, Mehmet Pasha grabbed her arms, setting her to rights.

They stood face to face, his gaze holding her enrapt before dropping briefly to her mouth then back to meet her eyes.

He still held her arms.

"I thank you, Excellency."

"You are very welcome, Miss Trent." He glanced at her mouth again, his tongue flicking at the seam between his lips. "And once you have exhausted the romance of dust and tents, I will arrange for an excursion to my palace."

"I look forward to it, Mehmet Pasha."

He straightened, his gaze exhibiting a touch of surprise. "I look forward to it as well." He finally released her.

Clarissa returned slowly to the excavation tent, suppressing utterly inappropriate thoughts every step of the way.

MEHMET DISMISSED HIS HAMAM attendants and leaned into the depths of the marble niche, letting the pile of cushions embrace him like a lover.

Imagining the embrace of a certain enchanting woman.

He had left the excavation site with the knowledge that rumors of impropriety were simply that: rumors. He would have to replace a few of the local men, men he had not hired personally, as they seemed to be the ones spreading untruths.

And he would not stand for any accusations of immodesty of the women he had just met, because each of them was a paragon of decency and correctness.

Which was a slight problem in that he was astoundingly attracted to Miss Trent. She made him burn with lust in a way he had not felt in a very long time.

There had been women over the years, including older European women during his youthful Grand Tour of Europe. Women of experience who had introduced him to the ways of the bedchamber. Widows who took lovers because they were free to do so, or married women who took lovers out of loneliness. What he hadn't learned at university or from a library, he'd learned from these women. And a very good pupil he had been, indeed.

But he had never himself been the teacher. Never took an innocent to his bed. He would have to marry one day, and the assumption was that he would marry a virgin, of course. A young woman Miss Smythe's age was expected. But what about an unmarried women of a slightly older age who might be considered, as the English said, "on the shelf"?

Someone like Miss Clarissa Trent.

Miss Trent inspired him in many ways, not just erotically, although his rather persistent erection of the last few hours would have him thinking otherwise.

She was beautiful, but her beauty was not merely in her golden-brown eyes and her plump, pink lips. She had a charming assuredness about her, a confidence in her own knowledge, and a desire to engage in discourse.

The appearance by Acker was most likely a ruse to make sure she was not left alone with Mehmet. He imagined the conversations they could have had. Conversations he was determined they would have one day very soon.

He truly did mean to invite the English to his palace, but he was mostly looking forward to showing off his palace to Miss Trent, wanting, needing to see the approbation in her eyes.

Then after a fine dinner and a discussion of classical literature in his library, he would make a request, a plea…

Just a kiss, one kiss from those tender lips of hers…

Except his cock had another idea.

And alone in his bath he was allowed to indulge his fantasies. The bath was his domain for private pleasure, and thoughts of Miss Trent were very definitely his private pleasure.

He grabbed his now throbbing cock and tugged, rolling the prepuce over the head slowly. He leaned back against the pillows to stare at the play of lamplight and shadows on gray-veined marble and turquoise tiles.

What would it be like to have a virgin?

Not a rabbity miss, but a woman clearly comfortable with her mind and body, a woman who just needed the experience of absolute pleasure to complete her.

He'd take his time, introducing her to the miracles of her own body, of what pleasures a tongue and fingers might elicit. And when she was thoroughly enraptured, he would open her legs a bit wider.

"Do you want this?" he would ask. She would have to be ready for him with her heart, mind, and body.

"Yes, yes, Mehmet."

He would enter her, the tightness like his firm grip on his prick. But unlike the frantic pumps of his hand, he would move in and out of her slowly, marking her expression for undue pain, hoping to witness the moment when pain dissolved into absolute pleasure.

After that moment, he would not be able to contain himself. As he thrust into her depths, he would suck at her pink-tipped breasts, his ear close to her heart, his orgasm jetting deep inside her as she wailed her own climax.

Mehmet stared at the trail of semen on his abdomen.

He'd have to pull out; he would not be able to experience that final joy in such a way.

Not with Miss Trent's reputation at stake.

DISCOVERING HER DELIGHT

* * * * *

ENSCONCED IN HER BED, her coverlet tightly around her shoulders, Clarissa stared at the cloth wall of her tent. The day had kept her busy, but the night meant her fantasies took hold.

Fantasies of a handsome, unmarried Turkish man who gazed at her far too intently and too often, and whose gaze she welcomed.

She'd been on edge since that morning when Mehmet Pasha had thrilled her with his charm. She had been perhaps a bit too curt with Althea, Cornelia, and Beatrice during tea, only because she wanted to be alone in her tent with wicked thoughts of the pasha.

And here she was in her tent with wicked thoughts of the pasha. But she was far from alone. Beatrice and her innocence slept on the other side of the space. Clarissa had never thought it would be she who would want to escape the confines of playing the chaperon, because she had not imagined there would be a devastatingly handsome pasha about which to fantasize.

If only Beatrice would have the sense to sneak out to visit William.

Clarissa exhaled, releasing a sound like a snore.

Behind her a rustling sound sent a chill along her spine.

She waited and listened. Was Beatrice getting up from her cot?

Possibly to merely use the chamber pot. No, no, just turning over in her sleep. Her heavy rhythmic breathing indicating she was utterly senseless.

And that Clarissa was free to indulge her fantasies of Mehmet Pasha.

His green eyes, his dark beard, his low baritone voice that had resonated lusciously in her core, teasing her sex, the memory of which taunted her still.

Clarissa rolled onto her back and hitched up her nightgown. She bent and opened her legs and slid her hand between her thighs to the hair of her mons.

She cupped herself for a moment, listening, before delving further, finding herself wetter than she'd been in a very long time. A very long time.

Because she'd not met a man as provocative as the pasha in a very long time.

She rubbed the aroused nubbin at the apex of her sex, each stroke eliciting an image of him, naked, kissing her, caressing her, touching her in ways she had almost forgotten.

This was no schoolgirl fascination because she was no schoolgirl. She was a grown woman with needs and desires, who'd only had a taste of men.

The pasha inflamed her, reminding her of what she'd had before. What she wanted again. This time with him.

That he was unmarried aroused her insensibly. It meant possibility, even if only for a furtive tumble at his palace.

It also meant his heart was free. Perhaps they could explore an intellectual connection as well as a physical one. Perhaps their friendship would grow, adding depth to the physical pleasures.

A twinge of ecstasy fluttered in her belly, beginning the climb to the peak. She pressed her lips together to keep herself from crying out. But in his arms, she would make sure he knew whatever he did to her was the most wondrous pleasure she had ever experienced.

She bucked up as she came, the iron bed frame squeaking. She let her body down gently, quietly and stretched under the covers.

As she exhaled, clarity descended. The pasha had known the Roman emperor Hadrian had taken a young man as a lover. What if the pasha were not married because he, like Hadrian, preferred the company of men?

Clarissa rolled to her side.

Would an intellectual friendship and sensual satisfaction by her own hand be enough with such a provocative man?

CHAPTER SIX

As she held the trowel and chipped away at the dirt, Beatrice felt a wave of triumph. Mehmet Pasha had reviewed the list of men who worked at the site, then had dismissed any whom he did not know personally. Those who remained had once worked for him in some capacity or another, or they were a family member of someone currently in his employ. The men who remained respected him and would abide by his directives.

And one of those directives was that Beatrice and Miss Trent be allowed access anywhere they pleased on the archaeological site. Mrs. Stanfield and Mrs. Acker were allowed the same access, but they were not so very interested in sitting on the ground and digging in the dirt. The pasha's interpreter at the camp, Sinan, was to immediately inform the pasha of any grumbling among the workmen about the presence of any of the women.

"I hope we find something."

Beatrice nodded at William, her excavation partner. "I hope so as well. Imagine uncovering something that has not been seen for well over a thousand years."

The workmen had cut a couple of deep trenches in strategic areas then set up shade tents so the archaeologists would be shielded from the hot sun.

She smiled to herself. She really was an archaeologist now.

On the other side of the mound Professor Stanfield and Mehmet Pasha worked under another tent, their chatter seemingly nonstop. Beatrice was just happy to be next to William in quiet companionship. And as Miss Trent was drawing in the artifact tent in clear view, Beatrice was still properly chaperoned.

Beatrice scraped away at the ground. "Did Professor Stanfield talk to you about Hadrian and the youth?"

William glanced up in the direction of the professor and the pasha. "He did."

"And? What did he say?"

"Did Miss Trent not talk to you?"

"She did. I just want to know if we got the same information."

William chuckled. "Well, he gave me a lecture about an ancient Greek social structure called pederasty where older men had intimate relations with adolescent boys, and how Hadrian admired the Greeks and so had such a relationship with the youth Antinous." He sighed. "He seemed to imply that this was a practice from ancient history, but I know of two men who have such an intimacy today. And they're both the same age."

"Miss Trent also mentioned the ancient Greeks. But she also said that some men don't want to have relations with women. She said I should guard my heart because it's very easy to become friends with these sorts of men who love men but do not want anything more than friendship with a woman. She also mentioned something about men with piercing blue eyes."

William leaned a bit closer to Beatrice. "It sounds like Miss Trent was relating her own experience."

"I thought the same." Beatrice glimpsed at Miss Trent who was pouring herself a cup of lemon water from an ornate enameled ewer. "Now I feel so sad for her falling in love with a man with blue eyes who did not, or, I suppose, could not, love her back in the same way."

"Maybe she'll find true love one day," said William. "She's very pretty and very amiable."

"And very intelligent."

William chuckled. "Yes, and very intelligent, as well."

WILLIAM HAD TO STOP HIMSELF from gazing at Beatrice while she worked. Her focus was positively attractive, her enthusiasm rousing, instigating him to perform his absolute best. He resumed his digging, so content that they were working together side by side.

After Mehmet Pasha had dismissed the men who had been deemed troublesome in some way, William had approached Professor Stanfield alone in the tent he used as his study. He had advocated for Beatrice to have a chance at "getting her hands dirty," to have a chance at chipping away at the rock and earth, to experience the thrill of discovery. William had said he himself would work with her and protect her if needed, and would arrange the nearby presence of Miss Trent if that were preferable.

The professor had let out a brief chuckle at that point. "I do believe all impediments to Miss Smythe's joining us on the ground have been removed. I think she will quite enjoy her new responsibilities."

Beatrice had been called into the study tent then, a little crinkle of worry marring her face as she'd glanced at William. But William knew what Professor Stanfield was going to tell her, and he could scarcely contain his grin. And when Beatrice had been told she was now free to do a bit of digging, her joy was apparent. She'd given him the most endearing smile, an expression revealing her satisfaction as well as her impatience to get right to work.

William had to restrain himself from picking her up, whirling her about, and kissing her.

He'd make sure to find a time and place.

Working so closely that he could hear her little grunts and breathe in her delicate perfume was proving to be distractingly arousing. If it had been just the two of them, he would have refrained from wearing the special binding around his groin, but he was in the presence of others and he had to present himself as a scholar, not a lover.

And now that Mehmet Pasha had finalized all the required bureaucratic documents and joined their camp, William felt the weight of even more scrutiny. He was not only a guest on the pasha's land and in his country, he was a representative of England and English culture. Which doubly meant he had to act respectably.

He and Beatrice could resume their love affair when they returned to England.

"Eureka!"

William and Beatrice stopped and turned at the sound of Mehmet Pasha's exclamation. The professor and the pasha were stretched out on their stomachs, clawing at the trench before them.

"It looks like they discovered something," said Beatrice. "Let's go see."

She climbed out of the pit and brushed herself off. William followed suit. She grabbed his hand, an act surely just out of elation, and they rushed to the other trench.

The professor and the pasha discussed the find with their heads lowered in the trench as they brushed and scraped away dirt.

"…Corinthian fluting, I should think—"

"Yes, the flat ridge between the carved channels—"

"Local marble, perhaps?"

"Once it is cleaned, I'll know for sure."

Miss Trent came up behind Beatrice. "Oh my, how exciting."

Beatrice squeezed William's hand. No one seemed to mind they were still holding hands. He squeezed back.

Professor Stanfield scrambled to sitting, then to standing, huffing a little. He noticed Beatrice and William. "Ah, my students have arrived. Have a look at what our patron has found."

Quickly unclasping their hands, they went to the edge of the trench and watched as Mehmet Pasha carefully scraped dirt away with a trowel. There, peeking through the earth was the side of a fluted marble column.

"Egads," muttered Beatrice.

William held his tongue as a stronger oath was at the ready. This was precisely what they had come for. It was, simply, magnificent.

"Mehmet Pasha, would you like me to capture this moment?" Miss Trent's voice held wistful admiration.

The pasha elegantly rolled over into a cross-legged position. "What a marvelous idea, Miss Trent. Especially as my photographer has failed to arrive in a timely manner."

Miss Trent blushed and sat on the ground.

"Shall I fetch you a chair?" asked the pasha.

"I'll be fine," responded Miss Trent.

If he hadn't noticed it before, William was quite cognizant of it now. There was something of a tendre between Miss Trent and Mehmet Pasha. How wonderful for them.

And for him and Beatrice, who could only benefit from a distraction on the part of Miss Trent.

Morning greeted Mehmet with a gorgeous golden light, a light profoundly suited to the blue-veined marble quarried on an island just off the coast of his land. The same marble used in the construction of the temple he had hoped—no, had *known* was buried under centuries of dirt.

From the entrance of his tent he walked over that very dirt. Two days ago, he had obtained proof of the temple. Since then, his men had worked diligently and carefully to unearth the section of column, finding more sections in the process. He now had almost an entire column waiting to be liberated from the earth.

Pride—mingled with relief—coursed through him, energizing him to continue the work he had too long put off. Father had always supported his obsession, but privately. Outwardly, he'd had to state the future was with the sultan, that the Greeks and Romans were an unfortunate part of the past. Mehmet had always thought knowledge of the past could inform the present, or at the very least, provide interesting stories.

A servant brought him a coffee with the obligatory obeisance. He downed the thick liquid in two gulps and handed back the ceramic cup. In the distance, a female figure examined the trench the university students had been picking away at. She knelt at the trench opening, bent down, reaching then quickly withdrawing as if in surprise.

A rodent? A snake? Something else? He would have to investigate why the lovely Miss Trent was up at dawn investigating an archaeological trench.

She squinted into the sun as he came toward her. The moment she recognized him, she stood, frantically brushing and smoothing her skirts.

"Excellency. Good morning," she said with a slight bow of her head.

"It is a good morning, Miss Trent. Have you had your coffee yet?"

She smiled. "I suppose I am up rather early. But Beatrice—Miss Smythe mentioned something last night that made me want to do a bit of exploring."

"I am intrigued. Please do show me."

Unexpectedly, Miss Trent clambered down the rope ladder into the trench. Of all the ways a woman could show a man something about his archaeological efforts, using her entire body to do so was very appealing. She stood in the trench and passed her hand over what appeared to be a ledge.

"Miss Smythe said she and Mr. Peel were reticent to chip away too coarsely so had been very delicate in their efforts. But as they scraped, a thin block form became apparent." She removed a small pick from her pocket and began scraping at the ledge. "As dirt accumulates, it clings in the crannies of whatever lies beneath." She scraped the dirt as if sculpting it. "The contour of the object is apparent before the object itself is fully uncovered."

Suddenly the brown of the dirt revealed a glimpse of white. She continued to scrape, exposing bits of marble and pockets of dirt. This was not a column.

"Part of a frieze?" he said with a gasp.

She smiled up at him. "Or a pediment." She returned to her work. "Well, that's what I'm hoping for, at least."

So the lovely Miss Trent was as invested in the temple as he was.

"I apologize, Miss Trent, that I do not have a photographer present for this felicitous moment. I received word yesterday that the chap has been called away to Istanbul for another opportunity."

Still working at the dirt, she grunted as if she had expected such a happenstance.

"Which means I will completely be beholden to your artistic skills to capture the important moments in this archaeological endeavor."

She looked up, resignation clouding her beauty for a moment before she gave him a smile once again.

"I think I would like my coffee now, Excellency."

He laughed and obliged her with a snap of his fingers.

CLARISSA WAS PROUD AND satisfied that her instincts had proved correct. When finally uncovered, the find was revealed to be a high-relief fragment from the pediment of the temple. The scene was simply magnificent—well, rather, the simple fact that there was a figural scene was magnificent.

What precisely the scene depicted was not clear.

"The lion skin hanging on a branch indicates Hercules," Professor Stanfield had argued.

"I think, rather, the presence of a female figure on the right points to the leopard skin of Dionysus," Mehmet Pasha had suggested. "It seems she might be holding an ivy wreath."

Of course all Clarissa could think about while listening to the two scholars was that the youth Antinous was sometimes depicted as Dionysus, but never as Hercules. And then once she began thinking about Antinous, her heart slumped in resigned awareness that the pasha was probably more like Antinous than Hercules in his sexual proclivities.

Clarissa had spent the morning sketching as the sculpture was uncovered, then had concentrated on quick sketches of the workmen shoveling the earth in the area where it was assumed the rest of the pedimental sculpture would be.

By midday, she was exhausted.

She sat in the shade of the artifact tent where bits of marble and ceramic waited to be cataloged. More work. Work that could be performed by Althea and Cornelia to give her a bit of respite. She dropped her head in her hands and rubbed her temples.

"I think luncheon might revive you, Miss Trent." Mehmet Pasha was before her, holding a metal cup of lemon water.

She took the cup. "Thank you, Excellency." She was parched. The water felt so good sliding down her throat.

"Mehmet, please. I insist you call me by my first name. Especially in the informality of a camp site."

She met his gaze, his golden-green eyes soothing. "It would be my pleasure, Mehmet."

God, his smile was devastating. She could not lose her heart to this man. She had work to do.

"Now, Miss Trent, while my men search for more of the pediment, I suggest you retreat to your tent where I will have luncheon brought to you."

He was so utterly handsome.

"And get some rest. You have been up since dawn."

She laughed softly. "As have you."

"I am used to the heat and have servants at my beck and call."

"This is true."

He offered his arm. "Your tent, Miss Trent, is waiting."

She stood and looped her arm around his. It took her mind a moment to register that they were touching. Exhaustion, however, smothered sensuality. He took her as far as the entry of her tent, where she let go of him and went inside. Somehow she ended up on her bed. Alone.

CHAPTER SEVEN

William took a moment to gulp some lemon water before returning to the trench. He surveyed the site, bustling with activity now that most of a column and a portion of the pediment had been found. A smile twitched across his lips. He and Beatrice had helped in the discovery of a spectacular find.

On the other side of the open artifact tent Beatrice consulted with Miss Trent on the latter's drawings. Beatrice exuded confidence and enthusiasm for her part in uncovering history.

He hoped they would be instrumental in finding even more.

Since the initial find, larger marble pieces had been unearthed—bits of molding, part of an ionic volute, fragments still encrusted with dirt. Professor Stanfield and Mehmet Pasha now had a better idea of where the temple had been situated. Miss Trent had sketched new plans. After the workmen had loosened and moved more marble from the ground, the plan was to dig deeper and perhaps find a mosaic floor.

Now *that* would be a spectacular find. William set his cup down.

"Mr. Peel?" Professor Stanfield still used the formal address when they were in public.

"Yes, Professor?"

The professor patted his canvas satchel. "It seems I have left my pick in my study."

"Albin," said Mrs. Stanfield. "I told you to check your worktable before you left this morning." Mrs. Stanfield had decided watching the temple be unearthed was far more interesting than whatever clerical duties and correspondence she had.

"I'm happy to retrieve it for you, Professor." Really he was. Professor Stanfield's study tent was a sort of magical, romantical space.

"Thank you, son."

William jogged across the dusty, weedy ground and halted at the entrance porch. He removed his sun spectacles, brushed himself off, then entered.

One would not know the marquee tent sat in a sunny landscape for inside it was heavily shaded, lending an instant coolness to the space. All the accoutrements for a scholar were present: books in bookshelves, desks, lamps, writing implements, journals. There was even a hammock for those days when the professor needed a nap. Probably hidden somewhere was a bottle of whiskey or port or whatever professors drank. William sighed. This was precisely what he dreamed of having one day.

He fought the urge to tarry. He should simply search for what it was he came for and leave. Mrs. Stanfield said the pick was on the worktable. Obviously that was the more ordinary pine table and not the magnificent mahogany desk.

"William?"

He turned abruptly at the sound of Beatrice's voice. "Bea? What are you doing here?" Had he lost track of time? How mortifying.

She stood in front of the closed doorway of the tent. "Professor Stanfield asked me to tell you he also needs his straw brush." She walked toward him.

He backed up against the worktable, glancing around as if they weren't alone.

But they were.

And she was now in front of him. "Kiss me."

His mouth was on hers instantly. *God,* she felt good. They were good together. They fit perfectly, arms, mouths. If only a kiss could last forever.

He parted from her, holding her gaze, her eyes reflecting the desire, the passion she'd just given him. They'd had their first kiss a week ago. He'd been wanting more every minute of every day since.

And now he had the chance. He pressed his lips to hers once again, opening to taste her, reveling in the sensation of her tasting him.

She moaned softly, a sound that seemed to awaken her body to writhe and press into his. Suddenly, with hands on his chest, she pushed back. "William," she said with a sigh, "I could do this all day. But we are expected back. We cannot continue." She reached around him to grab the tools, then gazed up at him. "I wish I could sneak into your tent again."

His entire body flushed with the memory of their furtive night together. "I wish you could too." He wrapped his arm around her waist and pulled her to him, kissing her one more time.

FROM THE CORNER OF her eye, Clarissa surreptitiously watched Professor Stanfield's tent. William and Beatrice were in there together. If they were there too long, she would make an excuse to leave the artifact tent and surprise the couple.

Relief washed over her as first Beatrice then William exited, the latter carrying the requested tools. Both looked a little flushed, but their clothing was tidy, so nothing too untoward had occurred.

Clarissa smiled. She was not opposed to the young couple having a furtive kiss or two. She just had her responsibilities to keep the precocious Beatrice out of trouble and return her to England *virgo intacta*.

As far as Clarissa was concerned, Beatrice could do whatever it was she wanted with William once they had returned home. Her charge just had to maintain propriety for the six weeks they were on this journey.

But could Clarissa maintain propriety herself? One glance in the direction of Mehmet Pasha weakened her resolve. He wasn't anywhere near her, and yet she felt his presence. He was in the distance under a shade tent talking with the workmen about how best to excavate when searching for a fragile mosaic floor of a temple.

Mehmet's temple.

Dedicated to Antinous.

Clarissa tried to not think about that part.

The rumbling of horses and a cloud of dust signaled visitors. Visitors who were rather motivated to arrive at the camp quickly. Perhaps some tragedy had befallen in the world outside of the excavation.

Professor Stanfield and Mr. Acker stepped outside the artifact tent to see what was going on. Sinan, Mehmet's interpreter, followed.

A Turk in an ill-fitting military uniform accompanied by three formidable men stopped outside the artifact tent. Behind them several carts pulled up, the peasant drivers keeping hold of their reins as if ready to leave.

The Turk's sword glinted in the sun. "Where is the man who leads this excavation? This Professor Stanfield?" he growled in heavily accented English, his dark eyes flashing in anger. His complexion was oddly brown, as if he spent a great deal of time in the sun—or wanted observers to think he did. There was a theatrical quality to his coloring.

The horses moved nervously as the two academics approached.

"I am Professor Stanfield. How can I be of service?"

The Turk waved at his entourage then dismounted, two of his men following suit.

"I am Durukan Fakir Pasha, the administrator of all archaeological activities in this part of the empire. I require the necessary permits."

Professor Stanfield glanced over where Mehmet still consulted with his crew.

"I have been informed all paperwork was filed with the Ministry of Education."

"There are complaints of courtesans in this camp." The pasha leered at Beatrice and Clarissa, the dark complexion garnering a red hue, a tiny dribble of saliva escaping the corner of his mouth to dampen his beard. Clarissa cringed in disgust.

"I can assure you these accusations are false, Excellency." The professor exhibited an uncharacteristic uneasiness. If the Ottoman bureaucracy was anything like the rumors implied, the whole campaign might have to be put on hold while proper paperwork was re-filed and re-approved.

Durukan Pasha circled around the tent until he was standing before Clarissa. Revulsion rippled through her. She stepped back, averting her face.

He cupped her chin and turned her to him. "What have we here?"

"That is Miss Trent, Excellency." Professor Stanfield's voice held a quaver. "She is our artifacts cataloger and artist."

"*Miss* Trent? An unmarried woman? And does she share your bed, Professor?"

Althea gasped.

"Good heavens. I am a married man, and Miss Trent is an honorable woman, I assure you." The quaver had steadied and turned to annoyance.

Clarissa's face hardened in defiance as she stared at this villainous pasha. He chucked her chin harshly, his fingernails surely leaving a scratch.

"And this other one?" The villain now pointed a thick finger at Beatrice.

No. He was not going to touch her. Every muscle in Clarissa's body coiled at the ready.

Behind her William tensed, also at the ready to defend his paramour.

"Lady Beatrice Smythe is a classical scholar and the daughter of a prominent English earl. I do not recommend offending her lest you want Parliament and the queen involved."

Clarissa chilled. The professor only called Beatrice by her title in exceptional circumstances.

The pasha grunted as he continued to regard Beatrice with an expression bordering on lasciviousness. "Just see to it that she is kept apart from the men." He swung around dramatically to face the professor. "I hear you discovered a cache of gold coins."

"Silver." Tension strained the professor's voice. "The coins were silver."

"Perhaps there was a problem with the translation."

"Do you have spies among us, Excellency?" Professor Stanfield said boldly.

Probably the men who had been let go by Mehmet.

"I see and hear everything that happens in my jurisdiction. I suggest you remain aware of that." He turned his beady eyes on Clarissa and Beatrice once again. "I do not want to hear of any more improprieties."

"Any *more*—"

Durukan Pasha held up his hand in the professor's direction. "I will inspect the documents and be on my way."

"Mehmet Pasha will be agreeable to oblige." Professor Stanfield gestured to where Mehmet was completely engrossed in the excavation.

With a dramatic turn, his sword once again flashing in the sunlight, Durukan Pasha stomped out of the shade of the tent, his men trailing behind.

"Something is very, very wrong here." Clarissa pressed her fingers to her lips. She did not mean to say her thoughts aloud.

Professor Stanfield stepped to her side. "I suggest we all be very careful and never be left alone." He placed a hand on her shoulder. "Especially you and Miss Smythe."

WILLIAM WATCHED AS Durukan Pasha marched over to the tent where Mehmet squatted and spoke to his workmen in a trench.

Apparently their patron had been oblivious to the whirlwind that was this sudden villain in their midst.

Mehmet stood and seemingly attempted an introduction. Durukan's rebuff surprised everyone. Such a reaction was not, as far as William understood, very Turkish.

But Durukan was not so very usual.

Sinan turned to Professor Stanfield. "I will attempt to listen and let you know what transpires."

"Thank you, Sinan."

The interpreter approached the two pashas tentatively, keeping his head bent in supplication. Mehmet noticed and said a few words to him. Sinan nodded, then turned away, listening as he shuffled off slowly.

To William's ears it sounded like the pashas were having a horrible disagreement. Miss Trent and Professor Stanfield stood engrossed as if they could understand what was transpiring.

Sinan returned to their tent and took his place beside the professor, an ear to the argument.

"Durukan Pasha is a new bureaucrat. A new province, Karasi Vilayet, has been established just this year, which includes Mehmet's land. Durukan seems to have some connection to this new provincial government. I've never seen him before, and Mehmet clearly does not know him. It is entirely possible that with the establishment of this new province, Mehmet failed to provide some expected document."

"I thought the sultan himself agreed to the final contract Mehmet and the Ministry of Education created," said the professor.

"Yes, he did. So this is why Mehmet is exhibiting signs of frustration." Sinan glanced at William and Beatrice. "I must explain. A decree several years ago established state ownership for all undiscovered antiquities, but allowed for arranging private ownership for legally excavated antiquities. This is our own system of what you call *partage* or division. However, any objects found in clandestine or illegal excavations can be seized by the state."

William understood. "This is the way the Ottoman government prevents outright confiscation of antiquities by foreigners."

"Like the Elgin Marbles," said Beatrice. "And if this new pasha is claiming our excavation is clandestine, then he can take everything we've found."

Sinan nodded. "An agreement with the government is called a firman. Mehmet's firman states he will pay the monetary value of one-third of the objects found on his land. Plus, the firman expressly specifies that indivisible discoveries shall not be divided, but valued as a whole and Mehmet will pay one-third the value of this whole."

Professor Stanfield nodded. "Meaning if we find a mosaic floor, the whole floor must be left intact and Mehmet must provide the government monetary compensation."

William stared at the marble slabs and fragments that had been uncovered and set aside in a pile, like puzzle pieces, for later reconstruction. "Does the definition of indivisible discoveries encompass a pediment? Columns?"

"Yes," said Sinan. "The whole temple, in fact. The government realizes it would be foolish to have one-third of a temple in Istanbul and two-thirds of a temple remaining on its original site."

Durukan Pasha raised his voice, his tone threatening.

"His accent is so very different from Mehmet's," Miss Trent observed.

William listened to the heated conversation. The inflections were different, but how Miss Trent could tell their accents were different in a language she did not speak was remarkable.

Sinan nodded. "I cannot place his accent. I admit it is very strange. But our empire is vast, so perhaps he is from somewhere I am unfamiliar with."

Suddenly Durukan shouted to his men who came forward. He waved his hands at the marble blocks and slabs, indicating they were to be taken away. The men called the peasants driving the carts forward.

William chilled. *No.* Not all their hard work. He moved to stop the outrage.

Beatrice grabbed his arm. "William, don't get involved. If Mehmet Pasha requests our assistance, we will give it."

She was right, of course.

A pang of helplessness weakened him as he watched random pieces of marble being loaded into crates then onto carts and carried away.

CHAPTER EIGHT

"Miss Smythe?"

Beatrice looked up from her cataloging entry and set her pencil down. The pleasant timbre of Mrs. Stanfield's voice always set one at ease. "Yes?"

"Albin—Professor Stanfield has a letter for you. In his study tent."

"A letter?" That was rather curious.

"Yes, it was sent alongside a letter to him from your father, our patron."

Beatrice held her tongue. Papa was not a patron of the excursion. Mr. Alistair Tubney was the chief financial patron, along with Lord Petersham. The best she could guess was that Mrs. Stanfield was speaking in some sort of code.

"All right, thank you. Shall I fetch my letter now?"

"Yes. You are expected." Mrs. Stanfield smiled. "I'll make sure your catalog does not blow away."

Rather, she would be making sure none of the cataloging ledgers disappeared. Beatrice nodded and walked casually to the tent that housed Professor Stanfield's study.

A few days had passed since Durukan Pasha had upset the excavation by plundering their best artifacts. Mehmet Pasha had left the next day. He had a staff of secretaries and clerks plus a telegraph machine at his palace. Without Mehmet's presence, the English company had been wary of the excavation workers, not quite sure if any of them were spies for Durukan.

Beatrice entered the study tent. William stood in the center. He offered a thin smile.

No one else was there. "Where is Professor Stanfield?" she whispered.

William stepped forward. "Bea—" Suddenly he took her in his arms, his mouth covering hers. She could kiss him all day, truly, but something was amiss.

She pulled back. "William, is this all just some sort of elaborate scheme to steal a kiss?"

"No, darling." He sighed. "Although I am going mad from want of kissing you."

"I as well."

He took her hand. "I wish we could tarry, but we cannot. Come." William quickly ushered her out the back and into the Stanfields' personal sleeping tent.

Professor Stanfield stood upon their entrance. "Miss Smythe, you must think this highly irregular," said the professor, his face darkened by unshaven stubble. "I apologize for the subterfuge." He waved at a chair indicating she should sit.

She sat.

"The appearance of Durukan Pasha was not expected. Our documents—or rather Mehmet's documents, his firman—are absolutely in order. But this new pasha is now requiring recompense in exchange for allowing us to continue."

"Recompense?" From what she had witnessed, the term seemed not entirely accurate.

"Extortion, really."

Which was certainly not an honest way to proceed.

"Not only has this Durukan Pasha taken some of the objects that were in the field as you witnessed—"

Beatrice's stomach had churned at the sight of marble pieces being carted away.

"He is now demanding we provide him with one-third of everything we have already excavated. We will not be proceeding with further excavations until Mehmet can obtain all the proof he needs that his firman with the government is in order." The professor shook his head sullenly. "Which means we will no longer attempt to uncover a mosaic floor."

"Because it is best it remains buried than cut up into pieces." Beatrice thought of the time in the British Museum she and William had seen an emblema of Atalanta, and how it obviously had been removed from a larger floor.

"I have grave concerns for our research," continued Professor Stanfield. "If we have to relinquish artifacts, we won't have the complete picture, as it were. We'll have missing pieces of the puzzle."

"The puzzle of ancient history."

"I knew you would understand, Miss Smythe—Beatrice. May I call you Beatrice? What I am about to suggest requires a certain level of confidence."

"Yes, of course, Professor."

"I don't suppose you wish to call me Albin." He glanced at her, and she offered him a quizzical look.

"You're older than my father. It would seem odd, I fear."

"All right. I understand." Professor Stanfield drew in a deep breath. "I'm doing something I never thought I would have to do. I am asking you to hide artifacts."

"Hide them? Where?"

"William and Clarissa suggested we hide artifacts among our personal effects."

"Oh. You mean in our luggage?"

"Yes." He gave her a worried look. "You understand, I hope."

"I do."

"Durukan Pasha is threatening to remove one-third of what we have already excavated. However, Durukan does not know precisely what we have excavated."

"So he'll confiscate one-third of what he sees, not what we actually have because we will have hidden some of it."

"Precisely," said the professor.

"Won't he request to see our catalogs?"

"Yes, this will be a problem."

Beatrice pondered the new arrangement for a minute. "Because if we found fifty silver coins and put twenty-five of them in our luggage, then what do I put in my catalog? How does Mehmet Pasha know what it is we actually have and what was taken?"

William chuckled and grinned.

The professor's smile seemed a mixture of relief and distress. "You are too clever, really, Beatrice." His expression relaxed. "No, not too clever. Perfectly clever. And this is why I called you here today."

"Oh?"

"Yes, we'll need a system in which we maintain two separate catalogs, one with the artifacts listed as we wish Durukan to review them, and one where we list the actual artifacts."

William straightened. "But in a sort of code."

"Ah, yes. In a code," agreed the professor. "That was William's idea. I am simply too burdened to come up with sensible ideas at present."

Beatrice cogitated for a moment. "So I need to hide artifacts, but I'll also need to hide a cataloging register as well."

The professor gave her a blank look before he paled. "Of course. This is all too complicated, isn't it? I could really use a brandy right about now."

"Does your wife keep a journal, Professor Stanfield?"

"My wife?" That got his undivided attention.

"Yes. Does she keep a diary?"

"I believe so."

"And Mrs. Acker? Can we ask if she keeps a journal?"

"We can."

"Very well. As I keep a journal, and I believe Miss Trent does as well, I think we can develop some method where we women maintain the correct artifact records among us. This will take a bit of organization on our part, but we do already have tea every afternoon together."

Professor Stanfield exhaled loudly. "I knew I could count on you."

"The complicated part will be to keep track of who has what artifact and which diary has the record of it," said William.

She caught William's eye and smiled. "And I am certain the women of this expedition can figure that out. Don't worry, Professor."

"Thank you, Beatrice. Thank you." A twinkle of gratitude shone in his weary brown eyes.

"Bea?" William gestured they should leave.

They retraced their steps back to the professor's study tent. Before she exited the proper way, William took her in his arms, kissing her once again, her flush of excitement heating more than just her face.

He pressed his forehead against hers. "Bea, you are simply brilliant."

She grinned. "Thank you." She pecked his lips. "I am so glad we are on this adventure together."

CLARISSA SIGHED HEAVILY in the artifact tent, the heat oppressive despite the shade. She had been hired to safeguard Beatrice, but now she was safeguarding antiquities, a task that was proving to be far more complicated than watching a lovestruck girl.

The reprehensible Durukan Pasha had removed only large chunks of the temple, leaving all the smaller fragments of marble and pottery behind. With William's help, Clarissa and Beatrice had separated what remained and moved the larger pieces—including the one piece of pediment that happened to have been in the artifact tent—to the Stanfield's bedroom tent.

Beatrice had invented an ingenious double classification scheme. One scheme was used for the artifacts that Clarissa and Beatrice worked on out in the open. The other scheme was for the artifacts cataloged by Althea and Cornelia. Surprisingly, the academic wives took to their clandestine enterprise with alacrity.

"I feel as if we are employed in some sort of espionage," said Cornelia. "So exciting."

The covert cataloging entries were incorporated into the two women's personal journals by including the classification number with each woman's other musings of the day.

But all this double cataloging was triple the emotional strain. At any moment Durukan Pasha could arrive.

In the meantime, Clarissa felt grief for Mehmet, who had lost not just archaeological objects but his raison d'etre. She thought about him far too much despite knowing he had no interest in her. Really, she was acting like a silly schoolgirl.

"Miss Trent?" Beatrice said just above a whisper.

They had been whispering a lot of late. An uneasiness had settled upon the camp. "Yes?"

"When you made your drawing of the coins, was it specific enough for someone to know how many coins there were?"

Clarissa's heart sunk. She prided herself on her attention to perfect detail. However… "Weren't there several stacks eventually dug out?"

"Yes. I think there was a total of fifty-two coins."

"There were only two stacks in front, then another that could be seen behind. I drew it so one could definitely count the coins. But perhaps thirty or so. Not fifty-two."

Beatrice sighed as she scribbled in a notebook. "I'm trying to figure out how we will handle such a find in the future. Would you have to make two drawings? I fear one blunder and that evil man will ransack our camp."

A gentle breeze blew a swirl of dust over the worktable. Clarissa closed her eyes as she held down the pages of her catalog and let the coolness of the air revive her.

The rhythmic thumping of hooves on the ground enlivened her even further. She glanced behind her. Mehmet Pasha on his gorgeous horse. Looking like a knight in shining armor.

She discretely watched him approach from the corner of her eye. His horse clip-clopped slowly to the artifact tent where he dismounted.

"Miss Trent, Miss Smythe, good day to you both."

Clarissa's heart picked up its pace at the sight of the handsome Turk now wandering through the artifact tent. She drew in a deep breath to steady her nerves and calm the beating of her heart.

Beatrice beamed ingenuously. "Good afternoon, Mehmet Pasha."

"How is the world of archaeological discovery today?"

"Very exciting, Excellency," Clarissa said swiftly, hoping she did not sound strangely curt or annoyed.

He smiled with a sort of knowing smirk. "I was looking for Albin—Professor Stanfield. He's not in his study."

Clarissa met his glorious green gaze shadowed by the brim of his hat and suddenly lost all ability to speak.

"He might be in his sleeping tent," Beatrice said in almost a whisper.

"Ah, I see." Mehmet nodded. "Thank you, Miss Smythe." With a touch to his brim and a smile he left in the direction of the professor's tent.

"He's very handsome, don't you think?"

Beatrice's words stunned Clarissa back to reality. Was she teasing her?

No. Her eyes held genuine innocence.

"More handsome than William?"

Beatrice blushed beet-red.

"I didn't think so." Clarissa smiled.

"But *you* think so," Beatrice said as she regarded her quizzically. "I mean, you think Mehmet Pasha is handsome."

Clarissa's face burned, her cheeks probably as red as her charge's a moment ago. Perhaps she'd find an ally in Beatrice. "Yes, I think he's handsome. But I feel a measure of concern for him and us in this strange situation."

"I do wonder how long we can keep this up. Eventually we'll run out of artifacts to catalog if we're not finding anything new. Would we just leave at that point?"

"I suppose so." Clarissa hadn't really thought that far ahead.

"But then you won't get a chance to kiss him."

Clarissa gaped at Beatrice. "I should chastise you for your presumptuousness."

A smile played upon Beatrice's lips. "But you won't. Because I'm right, aren't I?"

Clarissa heaved a sigh. "And you will keep such thoughts to yourself, young lady."

Beatrice chewed on her bottom lip and returned to her work. Clarissa tried to concentrate on her catalog entry, but her mind kept wandering to a fantasy of kissing Mehmet.

"Miss Trent? Miss Smythe?"

Professor Stanfield beamed with subdued delight. Just beyond his right shoulder stood Mehmet, devastatingly handsome, a devilish expression on his face.

"Yes, Professor?" Beatrice, at least, had the presence of mind to respond.

"How would you like to visit Mehmet Pasha's palace?"

The world started spinning.

"His palace, Professor?" Beatrice shot Clarissa a concerned look which set her firmly on the ground from her flight of fancy. "I think that would be lovely."

"My mother and my sisters love to have visitors," said Mehmet as he stepped forward. "And they especially enjoy meeting Occidentals."

Clarissa was finally able to focus her gaze. She flicked a glance up at Mehmet Pasha.

"I know you two ladies are scholars and scientists—"

A wave of pride rippled through Clarissa.

"So I apologize, but be prepared for my sisters to ask you all about Paris fashions."

"Oh, I have a magazine I brought with me," Beatrice exclaimed. "I would be happy to give it to your sisters. Do they read French?"

"Emine does. But if there are pictures, the others will be able to enjoy the magazine."

Beatrice blushed sheepishly. "Of course."

"And when will our visit take place?" Clarissa tried to maintain a coolness she did not feel.

"In two days' time. My mother and sisters are exuberant with expectation."

The pasha's own enthusiasm was so sweet. A genuine smile broke out on Clarissa's face. Mehmet caught her eye and grinned.

Good God, his smile, his expression were overwhelming. It was ever so wrong to be aroused in the presence of the professor and Beatrice.

"But, I must say that while this invitation to my palace is heartfelt"—Mehmet lowered his voice—"it is also a pretense for transporting some of the more valuable artifacts to my palace for safekeeping."

Beatrice and Clarissa nodded in understanding.

"Albin and I will pack what is in his tent among the Stanfields' and the Ackers' baggage." Mehmet lowered his voice. "Please feel free to take what you can from the artifact tent."

Clarissa glanced around even though the four of them were isolated from the rest of the camp. "Will the camp be secure when we leave?"

Mehmet nodded. "Yes. I have workers I trust, men I know personally, who will keep watch while we are gone."

"Good," Professor Stanfield muttered.

"However," Mehmet continued, "I am still afraid of any additional artifacts being removed." He shook his head. "I imagine what has already been taken languishing in some government warehouse, never to be seen again. Or traded on the illicit artifact market."

That was dispiriting.

He perked up. "We will leave the day after tomorrow. That should give everyone enough time to pack, but not make it look like we are fleeing with bundles of booty."

Clarissa offered a weary smile and a nod to the two men before they trotted back to the Stanfields' tent compound.

"I did not think my journey here would include visiting a palace."

Clarissa's niggling sense of dread was quickly quashed. Beatrice's excitement was infectious. Yes, they were going to a palace. Mehmet's palace.

A new adventure awaited.

FROM THE KNOLL OVERLOOKING the excavation, Mehmet stared at the archaeological site still covered in dirt. His men should be digging holes, uncovering the past. Instead they were merely pulling weeds and clearing brush, activities to keep them employed until he could settle affairs with the Ministry of Education.

He'd sent Sinan to the capital as his advocate. Sinan was not only his interpreter for the English. As a dragoman, he was Mehmet's ambassador to the sultan in Istanbul, as well as a good and trusted man. Mehmet hoped Sinan's advocacy would be fruitful and the original firman would remain in effect. He could have relied upon telegraph communications with the capital, but having a representative meeting face to face with officials would provide a more personal touch. Plus, Sinan had a portfolio of Miss Trent's preliminary drawings of temple finds which should prove impressive.

It would be a shame if Mehmet's workers were to uncover a mosaic floor and the government carved it up and carted bits away, most likely the more narrative elements, leaving behind decoration. Lovely to look at, but would it be enough to prove his theory that a temple of Antinous stood at this location?

He shouldn't be having this dispute with the government at all. He'd filed the correct paperwork and had been given permission. But then this Durukan mucked it up. Who was he, anyway?

Regret had ravaged Mehmet every day since Durukan's imposition. Mehmet hadn't bothered to reconstruct the pediment, because, of course, he'd assumed he'd have all the time in the world to piece it back together. He'd not foreseen the government wreaking havoc on his life's work. The only fragment of note he still retained was the original one found with a lion or leopard skin and a female figure. Luckily the block had been in the artifact tent covered with muslin as it had just been cleaned.

If that fragment had also been carted away, they would at least have had Miss Trent's very precise drawing. She was a marvel. She handled all tasks presented to her masterfully. Her talent with pencil and paper plus her knowledge of classical antiquities were certainly two reasons why he found her so irresistibly attractive.

But fantasies of seducing an English woman were suddenly an unproductive distraction, an impediment to clear thinking, when focus was what he abundantly needed.

Focus on a plan to prevent more artifacts from being taken, and getting what had already been seized returned. There was an inventive plan to hide artifacts, but this was not entirely sustainable as a tactic. Durukan or any governmental representative could insist upon an investigation.

Mehmet sighed as the figure of a woman in a wide-brimmed hat and a canvas apron over her plain dress made the view of his wretched archaeological site far more agreeable. And, as the woman climbed the low hill, it seemed the very much agreeable Miss Trent's trajectory was toward him.

At the summit she surveyed the surroundings with hands on hips. After a deep inhalation and exhalation, followed by a nod of her head, she sat on the ground next to him.

"The late afternoon breezes are a balm to a weary soul."

Dare he flirt? "And the tiled bathhouse at my palace will be a balm to a weary body."

The blush that livened her cheeks was endearing.

"I think I would quite enjoy a bath, Excellency."

"Your wish is my command, Miss Trent." He met her demure smile with a bold grin. "To what do I owe the pleasure of your company?"

"I needed some air." She stared at her hands. "Working in the artifact tent all day can be stifling."

She was probably feeling the stress of their situation just as he was—as they all were. The thought was both comforting and troubling. He could, at the very least, take her mind off their situation.

He gestured broadly at the archaeological site below. "If we were to dig down and discover a mosaic floor, what would you imagine the mosaic floor to depict?"

A smile was accompanied by a soft laugh. "As you are perched on this hill probably imagining such a thing, I offer the same question to you."

"Dionysus and grape vines."

"Oh." Her lips parted as if in surprise. "I was not expecting that."

He lifted an eyebrow. "An extension of the fragment of frieze we found."

"Yes, of course. You thought it depicted the leopard skin of Dionysus."

"Antinous was depicted as Dionysus at times."

Miss Trent nodded. "I suppose he was. And you expect the temple to be one dedicated to Antinous."

"I do." He tried to catch her eye but she was evasive. "And, Miss Trent, what do you imagine the mosaic to be?"

"I thought perhaps a Nilotic scene."

"With crocodiles and fishing boats?"

"Oh, yes, I should think so."

"Because Antinous drowned in the Nile?"

She pondered this. "Yes, I suppose I was inspired to think that because of your speculation. And to my eye the wreath looked like lotus or water lilies rather than ivy. Plus, the site is near the sea."

Mehmet considered this new idea. "We do not know where the coastline was two thousand years ago." He smiled at her. "Miss Trent, this is a compelling possibility."

"Thank you, Excellency." She took off her hat just then, as if suddenly overheated. A tendril of dark blond hair fell to brush against her cheek.

Instinctively, he reached out and tucked it behind her ear.

A moment later, mortification descended. "I beg your pardon, Miss Trent." He drew back. "My familiarity was inappropriate. Please forgive me."

She glanced around, as if making certain they were alone, then took his hand. Her palm was calloused, but not so very rough. He imagined she used a cream before she went to bed at night. Then he imagined her in bed. He shifted his position in a vain attempt to curb his burgeoning erection.

The fact that she was seemingly absentmindedly rubbing tiny circles on the back of his hand was no help in dispelling the fantasy—or his now fully developed stiff stander.

He enveloped her bedeviling hand. "Miss Trent, I look forward to all of us having a holiday at my palace."

Her blush glowed. Her mouth fell open again briefly, before she pressed her lips together as her hand retreated to her lap. She nodded, then stood.

"I must pack, and help Miss Smythe pack as well. Especially since we need to include precious objects in our luggage." She offered a smile before heading down the hill.

Anticipation washed over him. Well, there seemed to be hope in that direction. And his palace would afford plenty of opportunities.

CHAPTER NINE

Beatrice remained politely poised despite anticipation roiling within as the carriage approached Mehmet Pasha's palace. She rode with Miss Trent, Mrs. Stanfield, and Mrs. Acker and wanted to maintain some sense of decorum. As requested, the women and men were in separate conveyances. She'd see William at the palace soon enough.

Excitement welled as the outer walls came into view, the carved decorations of the reddish stone gilded by the late morning sunlight. A magnificent central portal with open wooden doors welcomed them into the entry courtyard. The walls surrounding the courtyard were punctuated with intriguing elements: pointed, Gothic-style arches lined with cobalt blue tiles; niches and doorways flanked by floral tiles and slender columns; carved wooden screens hiding what lay behind the windows on the upper story.

Despite the dazzling decorative details, the palace was more modest than what Beatrice had imagined a Turkish palace would look like. But Mehmet Pasha was not a king. He was merely the son of a wealthy landowner.

The carriage stopped, and Beatrice and the other women descended with the help of liveried footmen who averted their eyes and continued to do so even as they removed luggage from the back and roof of the carriage. Their expressions remained impassive as they handled the luggage holding heavy artifacts.

So strange that these men were deferential and dutiful, yet some of the workmen of the excavation were leering and practically mutinous.

The carriage conveying the men arrived. Professor Stanfield got out first, then Mr. Acker.

Then William.

She caught his eye, but he gave her an admonishing look. They'd agreed they would be as formal as they could bear, and attempt to find private time when they could.

Mehmet Pasha strolled into the courtyard from an exquisitely tiled archway wearing a striped and embroidered robe that looked like a dressing gown. He held his arms wide in welcome.

"Good day, gentlemen." He turned to the women. "And ladies." His proud countenance briefly softened with an adoring glow as he glanced at Miss Trent. "Welcome to Mavi Saray, the Blue Palace, my family's ancestral home."

Professor Stanfield came forward and shook the pasha's hand. "Thank you for your hospitality."

The pasha murmured his response then waved his hands and the courtyard was abuzz with activity. Luggage was taken away to disappear behind tiled archways.

Mehmet Pasha turned to his English guests and gestured at the entryway from which he had appeared. "Please, let me give you a tour of my humble abode."

He turned to Miss Trent, once again with a sort of besotted expression, and held out his arm. She blushed then looped her arm around his.

Oh, my. They were in love, weren't they? How wonderful. Beatrice kept her glee in check as she took William's proffered arm and entered the tiled portal.

"It's beautiful," said Mrs. Stanfield with a breathy voice.

"Indeed," said Mrs. Acker.

William looked up and gasped at the magnificent vaults covered in blue and green ceramic tiles. Beatrice had to tug him to follow along.

"This is the corridor to the public rooms," said the pasha. "Here is my study where I conduct official business." He waved his free hand at a door to the left. "My library, which is available to all to peruse"—he glanced around—"is just behind the study. The sitting room is through here." He ushered them through carved wood double doors into a vestibule, then through another set of doors into a room not unlike a well-appointed English drawing room.

He stopped, let go of Miss Trent's arm with a smile, then addressed the group. "This is the public sitting room where all may gather and converse and relax at any time, regardless of sex."

Beatrice flashed a panicked look at William. Were they to be separated by gender in other places?

William gave her arm a squeeze.

The pasha seemed to notice Beatrice's uneasiness. "All the public rooms are at everyone's disposal. And we will share meals together in the main dining room just beyond." He gestured to a door. "The outdoor terraces are also available to all, and I highly recommend spending an afternoon reading in the cushioned shelter of one of the many pavilions."

That sounded like heaven.

"But the sleeping and bathing areas are segregated by gender, as has been the custom since this palace was built over two centuries ago."

Mehmet Pasha extended his arm to the right. "The women's harem is to the right." He gestured behind him. "The apartments for married couples in the middle. And the bachelor quarters are on the left." He nodded at William.

"Mavi Saray has two separate bathhouses. The hamam for women is inside the harem. The hamam for men is next to the bachelor quarters. Married couples must follow this separation, I'm afraid."

The Stanfields and the Ackers indicated their understanding.

Mehmet Pasha gave a rhythmic knock on a large wooden door deeply carved with arabesques and hinged with equally decorative ironwork. The door opened, and four women stepped through, each of them strikingly beautiful, all dressed spectacularly in embroidered and brocaded robes. Three had green-brown eyes and hair as black as Mehmet's. The fourth woman wore a delicate silk head scarf, strands of graying hair slipping through. All smiled in eager excitement.

The pasha beamed as the women gathered around him. "These are my sisters, Emine, Verda, and Nadide." He turned to the older woman, his face beaming with love and respect. "And this is my mother, Beria."

Introductions were made all around. Surprisingly, the pasha's family all understood and spoke English, although they also gave their welcome—*hoş geldiniz*—in Turkish. Beatrice made an effort to respond that she was happy to be there—*hoş bulduk*—but she was certain her accent was terrible.

Mehmet Pasha clapped his hands together. "Now, I will continue the tour with our bachelor and married guests, while Miss Trent and Miss Smythe have their own tour." He bowed and led his tour through another carved wooden door.

"Miss Trent and Miss Smythe, if you will follow me." Beria smiled and gestured to the door she had come through.

An austere vestibule and dimly lit corridor were in utter contrast to what lay beyond. Suddenly they were walking along a breezeway with tiled columns separating them from a garden courtyard. Lemon and orange trees and flowers of all the colors of the rainbow perfumed the air. Couches and richly colored rugs filled the interiors of small gazebos. Servants lined the breezeway opposite.

Beatrice gasped. "Do the men have such a place as well?"

Emine, who seemed to be about Beatrice's age, laughed. "No. My poor brother has only the public gardens for his enjoyment."

"But we can go there too?" Beatrice so wanted to spend time with William. "We're allowed, I mean?"

"Beatrice," Miss Trent whispered in an admonishing tone.

Beria chortled. "Yes, yes. I know that there is a notoriety among the English about our Turkish harem."

A flush crept up Beatrice's neck. She did not mean to insult.

"The harem is not for the pleasure of a man, but rather, it is for the protection and privacy of the women. Even for the married women, when they want a break from their husbands, there is the refuge of the harem."

"Our eldest sister, Zeynep, has appropriated a room in her husband's house as her refuge," said Verda, who was probably a little younger than Beatrice.

"She lives in Bursa," added Nadide, who was perhaps thirteen or so.

Miss Trent nodded. "We also have the separation of the sexes in England, Beatrice," she reminded. "Such as at dinner when the women leave for the drawing room and the men stay in the dining room for their port and cigars."

The custom had always rankled, though.

"Well," Beatrice began, "I suppose in the harem if a woman wanted to smoke a cigar after dinner she could do exactly that."

That made everyone laugh.

Beria indicated they should continue the tour. "Come, let us show you to your rooms."

Beatrice would look for William later. The palace was large enough that surely they could find a hidden corner?

* * * * *

WILLIAM HAD NEVER SEEN such opulence. The Tudor-era ornateness of Harwell Hall in Lincolnshire certainly did not compare to Mehmet's Mavi Saray.

But the opulence seemingly ended at the bachelor quarters. Even Mehmet Pasha felt the need to explain once he had shown William to his room.

"I think the rustic austerity of these rooms was originally intended for traveling mystics and merchants. Or perhaps to encourage sons to marry." He chuckled at his own joke. "I myself merely sleep in my room. I spend most of my time in my study or outside on the terrace. I invite you to do the same. Please avail yourself of the library and lose yourself in a book under a pavilion."

"Thank you, Mehmet."

"I will take my leave. There will be a casual luncheon in the dining room during the afternoon, and we will have a formal dinner at six or seven. Please also avail yourself of the servants should you need anything. Most understand a little English."

Perusing the contents of a pasha's library was considerably enticing. Being with Beatrice under a pavilion was even more so.

But the tension and chaos of the last few days had drained him. A nap to reinvigorate his senses sounded like a better idea. William took off his shoes and stretched out on the mattress, the bed far more comfortable than what he'd been sleeping on in his tent…

William jolted awake with a start. Where the hell was he? A darkened room with a comfortable bed…

Right. Mehmet Pasha's palace. Apparently the bed had been a little too comfortable.

He lit a lamp, then grabbed his pocket watch still in his waistcoat hung over a chair. Five o'clock in the afternoon. Enough time to make himself presentable before dinner.

His stomach growled as he washed his face in the cold water poured from a pitcher by the basin. At some point, perhaps while he slept, a servant had hung up his clothes in a wardrobe and left out a pair of loose trousers, a fresh shirt, and a magnificent jacket embroidered with swirling vegetal tendrils in lustrous threads.

William dressed and combed his hair. One final check in the dressing table mirror gave him a bit of confidence. The jacket did rather compliment him.

He wended his way down corridors, trying door handles and latches, discovering the library which was not unlike any English gentleman's well-stocked library, then the bathhouse which was lavishly tiled and inordinately inviting.

Finally, a little further along, he heard voices. Another door, and he was in the drawing room, where it appeared everyone had just finished drinking some liquor from delicate glasses.

"Ah, Mr. Peel," said Mehmet. "Thank you for joining us." He surveyed William. "As I thought, the jacket looks very fine on you."

"Thank you—" Ugh. He should attempt to convey gratitude in Turkish. "*Teşekkür ederim.*"

The pasha grinned. His sisters giggled and blushed.

Beatrice stepped forward. She wore a blue and white dress that was the perfect mixture of Oriental and Occidental. Threads of gold set off her blond hair quite magnificently.

"Good evening, William." She slid her fingers along the shawl collar of his jacket. "So exquisite."

Blast. That awakened his cock. She should not touch him that way. Well, not in public anyway. Perhaps in the bathhouse…

He distracted himself by surveying the room. All the English were attired with some garment in the Turkish fashion. Miss Trent's gold and orange ensemble stood out as the most flamboyant.

"Now that we are all here, let us go in to dinner," announced Mehmet who wore a shimmering robe of olive and brown stripes.

They all followed him into the dining room. The seating arrangements seemed to be somewhat arbitrary, so William took Beatrice's hand and led her to one of two chairs side by side.

Really, he should avail himself of the opportunity to bridge cultural divides, to learn about the Turkish way of life and sit next to one of Mehmet's sisters. But he just wanted to be with Beatrice at that moment. He'd make an effort to talk to one or more of the sisters tomorrow.

"Where were you today?" murmured Beatrice. "I thought I might see you on the terrace, under a pavilion."

"Oh?" He should not have fallen asleep.

"Mehmet's mother gave each of the Englishwomen a gift of finely embroidered slippers for us to wear. Then I had a wondrous bath, and a snooze in the garden of the harem." She paused while a servant placed a bowl of soup before her. "Then Miss Trent and I moved to the terrace. We engaged Mehmet's sisters in conversation. They are so eager to speak English. And they are simply charming."

"That sounds far better than what I actually did." He remained silent while soup was placed before him and the servant had progressed to the next guest. "I am ashamed to admit I fell asleep."

Beatrice covered her mouth, but the upturn of her smile peeked above her hand.

"However, I did get a chance to explore while I was trying to find the dining room. You really must visit the library."

"Perhaps we could visit the library together," she said.

God, yes. Perhaps while no one else was there. "And the bathhouse." William almost choked as he swallowed. Did he really just say that out loud?

Well, not too loudly, for only Beatrice heard him. Perhaps Mr. Acker on his other side, but that staid man wouldn't understand such sensual insinuations.

Beatrice tore a bit of bread from the chunk in her hand. "That sounds like a delightful and daring idea." She chewed thoughtfully. "It would have to be yours, though. We have guards scattered about in the women's quarters."

All right, this was starting to be a plan of sorts.

"Mr. Peel," began Mr. Acker with unnecessary formality, "will you be joining our meeting in the pasha's study after dessert?"

The study? "I have not been informed of such a meeting. What is the purpose?"

"Ah, well, the pasha wants to review how to handle the artifacts kept in his palace. I'm sure if Albin has not requested your presence, then you need not be there."

Good. He could plan to spend time with Beatrice instead. "I'll ask the professor for a summary of the meeting in the morning." He nudged Beatrice under the table with his thigh.

She glanced at him, and he bent his head closer to hers. "The academics and the pasha have a meeting tonight in the pasha's study."

Beatrice nodded. "The wives usually retire early, but I'm not sure how I'll be able to evade Miss Trent."

The chaperon was very definitely the one to try to circumvent.

"But maybe she won't mind too much if we simply talk out on the terrace after dinner."

William once again leaned toward his love. "And perhaps she'll look away for a moment."

Beatrice's blush was endearing. But he should not taunt her so—or himself. Thoughts of being alone with her were beginning to tease not just his brain but his prick. His stomach reminded him to focus on his lamb köfte with rice pilaf while propriety insisted he pay attention to whatever pleasant dinner conversation was transpiring around them.

Mehmet's sisters were very interested in the archaeological site and were clearly pained for their brother's setback. Beatrice's and Miss Trent's enthusiasm for their work made the girls want to participate. Mehmet protested.

"You know your sisters would be very helpful, Mehmet," said Beria with a touch of admonishment.

"I could show them how to catalog," said Beatrice. "You'll need help after we return to England."

"Oh, please, brother, *please*." The chorus of pleas eventually wore the pasha down.

He waved his hands. "When I have settled all my business with the government, I will give my lovely family a tour of the site and consider their offer to help. But Verda and Nadide, you must keep up with your schoolwork."

"Yes, brother," Verda said through a grin.

The familial conviviality was heartwarming, making William feel at home. Only Mr. and Mrs. Acker seemed a little taken aback by what they probably perceived as a raucous display of overfamiliarity. All the other English seemed amused.

Finally, plates were empty, and conversation dulled. Mehmet Pasha stood. "I would like to give a speech, a toast, if you will, to our English guests." He held up his water glass. "Thank you for supporting my dream."

Everyone raised a glass and joined in the toast.

"You all have complete freedom in my palace." He presented a measured smile. "Of course within the boundaries that I presented today. The women deserve their privacy." He gave a subtle nod in Miss Trent's direction.

Miss Trent was positively moon-eyed. Of course, the pasha was—even William had to admit—a handsome man. It seemed Miss Trent had fallen for his attractions.

Good. Perhaps she would be distracted by romantic dreams tonight.

"I especially invite you to visit the terrace at night. Lamps illuminate the pavilions. Along the balustrade at the edge you will be greeted with a view of a vast sea of stars above a black void." Pride rang in the pasha's voice.

Beria stood as well. "Let us repair to the drawing room to enjoy some dessert with wine and coffee. There are double doors to the terrace. Those who wish to smoke a cigar may do so outside." She winked at Beatrice.

How odd. Perhaps women smoked cigars in Turkey.

William escorted Beatrice to the drawing room where the three sisters immediately surrounded her and began to ask all sorts of questions about cataloging.

His heart sunk a little. He wanted to steal Beatrice away, but perhaps tonight was not the night.

Mehmet approached and offered a glass of claret. "I did not see you all afternoon, Mr. Peel."

"I am mortified to admit I fell asleep. Despite the ascetic nature of the room, I must say the bed was overly restful."

The pasha laughed.

"Is it too late to visit the hamam?" William lowered his voice. "I never did avail myself of a bath, and I fear I may need one."

Mehmet's eyes lit up. "Oh, you *must* visit the bath. We missed you earlier today. Albin, Spencer, and I had a grand time of it. I will arrange an attendant to wait for you."

"Oh, I don't think I need anyone, thank you. Just some soap and a towel will do."

"Nonsense." The pasha called a servant over and gave him instructions in Turkish. The servant bowed and shuffled off. "Hamid will be waiting for you. He is the best."

How peculiar. An attendant really was not necessary, but it would be rude to refuse the hospitality. "Thank you, Mehmet. I will be there presently." He bowed his head. He should tell Beatrice he was leaving. She was still speaking with Emine.

He approached and cleared his throat. "Beg pardon."

Emine smiled and touched Beatrice's arm. "I will see you tomorrow, then." She left the two alone.

William took a gulp of claret and glanced around the room. "Where is Miss Trent?"

Beatrice fluttered her lashes. "Out on the terrace looking at the view, I believe."

An excellent turn of events. William downed the rest of his wine. "Darling, I have a plan."

* * * * *

CLARET IN THE DRAWING ROOM held no enticements. Clarissa was far too restless and edgy.

Spending a couple of hours in the presence of Mehmet Pasha could do that to a woman.

While self-pleasuring had its attractions, she had no interest in returning to her bedchamber at the moment. She wanted to explore the view from the terrace the pasha had effused about.

As she strolled across travertine pavers, she breathed in the spring night air, a touch of coolness imbuing the humidity. Lamps glowed dimly along a path then abruptly stopped leaving a semi-circular platform at the end cloaked in darkness. Clarissa let her eyes adjust then walked to the carved stone balustrade framing the periphery. Before her was a magnificent view of blackness surmounted by a firmament of twinkling stars. More stars than she had ever seen in her life.

The vista in the morning light was probably just as astounding. She'd have to rise early to enjoy it alone.

"This is my favorite place to be when guests are present."

The low rumble of Mehmet Pasha's voice was a welcome addition to the sublime surroundings. And as he approached her, his magnetic warmth and the intoxicating lure of his cologne were even more welcome.

"And why is that?"

He stood to her left at a respectable distance. "Because I discover who is enchanted by my description of the view."

"'A sea of stars above a black void'. Who would not want to witness such a phenomenon?"

"Everyone present at dinner." He turned to her in the darkness. "Except you."

She gazed out at the night sky glittering with stars. "It is beautiful indeed. At camp we can see the stars, but we must crane our necks to look up. Here, it is like someone has unfurled a tapestry of black cloth scattered with shining dots."

"The ability to see the stars is the precise answer I give when people ask why I do not live in Istanbul. Too many buildings."

"Have you ever lived there?"

"No. I have visited but not lived in Istanbul." He let out a clipped grunt. "But I have lived in many of Europe's great capitals."

"Oh? What about London?"

"Yes. For a short time."

Clarissa turned back to the view of the night. "But that's not where you learned to speak English."

It seemed he drew closer to her. "How could you possibly know that?"

"Your accent when you speak our language. It's not a London accent. More like an Oxonian accent."

"How very astute, Miss Trent." Mehmet chuckled. "I learned English from tutors here until I was about seventeen. Then I was sent to Oxford."

She turned to him. "That's a long way from home."

"My father always thought Turkey should look to Europe as an example, that we would one day be part of the West. Given his role as an official he could not voice this, of course. But he understood our shared history, such as our shared Roman heritage."

"Sent from Bithynia all the way to Britannia."

Mehmet laughed at the reference to Hadrian and Antinous. "Only a classical scholar would appreciate your sense of humor, Miss Trent."

"Thank you, Excellency."

"After finishing my studies at Oxford, I took the opportunity for what you Occidentals call a Grand Tour. Or, perhaps, in keeping with the metaphor, more like Hadrian's tour of his empire."

"So you really have lived in many European capitals."

"I do not deceive, even when hoping to garner the attention of a beautiful woman."

A shiver of acknowledgment riffled Clarissa's scalp. She remained silent as she looked at the stars.

"I apologize, I have made you uncomfortable."

"On the contrary, Mehmet. You have flattered me into speechlessness."

He chuckled. "I believe this is the first time in my life."

This was the moment to discover Mehmet Pasha's true predilections. "Surely there have been women who have inspired you?"

"Inspired me? In a superficial way? Yes. Plenty. Women who have had a deep impact on my mind and soul? Very few."

Was this more flattery? Or truth?

"At our first encounter, Spencer had been surprised to learn I did not have a wife."

As had she, but had not spoken it aloud.

"The women I met in Europe were…how shall I say this? Part of my experience there. Not one of them expected anything more than what we shared for a night or for a few days. I certainly did not expect much more than what we shared. I was young, living life for each moment."

He shifted on his feet, then turned his back to the view, leaning against the wall, angled in her direction.

"When I returned home, there were some political machinations by local leaders. Then my father became ill. When he died, the family, the palace, all his responsibilities fell on me. It has been a learning experience these last four years, with no time for romantic entanglements. Yes, daughters of officials have been suggested for me, but I was never interested."

Why was he telling her all of this? "You do not have to explain anything to me."

"But I want to." He sighed. "I should be married. But I have never been motivated until now."

The shiver tore through her again. "Now? Why now?" she dared ask even though her heart tried to stop her.

He took one step, two steps, toward her. His breath tickled her neck. "Because I have met an incomparable woman. A guest in my country. I am enthralled. And I now understand why a man might consider planning for his future."

Clarissa's lungs fought for breath. "A guest, Excellency? Who might this be?" She needed to hear it, to hear it plainly.

"You."

Emotion welled in Clarissa's eyes as a shudder rippled through her.

"Miss Trent, oh, Miss Trent, are you crying?" His hand on her shoulder loosed the emotions she banked back.

She turned away from him. She hadn't a handkerchief so she used the voluminous sleeve of the Turkish dress.

"Have I offended you?" His voice held a tremble. "I would never seek to do so."

"No, no." She wiped tears from both eyes. "I think I am overwhelmed with relief." She turned to face him.

He stood before her now, the heat from his body radiating comfort, his fragrance swirling in her head like a drug. He placed his hands on her upper arms. "Relief, Miss Trent?"

"That you enjoy my company as much as I enjoy yours. And that you are not like the emperor Hadrian."

"Hadrian?" Mehmet's tone was limned with incredulity.

"You understood his relationship with Antinous. I had thought perhaps you were of a similar mind."

He laughed with seemingly genuine amusement. "Oh, I have been considered many things, Miss Trent, but a man who does not desire women is not one of them."

Clarissa sighed in relief. "I suppose I should apologize for the insult."

"No insult has been taken." His thumbs stroked the thin fabric covering her arms, the caress arousing her core. "I did wonder why you seemed a bit distant when I thought I was being charming."

Her arms ached from want of touching him, like he was touching her. Could she? Dare she?

She slid her hands around his waist, under his jacket, the feel of him, athletic and lean, exciting every nerve, every pore in her body. For one moment, his breath hitched in his throat.

"I was being distant because you are a landowner and a government official, and I am merely a chaperon."

"Hmm, I would not say you are *merely* anything, Miss Trent." He released her shoulder to cup her cheek. "You inflame me, Miss Trent."

"Clarissa."

He leaned in closer. "Clarissa."

Her name had never sounded so provocative.

He brushed her cheek with a featherlight touch of his lips.

She tilted her head to give him more access, catching a glimpse of the stars above. He continued his sensual caress down her neck, the hair of his beard tickling, the sensations tightening her nipples. Her shallow breaths dizzied her, and she clung to the reality of this man before her, his touch delicate, gentle, as if she were precious. He held her head steady, his rapid breaths hot on her lips as his face remained poised above hers.

She closed her eyes and parted her lips, waiting…

Nothing.

She opened her eyes. He stared down at her as if mesmerized.

"Mehmet." Saying his name gave her a thrill. "Why do you not kiss me?"

"I am suddenly worried that I might be the first man who has ever done such a thing."

She tried not to smile at his reticence—it would seem too much like teasing. "And would that be a problem?"

"That is a tremendous responsibility. There is never a second chance at a first kiss."

"Would you be horribly scandalized to know you would not be the first to kiss me?"

"Not at all. I am relieved. Clearly the man who kissed you did not kiss you very well as you are still Miss Trent."

She laughed softly and wrapped her hands around his neck. "Then I have something to look forward to."

His mouth was on hers in a heartbeat. The play of his lips upon hers, the nimbleness of his tongue as it explored her depths utterly filled her senses. She clung to him as she melted in his arms, letting him take her on a sensual journey.

He was gentle yet commanding, his hands at her waist slowly sliding along her rib cage to remain poised under her breasts. His beard was a wondrous thrill, rough and masculine.

She pressed her body closer at the very moment he pulled back for air. She wanted more, she had never wanted a man so much in her life.

He kissed her temple, her hair, her cheek. "By all that is holy, I want you."

"Then have me."

He lifted a brow. "Am I to understand the man who kissed you was unsatisfying in other ways?"

She placed her palms against his chest, and smoothed the silky brocade of his waistcoat. "There was a perfunctory quality to his efforts."

"How disappointing for you." He continued to hold her close, gazing at her, lust curling his lips.

"You surprise me, Excellency. For a woman, the hint of an imperfect past is generally considered a stigma and a cause for censure."

"Yet moments before I revealed I have had lovers."

"But that is expected of men."

"Clarissa, I have wanted you since the moment we met, and knowing about your past does not change that. I am very much aware of the unfair dichotomy of how men and women are allowed to pursue their lives, and the level of freedom I have as a man. If you as a woman decided to pursue dalliances in your past, that is not for me to judge, except to say it is befitting an intelligent, interesting woman such as yourself."

"So you are not disappointed you will not be my first?"

"Deflowering virgins is not a letch of mine."

"And if I were a virgin?"

"I would have accepted the honor of being your first if you had chosen me." He sighed. "I would have been happy with mere friendship if that was all you would allow me. Now I am ecstatic that our friendship may be more intimate."

He dived in for a kiss once more, this time letting loose his passions, no longer gentle. He sucked her tongue into his mouth, entangling it with his own, holding her steady as he palmed and massaged a breast. Wetness pooled between her legs. She dared trail her hand down his torso wrapping around to cup a cheek of his bottom.

He growled against her mouth before pulling back, panting.

"Clarissa, my sweet, we must stop. I am a scoundrel for exciting both our passions tonight. Unfortunately, I have a meeting with Albin and Spencer in a short while. They will be leaving tomorrow as they do not want to be away from the excavation site too long."

"Oh. I see."

"There is great discontent in your voice."

"Of course there is. I was hoping for seduction."

He chuckled at her teasing tone. "I apologize profusely. Seduction will have to wait a day."

"I can wait, I suppose." She tugged on the lapels of his jacket pulling him in for a brief kiss.

Mehmet held her head and drew back. "Will I see you tomorrow?"

"I'm not leaving your palace until you have seduced me, Mehmet."

He kissed her forehead. "Then we are of one mind. Because I won't let you leave until I have done so."

* * * * *

Beatrice had tried to explain to William that a Turkish bath was nothing like an English bath or even an ancient Roman bath.

"There is no tub of water."

"Then how does one get clean?"

"You'll just have to find out. Trust me, you will feel cleaner than you ever have in your life."

Now, from her hiding place in the dressing room of the men's hamam, Beatrice tried not to giggle as William's *oof*s and *aah*s punctuated the humid air.

As she had learned earlier that day, a visit to the hamam was an experience beyond imagination. The first room was where she and the other Englishwomen undressed then covered themselves in luxurious towels. The next room greeted them with steam, fragrant with the scent of flowers and herbs. There, they lay on cushioned marble slabs while perspiration plumped their skin. Once they were ready, they were ushered into a heated room in the center of which was a raised, heated marble platform upon which they were requested to recline. The bathing part of the experience began with a soaping down and a vigorous massaging of the muscles. Next they were scrubbed with a fibrous sponge and rinsed until the accumulation of dirt from the excavation had been thoroughly cleansed from the skin.

The final room was one of repose and relaxation, where warm dry heat was countered by drinking cold sweet orange sherbet. Beatrice had held her mirth in check while Mrs. Stanfield and Mrs. Acker had expounded in utter incredulity on the experience they had all just shared.

The footfalls of wooden sandals on the marble floor signaled the attendant Hamid was finished with kneading, scrubbing, and rinsing William. The thud of a heavy door meant Hamid had left William to wallow alone in the afterglow.

Time to make her escape.

She scrambled out from behind the curtain in the dressing room and slid into the pair of *nalın* given to her earlier that day.

The wooden sandals were worn to prevent slipping on the wet marble floor. She hitched up the Turkish trousers that had been given to William which she now wore in her guise as his servant. Despite her every effort to be silent, the clopping of the soles resounded through the empty marble-lined rooms.

William was, as expected, lying on a towel draped over a cushioned platform in the octagonal room of repose. The soothing splash of water from a tiled fountain in the center of the room echoed off tile panels lining each of the eight sides, the patterns of turquoise tendrils and bright red flowers suggesting a garden.

The sensual glow of lamps lit her way as she crept closer, her heartbeat quickening with every step. He was nude—well, his hips and privates were covered by a towel. His face was awash in the bliss of one who had just felt ecstasy—that was the experience of the hamam.

She restrained herself from touching the finely sculpted chest, smooth as the classical statues in the British Museum. She had only imagined what he would look like nude. She had no idea her fantasy—sensual curves of muscles everywhere—would be reality. His countenance was like she had dreamed it would be after sexual intimacy.

Their sexual intimacy.

"William," she whispered, not wanting to startle him.

His eyes fluttered open. "Darling." He grinned. "You were absolutely right about the bath."

Egads, he looked utterly provocative. The heat of the room suddenly became more intense. "May I join you?"

"Please." He limply patted the space on the cushion next to him.

Should she also undress? The drooping trousers at least could go. Also, the velveteen cap which was just a bit too large for her. The shirt hung on her like a generous nightgown, so it would do for propriety's sake. Or William's gentlemanly qualms.

Wearing just the shirt, she joined him on the couch, gently touching his muscled shoulder.

He flinched. "Beatrice, not just yet, I beg you. I am still so very sensitive to the touch."

She understood completely. All the kneading, slapping, and scrubbing riled one's flesh into a frenzy while at the same time putting one's mind at ease.

"I should have believed you when you told me about the bath." He sighed heavily. "Distract me from my languor. I probably should not fall asleep here."

Even if he did, she would watch the rise and fall of his perfect chest as he breathed. "I'm sure the pasha has nighttime servants who roam the palace looking for slumbering guests."

That elicited an enervated chuckle. "How positively mortifying." He turned a smile to her. "Especially since I was asleep most of the day."

His lips were so plump, so ready for kissing. Beatrice shifted her position, feeling the arousal between her legs. When he turned back to look at the painted, domed ceiling, her gaze fell to his neck, his chest, his shoulders, every bit of him a delectable delight ripe for kissing, or nibbling, or licking—

"Do you think Mehmet Pasha will ever get his artifacts returned?" he asked her.

"I hope so. Did you ever get a chance to see all of them? I really only had a good look at the one we had cleaned."

William drew in a long inhalation, his gorgeous chest rising, then falling when he exhaled. "Yes, I did see the pieces when they were all in a jumble." He turned his face to her. "Bea, I think I saw an inscription to Antinous." Another breath. "In Greek."

He said the last words in such a whisper as if he did not want anyone to know.

"What did the inscription say?"

"I don't know. I mean, all I saw were the Greek letters for A, N, T, I, N. I really didn't get a good look, and then the piece was taken away."

"Did you tell Mehmet or the professor?"

He shook his head. "No. I didn't want to get hopes up. I know this is what Mehmet wants to see. But I have to be sure before I tell him." William sighed. "I'll make sure what I saw is real once we get the artifacts back."

The burbling of the fountain was the accompaniment to the ensuing silence.

William shifted on the cushions, turning to face her. "Bea, kiss me."

Her heart pounded as he slid on top of her, taking her in a glorious kiss. His soft skin invited touch along the spine to his nude buttocks. She squeezed and kneaded the muscular flesh as he thrust his tongue more deeply to tangle with hers.

He took a reprieve, his breath humid against her lips. "I guess you've realized I'm utterly naked."

She giggled as she squeezed his butt cheeks. "Yes."

"We've never seen each other stripped to the buff."

"No."

He kissed her one more time then clambered off the platform to stand before her.

Beatrice swallowed hard, staring at his perfect physique.

He met her gaze and blushed. Then grinned. "Are you terribly shocked?" He turned around. His buttocks was magnificent. More perfect than any statue in museum. And his front side—

So that's what a man looked like. "You're, er, bigger than what I imagined."

William's mouth twisted sheepishly. "Beatrice, darling, I'm..."—he cleared his throat—"aroused."

"Oh."

"I forget sometimes we've not seen each other undressed. We've been naked together in my fantasies."

She gazed at him in awe. "Mine, too."

"But I've yet to see you."

"Right."

She got up from the platform and stood before him. The shirt covered her almost to her knees.

"Shall I turn my back?" William asked with concern.

"No."

She pulled the shirt over her head. Despite the heated air, her nipples hardened and crinkled. Her natural reaction was to cover herself with her hands. But William's gaze was adulatory.

"Darling," he said with a sigh, "you are beautiful." He came forward. "I want to touch you. Every part of you."

"Yes, please."

He held out his hand and led her back to the cushions where they lay side by side for a moment, gazing at each other with wide eyes.

"I want to pleasure you."

"Oh, yes. Please."

He rolled on top, his potent erection pressing against her belly. She opened her legs, excitement for her deflowering coursing through her.

"No, love. Not like that."

Excitement was shattered by disappointment.

"I want you to have a pleasure beyond what you usually have by your own hand."

He slid to her side and cupped her sex before pressing a finger to her clit. A flutter of ecstasy jolted her against him. She spread her palms on his chest, tension in her fingertips.

"I think I found the spot," he murmured in her ear. "You're so wonderfully aroused." He kissed her cheek. "I want to watch you have your sensual crisis. But first I want to pleasure you in a new way."

After a peck on her lips, he commenced a trail of kisses down her neck, across her shoulder, pausing at her breasts, his breath fanning against her yearning nipples before he sucked each one, the warmth of his touch melting her. He kissed between her breasts, down her belly, down further still...

He urged open her thighs and pressed his next kiss on her most intimate place.

She bucked up against his mouth, his lips and tongue undaunted in their exploration. The sensations were glorious, but abashment retrained her. As each stroke of his tongue eased her trepidation, she gave in to lust. His hands cupped her buttocks, lifting her as she arched her lower back, thrusting into him for more.

More. She wanted more.

She rocked against him, his tongue sliding through her wetness. Her labia fluttered, wanting him further inside her, deep enough to squeeze him. As his ministrations increased, rapture coiled within. She relaxed, letting him take her on a sensual journey.

His rhythmic strokes matched her rapid breaths, matched the rise to ecstasy. She moaned as she drew closer to the culmination, her ecstasy echoing in the bath chamber.

A yelp escaped her throat before William clamped his hand over her mouth. She continued pressing into him as he sucked and licked her into oblivion.

She sank into the cushions, toppling from her moment of bliss into utter repose.

"William, oh, God, William, that was spectacular."

He slid alongside her. "I'm happy to give you pleasure."

She stared into his smiling eyes. "What about you?" She glanced at his rampant potency.

He met her gaze and grinned. "Yes, please," he said in the same manner she'd said it earlier.

What should she do? His member throbbed between their bodies. Something compelled her to wrap her fingers around the shaft. The feel of him was amazing, soft and yielding and yet with a strength.

"Slide your hand up and down," he said unsteadily.

She did, eliciting a tremor through his body accompanied by a low groan.

"That's right."

She continued. What she was doing to him must feel like what she did to herself.

What he had just done to her.

A frisson of delight coursed through her. Just like toward the end of her masturbatory session she increased her speed.

"Beatrice, oh love, Bea, that is so…oh lord, I'm…"

He jerked forward, wrapping his arms around her. She lost her grip on him, compelling her to look down to take him in hand again. The moment she did so, a white fluid released from the tip.

She let go, staring in surprise. "Is that what happens all the time?"

"Yes." His voice rasped as if he had just run across a field. "Oh, darling, beautiful Beatrice. That was wonderful," he murmured against her neck. "I just need a moment to catch my breath."

His hardness renewed between their bodies. She squeezed him. "I think you could have another go."

He laughed and gently pushed her away. "Don't you worry about me." He let out a satisfied exhale as he wrapped his arm around her shoulders. "Don't you just want to rest for a moment?"

"Yes," she said with a giggle. "But not too long. I fear I might fall asleep."

He kissed the top of her head. "One day we'll spend the night together."

She nuzzled against him. One day. Or maybe they'd spend a lifetime together.

What a magnificent idea.

CHAPTER TEN

William sipped his strong and flavorful tea in the sitting room as he paged through an ancient manuscript in Persian. The stylized script was somewhat incomprehensible but the pictures told stories of what looked like knights and ladies.

Surreptitiously he glanced up from the book to gaze at Beatrice, his heart somersaulting at the sight of her. The night before had been too daring and wonderfully magical.

She was perusing an oversized tome with Miss Trent on a large round table. Nearby, Mrs. Stanfield and Mrs. Acker chatted and sewed while seated in matching stuffed chairs. All had said their farewells to Professor Stanfield and Mr. Acker earlier that morning before the two men had returned to the archaeological site.

The door opened, and Mehmet strolled through. Miss Trent looked up from her book. A glimpse of familiarity passed between the two.

Well, perhaps something more than just a passing familiarity. William smiled to himself. Anything that distracted her would benefit his love affair with Beatrice.

The pasha took a seat on a divan near the academic wives. A servant brought him tea. "After tea, I would be happy to show my gardens to anyone who is interested."

"That would be lovely," said Mrs. Stanfield.

All agreed, Miss Trent with a very slight blush.

"Mehmet," William began, "what is this book I'm looking at?" He held it up so the pasha could see the cover.

"Ah." The pasha put down his tea and came over. "That, Mr. Peel, is the *Shahnama*, the Book of Kings. It is an epic poem of the history of the Persian empire." He paged through the decorated manuscript until he arrived upon a page with an image of a man with a bow and arrow riding a horse. "This is Bahram Gur, a Persian king who enjoyed hunting."

"Are these stories about real kings?"

"Well, perhaps. Legends were handed down over time, and illustrated in manuscripts such as this."

"Sounds like our Arthurian legend," said Beatrice.

"Yes," said Mehmet with enthusiasm, "but *Shahnama* legends have been adopted and reinterpreted across all Muslim lands."

William concentrated on the script. "I have made a study of Persian, but I find this difficult to read." He regarded the pasha. "Can you read this?"

Mehmet nodded. "Most of it. The script is overly fanciful given the nature of the book." He drew a finger across the arc of a letter. "I have the advantage as the Turks have the same system of writing as the Persians and many of our words are taken from their language."

"I confess I am finding learning Turkish to be quite a challenge."

"As am I," said Beatrice. "Especially learning a new system of writing."

William's empathetic nod turned into an adoring gaze.

Pounding on the door sent everyone to jump and stare dumbfounded as the doors flew open. A harried servant scurried through, followed by the heavy presence of Durukan Pasha.

Mehmet remained unmoved. The servant bowed his head offering what sounded like apologies. Mehmet held up his hand with a nod of understanding. The servant retreated to stand against the wall.

"Durukan Fakir Pasha, to what do I owe the pleasure?" Mehmet clearly seethed under his cool demeanor.

"I am displeased." Durukan eyed Beatrice and Miss Trent with a look that bordered not on displeasure but lasciviousness. He returned his attention to Mehmet and said something sharp in Turkish.

Mehmet responded coolly in Turkish.

With squinting eyes, Durukan let loose in Turkish, the tone of his words filled with anger, shooting fierce glimpses toward Beatrice and Miss Trent.

Miss Trent appeared alert and rather composed for such verbal vehemence seemingly aimed at her.

William went to Beatrice's side. He tried to understand the conversation. If Turkish held Persian words, he should be able to understand, shouldn't he? But it was one thing to be able to decipher and read a foreign language. It was something quite different to be able to speak it or understand it when spoken. Especially when spoken so harshly and rapidly.

Mehmet held his ground, responding curtly or not at all. After a final exchange, the two men stared at each other for a long minute. Durukan spun on his heel and left. Mehmet signaled to some of his servants to follow.

Beatrice gripped William's hand. "What was all that about?" she whispered.

Mehmet puffed out a breath as he stretched out on a divan. "Well, first of all, he is still unhappy with the presence of unmarried women in the camp." He glanced at Miss Trent, who paled and looked down at her hands folded in her lap. "And he suspects there is some deception as far as the artifacts are concerned."

Anxiety ate at William's gut. "What did you tell him?"

"I realize you do not understand Turkish, but I think you can at least see I did not tell him much of anything."

"Yes, I did catch that."

The pasha slid his palm over his face, scratching his fingernails through his beard. He sprung from the couch and began pacing. "I do not want to put any of you in danger. You are guests in my country, doing research not many wish to do, nor have the funds to undertake. I do not want there to be any hint of deceit. Nor of impropriety."

Beatrice squeezed William's hand again. "Miss Trent and I can leave under escort."

"We can leave with them," said Mrs. Stanfield. "Then there would be no women in the camp to complain about."

"No." The pasha responded swiftly. "Each of you is a valued member of the expedition." His gaze lingered on Miss Trent for a moment.

Miss Trent thinned her lips. "We can assess and rearrange how we process the artifacts. Perhaps Mrs. Stanfield and Mrs. Acker can perform their management tasks in the same tent as us. It would seem as if Miss Smythe and I were ourselves being chaperoned."

Mehmet nodded at the two academic wives. "How does that sit with you?"

"If it means my husband can continue his work," said Mrs. Stanfield, "then I will try anything. This research is so important to him."

"I concur," said Mrs. Acker.

"All right, I will leave it to you ladies to work out the logistics. Please explain to your husbands that this is a new approach to appease Durukan. I will increase security at the entrance of the palace and at the temple site to guard against any future surprises."

He placed his hands on either side of a silver tea pot. "Cold," he muttered. He shook his head, and glanced at all present with a new smile.

"I will meet whomever wishes to have a tour of the gardens in one hour." He left with a distracted look in his eye.

William glanced at Beatrice. She met his gaze with sympathy. Last night would remain a wondrous memory. Tonight they could sit together at dinner, but it was not a night to tempt fate again.

THE TERRACE GARDEN in late afternoon was always a treat. In the morning, the garden was serene, but the threat of sunset impelled birds and insects into a frenzy of activity. Every flower was abuzz with energy and vibrant with color.

Mehmet tried to focus on nature's resplendence as he strolled between the garden beds, but all he could think about was Clarissa. A walk through one thousand gardens alone with Clarissa would never be enough time spent with the woman.

She was beautiful, intelligent, and provocative. And was keeping a secret.

During the conversation—which was more akin to an altercation—between him and Durukan, Clarissa had registered reactions as if she understood what was being said. She had winced a bit when Durukan had snarled about the provocations of virgins while throwing a lascivious glance in her direction. Although, perhaps merely his leer made her wince.

Still, her eyes had darted back and forth between him and Durukan as each had made his assertions regarding the legality of Mehmet's excavations. The others in the room had kept their eyes cast down and only dared glance up when the boom of Durukan's voice matched his growing anger.

William had been clearly making an attempt at understanding—the crinkle in his brow had revealed his struggle with linguistic comprehension. But Clarissa remained calm, seemingly harboring no fear, just interest.

A tiny bee dusted itself with pollen in the well of a yellow flower, joyfully relishing its circumstances.

Could Clarissa be a spy? For Durukan or the government or even some British intellectual who fancied himself an archaeologist? He hoped not. He'd already kissed her, and, as she was an unmarried woman, there was indiscretion in that moment. If she were a spy, surely she would use that indiscretion to lead him further down a sensual path but only go so far, or perhaps go as far as she wanted—as he wanted—before disappearing from his life altogether.

He had to know. But he couldn't outright ask her. For if she were a spy of some sort she would simply deny it.

The chatter of women broke his thoughts. Mrs. Acker, Mrs. Stanfield, and Clarissa strolled toward him. Mehmet squared his shoulders and softened his expression.

"Ah, ladies, I see my offer of a tour of the gardens was enticing."

"Cornelia and I enthused over your garden while we made a brief survey upon arrival. You have some lovely specimens of tulips."

Mehmet bowed his head. "Thank you, Mrs. Stanfield. Several varieties were gifts from the sultan to my father."

Mrs. Stanfield's eyes widened. "Really?"

"Particularly the red tulips with yellow tips."

"They look like a field of flames," remarked Mrs. Acker.

"The very same variety is also grown at the palace in Istanbul."

"Oh my, such history," murmured Mrs. Stanfield.

"Spring must be your favorite time here," said Mrs. Acker. "Everything in bloom."

"Including my fruit trees. Yet, I cannot choose a favorite time of year in my garden. After spring blossoms fade, I look forward to enjoying the bounty of my trees in summer and autumn."

He caught a glimpse of Clarissa's smile.

"I, for one, love that the garden has pavilions," said Mrs. Acker. "They offer a pleasant refuge. I think I shall fetch my book and spend a quiet afternoon reading."

Mrs. Stanfield brightened. "Oh, may I join you, Cornelia? My husband left a book that I'm eager to read."

"I brought my own novels as Spencer's taste in literature is dull."

"You told me he didn't read novels."

Mrs. Acker laughed. "I admit I was being polite. Spencer's taste in literature is nonexistent."

While the women enjoyed their little joke, Mehmet turned his attention to their rather reserved companion. "And you, Miss Trent? Do you have a novel you would like to read in the shade of a pavilion?"

Clarissa blushed. "I fear I have finished all the books I brought with me."

Mehmet clapped his hands. "Then you must visit my library. I have so much to offer—"

One of her eyebrows twitched upward.

"History, literature, portfolios of art, and so much more. In many different languages." He smiled. "You read several languages, do you not, Miss Trent?"

"Oh, our Miss Trent reads ancient Greek and Latin," said Mrs. Stanfield with pride.

Mehmet maintained his attention on Clarissa. "I do have books in Greek and Latin. I invite you to explore all that I have."

Clarissa's blush deepened. "Thank you, Excellency."

"I can give you a tour now, if you like."

The blush faded. Had he distressed her? Was he being too forward, too obvious?

"Miss Smythe and I promised your sisters we would converse in English with them."

"How wonderful." It was indeed, as his sisters rarely had such opportunities with native English speakers. "After dinner, then."

Her eyes widened briefly. "Or whenever it is convenient for you."
He bowed. "I am at your service."

The lovely shade of pink returned to her cheeks. "Thank you."

He bowed to the academic wives. "Ladies, I will take my leave. Enjoy your respite in the pavilions." After a quick smile for Clarissa's benefit, he headed for his office.

And hoped he'd see the lovely Miss Trent in his library later that night.

CHAPTER ELEVEN

Clarissa had not bothered to prepare for bed. After Mehmet had practically invited her to visit his library that night, how could she?

He'd even reminded her at dinner. His library held all manner of tomes he'd said, equal to any library in Europe.

However, the implication was not that she would discover fine reading material on the shelves, but a pleasure of a different sort. Perhaps up against a bookshelf.

The mere thought excited her. So here she was, in Mehmet's library in the middle of the night, reading the spines of books by the light of a lantern, utterly overwhelmed by the quantity and breadth of the collection.

She leaned against the library ladder and ran her finger across the spines of a row of novels, the rhythmic click of nail across leather the only sound in the quiet palace.

Hmm... Alexandre Dumas, Victor Hugo, Honoré de Balzac... It appeared she'd found the French literature section. Jules Verne?

She'd never read Verne but had heard his stories were rather fantastical.

"Miss Trent." Mehmet's gentle baritone startled her even though she'd expected him. "Have you found something of interest?"

He was right behind her, his hand at the small of her back, his breath hot on her earlobe. Her whole body reacted to his touch, his presence, the promise of what might be.

"Perhaps" was all she could manage.

His lips grazed her neck while he murmured something. She endeavored to understand.

A chill ran up her spine.

Mehmet spoke in Turkish. The filthiest, most seductive words she had ever heard.

"My beautiful harlot. I will take you to my bed and do indescribable things to you..."

Heat replaced the chill.

"...hold you down and fuck you hard. Your cunt will not be enough for my appetite. I will turn you over and move on to darker pleasures."

She turned to face him, meeting his sultry gaze with eyes wide in shock.

He chuckled. "I thought you might understand." His hand still clung to her waist.

"How did you know?"

"During my exchange today with Durukan, you seemed to follow along. When Turkish is spoken around you, you have an air of one who knows, who understands, who does not fear. Most English fear a language they cannot understand, especially when immersed in a culture they cannot comprehend. They fear they are the subject of conversation and not in a favorable light."

"But I *was* the subject of conversation earlier today. Miss Smythe and myself."

He nodded. "Yes, you were."

"Mehmet, please understand, I did not mean to deceive. Least of all you."

"Yet there is a reason you've kept your knowledge of the Turkish language a secret."

Clarissa sighed. "Miss Smythe's father needed assurance that she would be safe. We thought it best I pretend to not understand, then the locals would feel free to speak candidly in my presence." She tried to contain a smile. "The workmen use very colorful language."

"I will suggest they converse as if their mothers were present."

She laughed softly.

"I suppose Mr. Smythe was correct in his estimation of a chaperon for his daughter."

"Oh." Clarissa looked guilty.

"What is it?"

"Beatrice's father is the Earl of Ryburgh."

Confusion clouded Mehmet's eyes. "So shouldn't she be styled Lady Beatrice?"

"Properly, she is. But the earl is a Radical and has let his daughters decide how they want to call themselves."

Mehmet chuckled and shook his head. "With ideas like that in her brain, I see why she needs a chaperon."

"That, and she's utterly in love with William."

"William Peel?"

"Yes."

"Ah. So, Miss Trent, is there anything else you would like to disclose?"

"I have not been keeping anything from you—well, except my knowledge of languages. But that's it. And I'm surprised Professor Stanfield did not explain Beatrice's parentage to you."

"Does the professor also know about Beatrice and William?"

"Oh, I don't know. I just assumed everyone did. They are not very discreet."

"I thought he was merely being protective. Like an elder brother might be."

Clarissa could not contain her amusement. "Oh, I assure you, it is not brotherly affection he feels for her."

Mehmet looped his arms around her waist and pulled her close. "As far as your language abilities, what do you know?"

She plucked the buttons of his dressing gown. "I can understand Turkish, Persian, and Arabic. I can speak a little—"

He lifted an eyebrow.

"Although I fear my accent is atrocious. I cannot write your script, and I can only read a little. I was taught to read Arabic using the Qur'an."

"The Qur'an? And do you agree with what you've read?"

"Religion is more interesting to me for its historical component."

"Yes. I quite agree." He nibbled on his lower lip. "So, you understood every word spoken by Durukan?"

"I did. He has an unusual accent, does he not? It sounds somehow flat to my ear. Do you know where he is from?"

"I do not. His accent is indeed peculiar. I can only gather he worked his way up from a lower class, or he's from one of our far-flung provinces. And I admit I do not know enough about either to pinpoint his origin."

She smoothed her hands across his chest. "Mehmet, I did not mean to cause distrust between us. I struggled with the knowledge that with our growing intimacy, I would have to tell you eventually. But my language abilities would be yet another secret for you to keep when we have so many already."

"You're right. But I am to blame for all the secrets regarding the excavation." He leaned in, tickling her neck with his beard. "My heart is willing to forgive you. As is my body." He grazed her sensitive skin with his lips.

She tilted her head to give him more access. A moment later he sought her mouth and gave her a lingering kiss.

He drew back. "And now I know your secret, I need you to be attentive while at the camp."

"I have been, but with little to mention. Your workmen seem to be simply that, workmen."

"Yes, but now I suspect Durukan may try to insert one or two men into my crew. I have already dismissed a couple who were probably spies." He grinned. "And can you tell one Turk from another?"

She scowled. "I do recognize the few I see regularly." She stroked his cheek above his beard. "It would help if they would shave every once in a while."

Mehmet seemed dejected. "You don't like the beard?"

She pecked his lips. "I like it just fine on you, Excellency."

He dived in for a deeper kiss. She was eager, too eager, really, to be in his arms, kissing him, stroking his back, gripping his gown, pressing against him.

"You are perfect." His hands hovered near her breasts, not touching, his heat penetrating her clothes. "Your breasts precisely sized for my palms." He moved lower. "Your waist perfect for my embrace." Even lower. "Your hips perfect for the clasp of my thighs." He kissed her neck. "Your body perfect for my kisses."

He urged her against the library ladder. "Up."

She gave him a quizzical look "You want me to climb up?"

"Yes."

Clarissa turned to face the ladder.

"No." Mehmet pressed on her shoulders. "Not that way. Backwards. Your back to the ladder."

How strange. She did so. He halted her after she had stepped up a few rungs.

"Perfect."

He pulled up her entari revealing the fine linen gömlek under the robe. He lifted the gömlek to her waist and tied a knot at the hem, securing it. He then untied the drawstring holding up her şalvar, and slid the baggy trousers down to her ankles.

Her crotch was utterly exposed to him. Instinctively, she clamped her thighs together.

With his hands wrapped around her thighs, Mehmet urged her legs apart. He leaned closer, licking his lips, his breath fanning the hair of her mons. He opened her further and dived in, his mouth…his mouth…

Good God. His mouth was pressed against her sex. And his tongue…

Heavens above.

He licked and sucked and thrust his tongue into her depths. She grasped the ladder, her hold on the wood her only grip on reality.

Her muscles and bones threatened to melt, as if her body were wax in a furnace of utter carnality. Mehmet held her fast against the ladder, keeping her steady while he worked her into a lust-filled frenzy. The hair of his beard and mustache tickled her tender flesh as his lips and tongue pleasured her in a way she had never imagined.

His attentions elicited more familiar sensations, the climb to the peak of ecstasy, but this new path was distracting. She closed her eyes, concentrating on the wondrous feelings coursing through her, focusing on that one spot he was tormenting.

She cried out, undone. Relaxation and energy simultaneously overwhelmed her.

"Mehmet, that was"—*indescribable*—"spectacular."

"Darling," he said as he propped up her enervated body, "from this library there is a private corridor to my bedchamber."

"And are there other private corridors throughout your palace? Perhaps to *my* bedchamber?" She tugged on her lower lip with her teeth.

Mehmet grinned. "Alas, no. The harem is quite contained. We would have to walk along public corridors to arrive at the entrance."

"So, your bedchamber it is, Excellency."

After she tottered down the ladder, he lifted her pleasure-addled body in his arms. He grabbed the lantern and went to a bookcase behind them. He slid his hand behind some books and clicked a latch. The bookcase opened as a door to a corridor. They made their way down the darkened space, and after a few turns, he opened another door leading to his apartment. He glanced around.

"No servants. We're alone."

Meaning her reputation was safe.

Still in his arms, they continued to his bedchamber where he locked the door behind him.

She stared at the closed door. "Am I your prisoner?"

"Would you like to be? I mean, as a lover's charade?"

The notion surprised her. "Mehmet, I may not be an innocent in body, but I think I might be one in experience."

"Ah. We will leave such games for another time, then." He set her down, her şalvar bunched around her ankles. "There will be no untoward surprises tonight, just a man and a woman discovering each other—our hearts, our minds, our bodies."

Clarissa's heart pounded. She was ready for this wonderful, interesting, attractive man.

MEHMET COULD NOT BELIEVE his good fortune. The wondrous Clarissa was before him, in his bedchamber, willing— and perhaps eager from the blush on her cheeks—to be his lover.

He searched her chignon for pins, taking them out one at a time until her hair spilled over her shoulders. He threaded his fingers through the silky tresses. "Glorious," he said before pulling her in for a kiss.

Her willing lips, her hungry mouth, her questing tongue were such a treat. What other treasures did she have to offer?

He broke free, and she stumbled forward into his arms.

"I fear I am tangled in my trousers," she said, her lips hovering over his.

"Easily remedied."

He lifted her up and sat her down on his bed. He took off her shoes and slipped off the trousers.

She met his gaze with a raised eyebrow. "Your turn." A surprising coquettish challenge.

"With pleasure."

He toed off his shoes, then turned his back to her so she could not see him untying the drawstring of his şalvar. When his trousers had fallen to the floor, he stepped out of them and turned back to face her. "What's next?"

"Come here. I want to unbutton your kaftan."

"While I unbutton your entari?"

A flirtatious smile flitted across her lovely lips. "Of course."

Their hands and arms interwove as each unfastened the other's buttons then tugged sleeves off the other's arms.

They stood face to face undressed down to their gömleks. The fine cotton fabric clung deliciously to the curve of her breasts.

"Shall we disrobe our final garments together?"

She nodded and pulled her chemise over her head at the same time he dispensed with his.

Clarissa gasped.

Mehmet had a similar reaction. The naked woman before him was simply magnificent. Perfection personified.

His heart furiously pumped blood to his one body part that was not experiencing stupefaction. Instinctively he covered his crotch. This beautiful woman deserved more than just unbridled lust.

From the glazed, stunned look in her eyes, she, too, was seemingly experiencing some sort of lewd mania as she stared at his body.

"Clarissa?"

She met his gaze and blinked. "I…Mehmet, I confess, I've not seen a man such as you."

He took a step forward, tentatively. "And I have not seen a woman such as you."

"I had imagined—well, fantasized, really—you as a muscular man as you have a good seat on your horse." She swallowed. "And I have seen the Farnese Hercules and so know muscles could be in interesting places on a man, but, well, you're flesh, not marble." Her gaze traveled back up to his eyes. "I'm a little surprised. Pleasantly so."

"And I am pleasantly surprised to have Aphrodite in the flesh before me." He held out his hand.

She pulled him to her for a kiss.

He melted into their embrace, their naked bodies crushing together, his fingers dancing over her soft skin, hers pressing into the muscles she so admired.

With both hands under her glorious bottom, he lifted her onto the mattress. She scooted back, making room for him as he climbed over her. He urged her legs open to let the yearning head of his cock prod her welcoming entrance.

"Clarissa…love…?"

"Yes."

And then he was inside her.

He lost all hold on the world around him. Each thrust took him out of the realm of reality, into the realm of a lover's fantasy.

The burn of her nails digging into his back centered him to their connection. The music of her moans and heated breaths lifted him once again into a sensual heaven.

She repeated his name, that much he knew. Perhaps he murmured hers as well between moans of ecstasy, an ecstasy that built continuously to take them to the precipice—

No. He had to hold back. He willed himself back to earth, to focus on her pleasure and hers alone. He kissed her neck, her shoulders, her breasts, as she undulated under him. He reached between them, pressing a finger to her clit, knowing he'd found the right spot when she gasped. She rocked enthusiastically against his hand, his cock, then suddenly raised her hips, hovering for a moment until she came with a yelping wail.

He pulled out and rolled onto his back, grabbing his cock, frigging frantically, his need for release overwhelming the ardor melting his heart. He bucked up, jetting his seed onto his stomach.

Mehmet stared at the wooden beams of the ceiling as his body and mind calmed from their moment of utter bliss.

A rustle of sheets drew his attention to the woman on his left. She stared at the spatters and rivulets of his emission as if mesmerized.

"I've never seen a man have his culmination." She tentatively touched the fluid then stared at her wet fingertip before placing it in her mouth.

"Somewhat brackish, isn't it?" he said.

"I suppose it is." She gave him a curious look. "You've tasted it?"

"Yes. Not mine."

She gaped.

He got up and fetched a towel from his bedside table to clean himself. "As you have confessed your secret, I would like to confess one of my own."

"Oh?"

He beckoned her to join him under the covers. "You had thought my fascination with Hadrian was because I was like him. That is not so far from the truth."

She slid alongside him.

"When I was making my Grand Tour, it was not only widows and dowagers I bedded. In Italy I had an affair with a *conte*—an older man for whom I suppose I was like Antinous."

"In the prime of youthful vigor." She ran a finger down his chest.

"It was he who told me details about the relationship between the emperor and his beloved, information the professors at Oxford deftly skirted around. This count even had a bust of Antinous— although I have no idea if it was genuine. He did feel that classical scholars of late had buried the beauty of the relationship. He wanted it to be revealed and reveled in."

"That's why this temple is so important to you."

"Yes. If my theory is correct, then I will have found a legacy, a celebration of the love between two men." He pulled her more closely. "Have I scandalized you utterly?"

"On the contrary." She raised her chin and offered a smile. "The reason I was worried you would be like Hadrian is that I once fell in love with a man who loved other men. He knew his desires but wanted to see if being with a woman held any appeal so he could please his parents and live a conventional life. I was already half in love with him, so I agreed. One night of intimacy and he understood more fully that his desires were not for women. Rather than try to convince his parents he needed to remain unmarried as a condition of his university fellowship, he joined the diplomatic service. Somewhere in the Mediterranean, I think. I was left behind, brokenhearted."

"This man was not your first, was he?"

"No. That was why I agreed to his proposition and why he asked me. I already knew how a man and a woman could be intimate."

Mehmet kissed her hair. "Clarissa, my sweet, I would like more than one night of intimacy."

She nestled against his body, her fingers threaded through the hair of his chest. "I would like that as well."

A warm, comforting sensation washed over him, lulling his drowsy eyes to shut.

A moment later, he jerked awake.

Clarissa sat up in the bed. "What time is it?"

Perhaps they had been asleep longer than a moment.

"Does it matter? Stay with me. Sleep in my arms until morning. I'll have a female servant escort you to the harem. I promise there will be no disgrace or dishonor."

"Darling, believe me, I would love to spend the night with you. But I need to check on Beatrice. She is my first responsibility. Our desire to be together will have to wait."

"I understand." He got out of bed and sorted through their clothes.

"Mehmet, is there, er, a..." She looked about the room. "Necessary?"

An interesting euphemism. "Will a commode do?"

She nodded.

"Under the bed." He moved the commode into position, then turned his back to give her some privacy.

That she felt comfortable enough to perform such a task in his presence was gratifying. Perhaps camping had broken down some barriers of polite society.

Finished and with a blush on her cheeks, Clarissa dressed. She braided her hair, then picked up a few of her hair pins scattered on the ground and fashioned a loose chignon.

More informality. His heart beat in happiness.

She grabbed the lantern then kissed him. A long, lingering kiss that held promise. Not for that night, but some night hence.

"I'll return to the women's quarters the same way I came."

She exited through the private corridor that led to the library and the harem.

Mehmet smiled, confident that yes, indeed, there would be more nights of passion with the glorious Clarissa.

ONCE OUTSIDE THE LIBRARY, Clarissa slunk down the corridor, knowing she was being watched by servants.

They would know what she'd done with their master. What she enjoyed doing and would do again whenever she got the chance.

Mehmet was a fabulous lover. Not that she had much to compare him to, but just one tumble and she could tell.

Her body responded with the memory of what they had done. She would've loved to have spent the night with him, but she had her duties.

She wended her way to the harem. How odd there was no guard at the door. She pressed the handle. Even more odd that the door was unlocked.

Clarissa entered the still and dark corridor.

The harem was devoid of servants. It must have been later than she thought. Perhaps that eerie time between darkness and dawn.

She placed her hand on the knob of the door to Beatrice's room and slowly turned, cringing when the metal creaked. She slowly pushed the door open and slipped inside the room.

She let her eyes adjust to the dark before moving toward the bed.

Empty.

The covers were tossed back, the sheets were rumpled as if someone had occupied the space that night. She touched the mattress.

Cold.

"Beatrice?" she whispered.

No answer.

Her heart sunk. She'd failed her charge. Or, rather, her charge had eluded her.

She was probably in William's bedroom. In his arms.

Of course, Clarissa was no example, having just spent most of the night with a man she, admittedly, did not know as well as she should if she were going to continue spending nights with him.

She plopped down on the bed, her head in her hands, admitting defeat as a chaperon.

A dark shadow on the dressing chair opposite drew her attention. She went to it, finding Beatrice's dark green dressing gown draped over the back. She bent over. Beatrice's slippers lay side by side, tucked under the seat.

Did she change before venturing off to William's bedroom? Where was her nightgown?

A rustling behind startled her.

"Beatrice?" This time she whispered more loudly.

No response.

Panic ripped through her for a second before a thick set of arms gripped her body and a calloused hand clamped over her mouth.

CHAPTER TWELVE

Beatrice rubbed the back of her head, then pressed her palms against her temples.

No, it wasn't a dream. She really was sitting on a camp bed alone in a clammy stone room, a sliver of sunlight shining through the metal grille of a high window.

Sudden apprehension signaled she wasn't alone.

A moan from the pile of straw on the opposite side of the room revealed another in the room with her. The figure stirred. A woman.

Egads. Miss Trent.

Beatrice went to her, kneeling at her side. "Miss Trent? Are you all right?"

She was wearing the same clothes as the night before, and her hair was disheveled, as if she'd fallen asleep somewhere without bothering to undress.

"Beatrice?" Miss Trent sat up and looked around. "Where are we?"

"Truthfully, I don't know. But I suspect some mischief is afoot."

Miss Trent paled. She looked Beatrice up and down, right to left, then palmed her cheek. "Oh my dear, you weren't with William at all. They ripped you from your bed."

"They? Do you know who took us?"

She shook her head. "No, no. I was with…well…I just decided I should check on you before I went to bed, and you weren't there."

"You had gone to Mehmet's library."

"Yes."

"How did you end up here?"

"I was in your room, and I was grabbed. That's all I remember."

Beatrice saw the fear in her guardian's eyes. "We're not in Mehmet's palace, are we?"

"No, dear. I don't think we are."

She stood and held out her hand to help Miss Trent up. "Well, then, we should attempt to figure out where we are."

Once standing, Miss Trent began to examine their surroundings. "What do you notice about the stonework?"

"Old—"

"But not as old as Roman."

"No." Beatrice ran her fingers across the cold damp rock. "Are we near water?"

"A good observation. I think so."

"So we're on the coast. There are no rivers near Mehmet's palace."

"That's right," Miss Trent said thoughtfully. "Beatrice, where does Durukan Pasha live?"

"I don't know—" Beatrice stopped. "Is that where we are? Why?"

Miss Trent took her hand. "I don't know, dear." She led her to the bed, and they sat. Miss Trent wrapped her arm around

Beatrice's shoulder. "You're only wearing your nightgown. You were asleep when they took you? Were you…" She paused. "Were you hurt in any way?"

"My arm, I think they bruised it." She looked at her ankles. "They might have scratched my legs."

"But nothing else?" Miss Trent asked gently.

Beatrice suddenly realized what she meant.

"No, Miss Trent. No. They did not take liberties, if that's what you mean."

Miss Trent gave her shoulders a squeeze. "I am relieved to hear. And please call me Clarissa. I fear we have discovered ourselves in quite an unusual situation."

A clanging behind the wooden door made Miss Trent—Clarissa—hold her more closely. The door creaked open. A servant appeared, perhaps a woman, covered from head to toe in pitch-black cloth, only the eyes showing.

She gestured they should follow her. Clarissa began to move. Beatrice held her back.

"There's just one of her," whispered Beatrice. "We could do something daring."

"We need to figure out where we are and why we are here. Don't do anything rash, Beatrice. Follow my lead."

Of course her chaperon was right.

And as soon as they stepped over the threshold, there were two large and ominous-looking men, swords flashing at their sides.

So much for attempting anything daring.

The woman led them down a dark corridor, the two men following behind. The floor was cold under Beatrice's feet. They went up stone stairs, at the top of which was a heavily bolted wooden door. The woman unlocked and opened the door then stood aside beckoning them through.

Another corridor. This one with a checkerboard floor of large terracotta tiles and a narrow carpet down the middle. The walls were covered in blue and white tiles, dabbed with red flowers. Carved dark wood molding added a layer of opulence.

They were most certainly in a palace. But whose?

Durukan Pasha. Of course. It had to be.

A chill seared Beatrice's flesh. She was suddenly more aware that she was naked but for her nightgown. Clarissa gripped her hand more tightly.

They walked down the corridor, Beatrice grateful for the carpet underfoot. They finally reached a set of deeply carved dark wooden doors. The woman dressed in black opened one and proceeded through. With the men at their backs, Beatrice and Clarissa had no other recourse than to follow her.

If the palace could have been more opulent, then this room was it, with gilded woodwork, shiny brass lanterns, plush red carpeting, and gleaming green and blue tiles. A throne room perhaps, but from some distant time long ago.

The woman in black halted, spreading her arms out at her sides to motion for Beatrice and Clarissa to stop behind her. They remained in place as the woman moved to stand near a tiled wall, where other servants were lined up at the ready. The guards behind them also moved to the wall leaving Beatrice and Clarissa alone in the huge hall.

A flutter of robes drew their attention. Durukan Pasha strolled from behind a gilded wooden screen carved and pierced with arabesques, through which he had most likely observed their entrance.

"Ladies, welcome to my palace. Your beauty heightens the artistry and workmanship of my abode. Do you not agree?"

"What are we doing here?" Clarissa's query was said with a clenched jaw.

"Why, you are my guests, of course." The pasha offered a somewhat disingenuous smile.

"Dragged from our bedrooms?" Clarissa was bold.

"I apologize for the suddenness of your summoning." Durukan regarded Beatrice as if she weren't wearing anything. And truly the thin cotton of her nightgown was not much of a barrier between her body and the pasha's lascivious gaze.

"My man returned to Lady Beatrice's room to retrieve her dressing gown and slippers, and we found an even better prize." His mouth stretched in a triumphant smirk. "Miss Trent."

Even Beatrice felt Clarissa's shudder.

"But I am not a cruel man," he said as his gaze continued to sweep over Beatrice.

He snapped his fingers, and the woman dressed in black came forward. Beatrice's dressing gown was draped over outstretched arms. In her hands, she held the pair of finely embroidered slippers given to Beatrice by Mehmet's mother as a welcome gift.

Clarissa grabbed the articles of clothing. Shielding Beatrice from Durukan's gaze, she helped Beatrice into the robe and buttoned every button. Then she gave Beatrice the slippers. The soft but sturdy footwear added much needed warmth to her cold feet.

"I'm certain you will find that more comfortable, my dear," said the pasha.

Ugh. She was most definitely not *his dear.*

He began shouting commands in Turkish to his servants, who scurried this way and that, some leaving the hall but only after they had genuflected before his presence.

Through the distressing chaos Clarissa watched the pasha with intent, her expression changing subtly as if she could understand what he was saying.

She pulled Beatrice into a tighter embrace. "Beatrice, I need you to pretend to cry, so I can pretend to offer comfort to you. Do you understand?"

"Yes." It wasn't too difficult, really. The pasha's evil lascivious gaze was unsettling. And certainly William must know she was missing by now—

A sob overtook her. She gulped air and broke down into tears.

"What's all this?" Durukan's yelp sliced the air.

"She's upset, my lord," said Clarissa. "She's just a young girl."

There was that horrid smirk again. "Yes, I know."

Clarissa wrapped her arms around Beatrice, tucking her head against her chest so Clarissa's mouth was near her ear.

"Listen carefully. Durukan speaks Turkish with a foreign accent."

A chill overtook the sorrow. How did Clarissa know this?

As if understanding Beatrice's thoughts, Clarissa continued to whisper in her ear while she stroked her hair in consolation. "I am familiar with Turkish, as well as Persian and Arabic."

Beatrice looked up with crinkled forehead at Clarissa through teary eyes.

"Excellency," said Clarissa to the pasha, "Lady Beatrice needs a moment to sit. Please, she is so very upset."

Durukan waved to the woman in black who led them to a bench along the wall. The two burly men stood on either side.

"Shh, shh, darling. I'm here for you." Clarissa wrapped her arm around Beatrice's shoulder as she said those words aloud. She bent her head lower. "I was hired by your father because of my linguistic skills. He wanted to make sure you were safe in a strange land."

Her expression relaxed. "Oh." Papa was sweet to be so concerned. "What do you mean the pasha has a foreign accent?"

"Well, that's the trouble, see? He's got an accent as if…I mean it's strange, but it sounds like he's from the East End of London."

Beatrice smothered her shock with feigned sorrow for show. "The evil pasha is Cockney?"

"Seems like it, yes. As ridiculous as that sounds."

"Do you think Mehmet knows?"

"I know for a fact he does not."

Something about how she spoke those words was revealing. "You're in love with him."

"Beatrice, now is not the time to discuss such things."

"But if he loves you back, he'll want to rescue you."

Clarissa kissed the top of her head. "I think we need to figure out a way to escape before then. I'm worried about what Durukan plans to do to you."

Beatrice felt sick to her stomach.

"Beatrice, darling, are you still a virgin?'

A chill raced through her. "Yes. William's been such a gentleman." And now she wished he hadn't been.

"Please do not react too strongly, for I do not want to draw attention to us. But Durukan said he intends to make you his bride."

"His bride?"

"Yes. That is the polite way of saying it, I fear."

"You mean he wants to…to—" *Oh, God.* To do what she had wanted William to do.

"I am so sorry, darling. And that is why I don't think we should wait to be rescued."

WILLIAM SIPPED HIS TEA and looked over his cup at the two empty chairs across from him. It really wasn't like Beatrice to be late to breakfast. Nor Miss Trent, for that matter. Especially Miss Trent.

"I wonder what is keeping the ladies," Mehmet said casually, his words edged with concern.

"Perhaps Miss Smythe has needs that only the counsel of another woman can manage," said Mrs. Stanfield.

William flushed. Of course. Womanly issues. He gulped the rest of his tea a little too quickly.

A female servant rushed into the breakfast room, curtsying to Mehmet, seemingly muttering apologies. The pasha offered calm words, the woman answered him slowly at first then picked up the pace until she was speaking so rapidly it was a wonder the pasha could understand her. Something was wrong.

Mehmet paled, then slid his seat back to stand. "Mr. Peel, will you accompany me, please?"

"Certainly."

Mehmet left the breakfast room nonchalantly, and William followed in the same manner. As soon as they were much further down the corridor, Mehmet gathered speed to almost running.

Beria waited for him at the entrance to the harem, her face streaked with distress.

Something was definitely wrong.

The pasha said something to his mother, and she bade William follow her. Mehmet fell in behind but soon disappeared into a room. William trailed Beria into the room across the hall.

Instantly he knew it was Beatrice's room. The bed was in terrible disarray, the covers pulled onto the floor.

"We found the room like this," said Beria, her voice shaking.

"Where is Beatrice?"

"Clarissa—Miss Trent is gone as well," Mehmet said from the doorway. "But her room is tidy."

"May I see?" asked William.

The pasha hesitated a moment, then allowed William into the room across the hall. The scene there was very different.

"The bed is made. Did the servants do this?"

"No."

"It's as if Miss Trent did not sleep in her bed at all last night."

A subtle shade of pink crept across the pasha's cheeks above his beard.

"It does appear that way," he said.

"Perhaps she was concerned for Miss Smythe and stayed there."

Mehmet remained silent, his reticence broken by a scream down the hall.

They ran in the direction of the outcry. A maidservant waved at Mehmet. She stood before an open door to what appeared to be a linen pantry. On the floor was an elderly maidservant bound and gagged. Mehmet and William quickly set to freeing her.

The pasha spoke to her gently as he helped her up. They took her to a sunlit room with small wooden tables and divans overflowing with pillows. He sat her down on one of the divans, and they conversed.

The pasha looked up at William. "This is Hafza. She says two very large men entered the harem, dressed as women. She thought there was something unusual about them. They took Miss Smythe first. When Hafza confronted them, they tied her up. She thinks they took Miss Trent as well."

The old woman rattled on, pointing out the window.

"She says the men talked about Eski Saray, the old palace by the water."

"Whose palace is that?" asked William.

Mehmet seethed. "Durukan. It's where he lives." Mehmet pressed his lips together as if in thought. "I thought nothing of his presence here yesterday, except as an official visit. I increased security on the outside of my palace, but not the inside. He must have secreted his kidnappers in my palace upon his arrival." He met William's gaze, his expression determined. "Do you know how to fire a gun?"

"I do."

"Good. We'll also bring knives just in case we don't want to make any noise."

The idea of having to commit violence was alarming, but necessary.

"Can you ride a horse?"

"Of course."

"We'll get you one, and two for the women. My groomsmen will follow and be ready to ride back with them."

William's heart beat a little too rapidly. *Beatrice, darling Beatrice. Hold on. We're coming to rescue you.*

BEATRICE WAS GLAD FOR Clarissa's presence at her side. As they were led down a corridor decorated with silk carpets and exuberant tile work, they paid very close attention to their surroundings. Whenever one of them spied a possible doorway or means of escape, she squeezed the hand of the other.

Beatrice also made note of their route, the people around them, landmarks along the way. It was curious to see both men and women servants in the same corridor. Mehmet's palace was rather segregated, not because he thought that the best way, but because of tradition. His servants wanted it that way.

Which seemed to give credence to Clarissa's ascertainment of Durukan being not Turkish, but English.

The whole situation was so utterly odd, really.

The entourage stopped before a set of double doors. A servant opened the doors, and Beatrice and Clarissa were pushed through. A bedroom. But the most opulent bedroom Beatrice had ever seen, in the center of which, behind a pierced screen, was a large four-poster canopied bed covered in silk quilts, with fur rugs strewn about on either side of the bed so the occupants would descend on softness and not cold tile.

A male servant grabbed Clarissa and took her forcibly from Beatrice's side holding her roughly. She offered Beatrice a consoling look.

With a flurry of angry Turkish, a burly man ripped Beatrice's dressing gown from her body, buttons falling to the floor. After the haze of astonishment subsided, she tried to run free, but was grabbed by two robust men harshly gripping her kicking legs and flailing arms.

"You brutes! Let her go!" Clarissa protested. A hand was slapped over her mouth.

A female servant threw back the quilts to reveal starched white sheets. Beatrice was lifted up and placed onto the bed. Once again, she struggled, trying to break free, to no avail. Four male servants each grasped a limb and wrapped leather ties around her, securing each limb to a bedpost.

She was a prisoner. She squirmed despite her bindings, hoping to find a weakness, only to discover the burn of leather against flesh.

The men chuckled as they watched her, making comments the meaning of which she did not understand, but the dark tone she very much understood.

Then the four men lifted a wrestling Clarissa and left through the double doors.

The woman in black lowered her gaze as she closed the doors, leaving Beatrice very much alone.

And her mind racing with possibilities of how to free herself.

THE MEN DEPOSITED Clarissa unceremoniously in the corridor. She lay limply on the silk carpet, assessing the situation.

As far as she could tell, the woman in black was her only captor. But servants could be tucked away in the shadows. She had to be very careful.

The woman gripped her wrist and jerked her to standing, apparently in an attempt to signal Clarissa should obey. All right. She would obey. For as long as she needed.

She glanced back at the doors to the bedroom where Beatrice was held captive. Two imposing men guarded the entrance.

With hunched shoulders Clarissa followed the woman, who every once in a while would turn around and give Clarissa a swat. They were backtracking through the same corridor whence they came. Luckily, Clarissa had mentally cataloged every decorative urn, every piece of furniture, every doorway and niche.

And one was coming up.

She grabbed the woman and slammed her into a tiled niche. Horrified eyes gazed up at Clarissa, but Clarissa remained undaunted.

The only way out of the palace was in disguise. And this woman, with her head-to-toe covering, had the best disguise.

With all her might Clarissa hit the woman's cheek with her fist. The woman appeared dazed for a moment, so Clarissa pushed her skull against the tile and hit her one more time. And then again.

The horror of it all sickened her. The woman weakened, slackening to the floor, giving Clarissa her chance.

She tugged at the woman's clothing, untucking and unwrapping her veil and shawl-like cloak until Clarissa had enough black cloth with which to conceal herself. As she fashioned the cloth around her, she felt only a little remorse for the aged woman heaped in the corner of the niche.

In the unfamiliar surroundings she had to act naturally, as if she knew her way. She couldn't go back to Beatrice. An old woman was an easy opponent. Not so much two hefty guards.

Clarissa hugged the wall, and headed down the corridor to find any place in the palace that might grant her exit. She restrained herself from running, trying to gain confidence in her costumed masquerade.

The ornate door to the throne room was a landmark. So she was close to the stairs where she and Beatrice had emerged. Beyond that spot, she was not certain what lay ahead.

Two men stood in the corridor, their stances revealing apprehension. Perhaps unwilling compatriots of Durukan.

She studied them closely. One had reddish-brown hair.

Good heavens.

Mehmet and William.

They were, as was she, attempting to act naturally as if they belonged in the corridor of this Turkish palace.

Clarissa wanted to run to Mehmet, throw her arms around him, kiss him. But that would not be prudent. How should she reveal herself?

She could speak to him. Some personal message. Perhaps he would understand the layers of meaning.

She approached. "*Mehmet pasha, your library holds many literary treasures,*" she said in English-accented Turkish.

Mehmet paused, holding William back. He looked at Clarissa, meeting her eyes with suspicion. She carefully unwrapped her veil. A moment later, realization melted his stern gaze.

The happiness, the desire, the love on his face said everything. He glanced around the corridor, then gave William a pat on the shoulder before taking her in his arms and kissing her mouth.

"Darling, oh my darling," he murmured against her lips.

"Mehmet, we may be seen."

He stepped back, casting a glance at an utterly shocked William. "We gained entrance through the stables."

"No one seemed to notice," added William.

"Clarissa," Mehmet said quietly, "do you know where Beatrice is?"

"Yes, down the corridor. She is tied to a bed. I fear Durukan has brutish intentions." She lowered her voice. "He wants to make her his bride, if you understand my meaning."

William paled. "Show me."

Clarissa slowly retraced her steps, as each kept a look out. When they came across the crumpled old woman, Mehmet raised a brow in Clarissa's direction. He reached down and picked something out of the woman's boot.

A knife. The metal hilt was decorated with enamel. The blade was small but would have been quite effective.

"You were brave," he murmured as he pocketed the knife.

"Foolish and lucky, rather," she said.

They continued on their way until she saw the double doors to the room where Beatrice was held.

And the two burly men stationed at the door.

She pulled Mehmet and William into a niche, behind a palm in an oversized metal pot. "She's in there. But the doors are guarded."

"I'll kill them," hissed William.

"We don't want to create a commotion and draw attention to ourselves," counseled Mehmet.

William seemed disappointed yet relieved.

"Well," began Mehmet, "we have either distraction or violence to aid us."

Clarissa was not looking forward to more violence. Her stomach was still unsettled from harming the old woman.

Mehmet clasped her hand. "Can you act as a bent old servant and accompany me?"

"Will these men know who you are?"

"I doubt it. But even if they do, how do they know that Durukan and I do not see eye to eye?"

"You have a point. Do you have a plan?"

"Sort of. If they do not recognize me, I will claim to be a doctor ordered to confirm the bride's virginity—"

William growled.

"If they let us in, we will proceed to free Beatrice. If they don't, we'll have to come up with another plan."

"And if they want to accompany us inside the room?"

Mehmet scratched his beard a moment. He weighed the old woman's knife in his palm, then handed it to William. "William will provide a distraction."

Clarissa was incredulous. "By stabbing the guards?"

"I was thinking perhaps of creating a racket by throwing it against one of those large porcelain urns." He pointed down the corridor.

Which might break or, at the very least, make a loud noise. The handle was rather hefty.

"And when they see it's a knife, they'll go looking for the assailant," added William.

A diversion was their only strategy really because the two guards looked rather formidable.

Clarissa rolled her shoulders and covered her head. "I am ready to play the part of an old woman inspecting a young woman's innocence."

Mehmet squeezed her hand before leading the way to the doors of Beatrice's room.

DISCOVERING HER DELIGHT

* * * * *

TUCKED BEHIND THE potted palm inside the tiled niche, William watched as Miss Trent and Mehmet approached the guarded door beyond which was his Beatrice. That the pair had advanced their relationship to the point of kissing was a delightful shock.

The guards straightened to attention. Mehmet was uncharacteristically animated as he spoke with them. The ruse seemed to be working. The guards nodded solemnly.

Miss Trent, in the meantime, had leaned her ear against the seam of the double doors. She turned and looked in William's direction, nodding as she took her place at Mehmet's side.

Which probably indicated Beatrice was still in the bedroom.

Good.

The guards approached the door, one with a large metal key in his hand. He slid the key in the lock and turned.

There was only one moment to consider his options. Create a distraction now, with Mehmet and Miss Trent on the outside of the door and able to help him, or wait until the two were inside.

He would definitely need help against a pair of burly men.

William grabbed the knife and heaved it at a large ceramic urn with such force it shattered.

Behind him a woman screamed.

Damn. The old woman had revived. At the wrong bloody time.

The burly guards separated, one running toward the urn, the other coming toward him and the old woman.

William ducked behind the metal urn containing the potted palm, crouching down as far as he could to be shielded by the urn.

He had one chance. He ran toward the bedroom doors. Mehmet and Miss Trent had already slipped through. He glanced to both sides to see if he'd been followed, then sucked in a steadying breath as he gripped the door handle and let himself inside.

The room was overly decorated, colors, patterns, materials everywhere. Where was Beatrice?

Mehmet pressed his weight against the door. "Did they see you?" he asked barely above a whisper.

"No. I don't think so. But the old woman woke up. The two guards are on either end of the corridor."

"All right." Mehmet thinned his lips as he thought. He gazed at Miss Trent. "They still think me a palace doctor. We should see how far that will take us."

"Yes," agreed William. "Get Miss Trent to safety. I'll see to Beatrice."

Mehmet nodded and cracked open the door. He grabbed Miss Trent's arm as he assessed the situation, then opened the door and pulled her into the corridor.

William was alone. He examined the door lock. There was no way to lock it from inside. He had to act quickly.

In the center of the busy array of textiles and tiles, behind an elaborately carved wooden screen, was an enormous four-poster bed.

He stepped forward gingerly, looking around. "Beatrice?" he said softly.

She was on the bed in her white nightgown, her limbs impossibly stretched out against white sheets, the absence of color in stark contrast to the colorful pattern everywhere.

Beatrice flinched, then raised her head. "William? Oh, God, William." She squirmed against her bindings.

He looked about again.

"I'm alone," she said. "I'm pretty sure I've been left here on my own."

Perfect.

"I heard voices though. Just before you arrived."

"Mehmet and Miss Trent."

Beatrice's eyes widened, the green clouded by gray. "She's safe?"

"Yes, my love, but you are not." He went to her right foot, examining the bindings holding her to the four bedposts. The knots looked complicated.

Her body was barely obscured under the sheer fabric of her nightgown, her nipples erect from the chill in the room. He shouldn't feel aroused, but he did. Abashment should not deflect him from his main purpose. He went to work on the bindings.

"Bolt the door," she said.

"I can't. It won't."

"Put something heavy against it?"

He grabbed an ornate chair and shoved it against the door, angling the top rail under the door latch. The stratagem should delay the guards for a bit, at least.

"Free me." Beatrice sounded enervated.

He worked at the knot of the leather strap attached to her left arm.

"Is there anything sharp in the room?"

Of course. He almost forgot. Mehmet had insisted he keep a dagger in his boot. He slipped out the knife then proceeded to work on Beatrice's bindings, cutting them well away from her flesh.

Moments later she was free.

Still, she hesitated, remaining sitting on the bed, the sheer fabric clinging to her perfect body. Her dressing gown lay in a heap on a fur rug, her slippers tossed not far away. He handed the gown to her.

After she dressed, he took her hand and gave a gentle tug. "Darling, let's go."

"No."

"*No?*" Did she not understand the danger they were in?

Beatrice sat up on her knees. "William, you have to do one thing for me before we leave."

"Anything. Then we *must* leave."

"You have to relieve me of my virginity."

CHAPTER THIRTEEN

"What?" William paled, his expression not merely astonished but incredulous.

"I was tied up and left here like an offering because Durukan wants my virginity." Beatrice could not keep the tremble from her voice.

William's pallor turned a reddish tinge.

"And if I am captured again I'm certain he will dispense with any pretense of courtship and do it in front of his guards."

"I hardly think tying you to a bed could be considered courtship."

She cupped his cheek. "Will you do it for me? Please?"

"It's not what I wanted for us." His voice quavered. "But I will do what you need me to do."

"Nothing romantic. Just do the deed as it were."

He slowly unbuttoned his braces at the front of his waistband.

"William, hurry, we cannot delay."

He unbuttoned his fly, then untucked his shirt. He reached into the front of his trousers and pulled out his manhood, erect and ready.

A flush stained his cheeks. "I admit seeing you in your sheer nightgown provoked my desires."

So sweet. She kissed him, then lay down on the mattress and rucked up her hem.

"Beatrice, are you ready for me? You have to be ready, or it will hurt."

"I've heard it will hurt anyway."

He lengthened himself over her. "No, listen, I know I'm not a girl, but I was told by…by…"

"By your lover."

"Yes, by my last lover, that a woman needs to be pleasured first."

"William, we don't have time."

"Yes, we do."

He spread her legs open and dived his face between them. His tongue thrust inside her, then he began licking her.

Oh lord, that was incredible.

Beatrice relaxed on the mattress, as much as she could with her mind wondering if the door would be breached soon.

Like her maidenhead.

But William's tongue stroking her was enough to make her forget for a moment where she was and why she was there.

She threaded her fingers through his hair, gripping the strands, drawing him closer to her as she pushed into him, undulating with each movement of his jaw. His attention focused on her clit, thrilling her until a wave of pleasure overtook her, threatening to crash in a wail.

Beatrice checked herself. They should not make a sound.

"William, love, please."

He lifted his head, his mouth wet with her desire. "I think you might be ready now." He clambered on top and nudged open her legs. He grabbed his manhood and positioned it at her entrance, prodding her.

"Darling, there may be some pain—"

"I don't care, William."

He held her gaze and pushed through.

A painful pinch. She tensed then flinched at the sensation of stretching. He kissed her mouth and began to move in and out of her, slowly, deliberately.

Wonderfully.

"My God, Bea, this is glorious."

Yes, yes, it was. She tried to choke back tears of relief and joy, but could not restrain herself.

He slowed, then stopped. "Darling, am I hurting you?"

"No, no. William please, we must—"*just get this over with*"—not tarry."

He once again resumed his languid rhythm. "I suppose you are no longer a virgin."

True. "But I want to leave evidence."

"Evidence?"

"A stain on the sheets."

"Oh, yes, I see." William picked up his pace, plowing ahead. He bent his neck, no longer holding her gaze, but immersed in his own drive to culmination, his sharp breaths echoing hers.

Despite the pinch, which had grown into a dull ache, pleasure overtook her, a different sensation from when William had used his mouth, a deep voluptuousness, centered in her core, radiating outward to tingle her toes. She held on to the feeling, wanting, needing more. With a clipped yelp William tore himself from her, leaving her unsatisfied, holding his cock as it jetted milky fluid onto the sheets.

Beatrice scooted back as he finished, leaving a trail of slimy blood to mar the white sheets.

William grabbed the top sheet and wiped himself, offering a corner to Beatrice. She wiped herself clean, shaky and in awe of what their bodies had done together.

And what she had denied to her captor and made damn sure he knew it.

He handed her the slippers. "Put these on."

They needed to leave. Now.

WILLIAM FRANTICALLY SURVEYED the room for an exit.

Beatrice sighed. "We'll have to leave the same way we both arrived. I only know how to get back to the throne room. Do you know how to get us out?"

"Yes," he said. He went to the double doors, removed the chair holding the latch, and pressed his ear against the crack to listen.

Then slammed himself against the wall.

"He's there," William hissed.

Rustling sounds and low murmurs came from outside in the corridor.

Panic gripped him as Beatrice paled.

"The bed." She met William's gaze. "Under the bed."

It was the only possible hiding place.

From either side they each rolled under the bed as quickly as possible, meeting in the middle on their backs, grasping hands. William drew in a deep breath to calm his pounding heart. Beside him, Beatrice stiffened.

"Lady Beatrice, I am here." Durukan Pasha's voice rang in a lighthearted melody as if overjoyed to see a sweetheart. He spoke in undertones with someone in Turkish, his words light as if he were happy, a chuckle at the end of his sentence.

Then silence.

"What the bloody hell?" The Turkish accent was gone, replaced by a working-class English accent.

How utterly strange.

William froze as the pasha's feet were planted inches away from him. Beatrice gripped his hand harder.

Above them, the pasha tore at the bed covers, growling oaths in English. A deep red coverlet fell off the side of the mattress to obscure William's view.

"Where is she?" Durukan yelled to whoever was with him in the room. "I want her found."

The other occupant of the room spoke softly, obsequiously.

"Now!" Durukan screamed.

William gripped Beatrice's hand tighter, and tugged her to him. She poked his chest and pointed to the view from her side.

He caught a glimpse of the servant slipping through a door hidden by the cacophony of ornament on the wall.

Their escape.

If the pasha ever left.

Durukan snapped commands, once again speaking Turkish to whomever else was in the room.

Good God. Beatrice would have been strapped to the bed under the gaze of all of these men. William strained to contain his anger. Beside him, a tear slid down the side of Beatrice's face.

Frenzied footfalls indicated the servants were scattering to do the pasha's bidding.

A crash, like a ceramic urn shattering against the wall, and the slamming of the doors indicated the pasha had left as well.

William pressed a finger to his lips. Perhaps it was all subterfuge and someone was still in the room. They couldn't be certain. In the tight confines of under the bed, William twisted awkwardly to reach his ankle. He fumbled with the leg of his trousers, then stretched back to normal.

With a gun in his hand.

He pointed to the side he was on, that Beatrice should follow him after he slid out from under the bed and made sure their path was clear.

He poked his head and the gun out from under the bed, then slowly extracted himself, using the red coverlet as a shield.

"No one's here," he whispered, motioning for her to follow. "Come."

Very carefully she inched along until she was at the edge. William pulled her out from under the bed and up to standing. They hurried to the wall where the hidden door was, sliding their hands along the tile searching for the opening.

"Here," she said, gripping a diminutive latch right above the tiled wainscoting.

"Me first." William pressed the latch. The door opened silently, the hinges probably well-greased because it was a secret door. He peeked his head inside, then took her hand and led her inside, closing the door behind them.

Behind the wall was a narrow and dark corridor. They both looked side to side. A faint light to the left enticed them to go in that direction, treading gingerly, their steps measured.

The light was from an open door at the bottom of a narrow stone staircase, the steps shiny from decades of use. William bade Beatrice grip the rope handrail as she followed him. Her soft slippers would be unsafe against the slick steps.

He stopped at the bottom, stretching out an arm to hold her at bay. He very slowly glanced through the crack in the door and around the corner to the other side.

The way was clear. Where were all the people?

Probably trying to find them.

Beatrice tugged on his jacket then gave him a questioning look. Which way?

He shrugged. Her guess was as good as his. She pointed to the right. That direction would be away from the public rooms, but also away from the main entrance. Perhaps there was a sort of back door. Didn't palaces have servants' entrances and exits?

This was definitely a servants' corridor, lacking the opulent decoration of the main palace, with just a simple ornamental frieze along the wall.

The clicking of shoes on the stone floor indicated there was a servant coming right toward them.

Perhaps two.

Yes, two men.

William grabbed Beatrice by the arm. "Follow my lead," he murmured, his lips pressed to her ear. "Please. Trust me."

She tossed him a worried glance.

As the two servants passed by, William made a show of brandishing the gun, then held it against Beatrice's ribs as his other hand held her by her wrists. He hardened his expression, trying to convey that he was not to be challenged. Beatrice feigned fear. With a real gun at her side, she probably did not have to pretend.

The servants regarded them with curiosity and unease, perhaps a bit of suspicion.

Still, they continued on their path.

William marched Beatrice along as if nothing would get in his way. He continued marching until they were well enough around a corner and alone.

He stopped and relaxed at her side. "I apologize, darling," he said, slipping the gun in his jacket pocket. "We need disguises if we're going to wander about the palace trying to find a way out."

She trembled. "We have to get out of here."

"Let's keep going and hope we find something along the way."

MEHMET AND CLARISSA HAD been hurriedly walking, practically running down corridors. Why hadn't they been seen? Was Durukan that unobservant? Or was he letting them get away?

Or had he put all his resources in capturing Beatrice?

Mehmet shuddered.

He had kept his hand on Clarissa's arm the entire time they were fleeing. He would not let her out of his sight. She'd been taken from his palace as he'd slept in his own bed unaware. He would never put the woman he loved in such danger again.

They came to the door he and William had initially entered, a solid wooden door that led to the stables.

As they huddled against the wall, Clarissa pressed herself against him.

"He's letting us go," she murmured.

"I don't even think he knows I'm here," Mehmet said.

"But he knows *I'm* here," she said. "Somewhere."

"It was never you he wanted."

"No," Clarissa agreed. "He wants Beatrice for her virginity. I was only in the way, really."

Which meant William and Beatrice would be in grave danger. Mehmet would have to stay behind.

He opened the door slowly and glanced around.

Nothing. No one. Only a porch leading to a muddy yard where servants managed the animals.

Beyond was the field he and William had traversed. Where his groomsmen were waiting for him with horses at the ready.

"Darling," he whispered in Clarissa's ear, "are you ready to cross a quagmire, partly in the guise of an old woman?"

She drew in a deep breath. "I'm ready."

He led her out of the door and walked calmly, but with purpose, not turning around, assuming—and hoping—Clarissa was following him as a bent old woman.

But when they arrived at the field with tall grasses, he picked up speed, Clarissa meeting his pace until she could grasp his hand. Together they moved swiftly until they reached the groomsmen Iskender and Cahit standing at the ready next to Borysthenes and three other horses.

Now was the time to let her go. As much as he did not want to be parted from her.

"Clarissa, my sweet, can you ride a horse?"

For one moment, she looked stunned. "I think so. It's been a long time."

"You will ride with my groomsman, Iskender. He will take you back to my palace. Cahit will wait with the remaining two horses."

Her expression pained. "What about you?"

"I need to wait for William and Miss Smythe."

"Mehmet, no—"

He pressed a finger to her lips, the simple touch exploding his erotic sensibilities. "My sweet, I need to be assured that you are safe."

She placed her hands on her hips. "And I need to be assured that *you* are safe."

He bent over and lifted both legs of his trousers revealing a dagger and a pistol.

Clarissa gasped.

"Does that reassure you somewhat?"

"It makes me fear for you even more."

"We can argue about this later." He nodded to his groomsman. "Please, go with Iskender. You need to rest."

She gave him a perturbed look.

"Please." He placed his hands on her cheeks and leaned in, kissing her. "Darling, please."

Her expression was pained resignation.

Mehmet snapped his fingers at Iskender and gave him instructions.

He stood back and watched as the groomsman helped Clarissa mount a horse then take the reins. The horse walked away slowly, so as not to draw attention. Their pace would increase the further away they were, when Iskender would take his place in the saddle.

As he approached Borysthenes, Mehmet combed his hair with his hands and smoothed down his clothing. He'd return to Durukan's palace but this time enter through the front door to see what the hell was going on.

CHAPTER FOURTEEN

"William, look," Beatrice whispered, nodding toward a door left ajar up ahead on the right. Could it be a way out?

He took her hand in his, and together they went to the door. He peered inside, while she looked over his shoulder. Darkness welcomed them.

The drumming of rapid footfalls nearby meant they would have to take their chances inside the dark room. Beatrice pushed William inside.

Heart pounding in her ears and William's under her palm, they waited as what seemed like a dozen men ran down the corridor.

Durukan Pasha had finally marshaled his minions in the effort to find her. But it was possible they had no idea William was with her. Likely they assumed Beatrice was being helped by Miss Trent instead, which could be why Durukan's men had not stopped William when they saw him with the gun.

William leaned against the door, listening intently. Silence meant they had a moment to think.

"Bea," he said quietly, "I suspect Durukan believes you are escaping on your own or with Miss Trent."

"Yes, I considered that. So we can maintain the charade of you as my captor to his servants?"

"I suppose for a little while at least," William agreed. "Durukan has seen me before, so we mustn't encounter him or his immediate staff. And it might eventually seem odd to his men that a tall non-Turkish fellow was guarding you, don't you think?"

"Not necessarily. Miss Trent thinks Durukan is from the East End of London."

William's jaw dropped. "Hence the stream of expletives when he discovered you not tied to his bed?"

"Exactly. And who knows how many of his servants are English?"

"Which means we have to be careful of what we say aloud when you are my captive."

Beatrice's eyes had finally adjusted to the darkness. On the other side of the room was a railing for a staircase going down. "William, look, over there. Perhaps our way out?"

William ruminated as he regarded the railing. "Bea, do you know how many stories the palace has?"

"Three, I think."

"And that bedroom you were in was on the first floor, correct?"

"Yes."

"And we've already gone down one flight of stairs. Shouldn't we be on the ground floor?" He pointed to the staircase.

"Ah," she said. "Perhaps some parts of the palace have more stories than others?"

"Well, if we are not already at ground or sea level, I say we continue down."

He was correct in his assessment. "All right."

William took her hand, and together they moved slowly in the dark to the first step down. He felt each stair with his toes before letting Beatrice follow him. Darkness swallowed them as they descended.

The lack of a next stair indicated they had reached the bottom. The pitch-black bottom.

"Maybe we should go back," he said.

"No," she said, letting go of his hand.

"What are you doing?"

"Feeling the wall for some sort of opening. A latch, a knob. If you think about it, why would there be a staircase to nowhere?"

"Perhaps where it leads to has been blocked off? Maybe there was some sort of renovation—"

"Ah-ha!" Beatrice exclaimed in a whisper. "A lever."

"Bea, darling, let me go first."

"But—"

"Don't quarrel, darling. I have the gun."

Beatrice stepped aside. William pressed down on the lever slowly, as she said a quiet prayer that it was not some sort of trap. The latch clicked free from the jamb, and he nudged the door open.

An ill-lighted corridor. At least it wasn't complete darkness.

"This palace is a maze," Beatrice whispered.

"Truly."

They looked side to side before leaving the darkness. They hugged the wall as they proceeded down the corridor to the left.

Shouts and the thunder of footfalls came from behind them, just beyond the door to the darkness. There was no retreating back. They had to move forward.

Beatrice pointed to a tiled niche across the corridor, a deeply inset archway with narrow alcoves on either side. Each shadowed alcove was big enough for two to hide.

William pulled Beatrice across the corridor and into the alcove on the right, the same direction as the shouts. Anyone running down the corridor would have to stop and turn around to see them. They pressed inside the tiled alcove as flush as they could, Beatrice's heart thundering anxiously.

Half a dozen men ran down the corridor intent on getting somewhere and not looking back. The pair stayed flattened against the tiles until the sounds of running had completely faded away.

William let out a breath only to suck it in again. "There might be more coming in the other direction."

"I already thought of that." Beatrice ran her hand over the tiled wall and found a length of metal between two tiles. "A hinge."

"Another secret door." He kissed her. "Beatrice, you're brilliant."

Together they ran their hands over the tile wall searching for a way in.

A small hole big enough for a finger held a metal latch. Beatrice pulled, and the latch clicked open.

William pushed the wall gently, and they slipped inside.

Boxes and crates and straw were everywhere. They had stumbled upon a storeroom of sorts.

William looked around the room, keeping Beatrice at his back. They were alone. But the disarray made it seem like someone had recently been in the room and had left in a hurry.

Light spilled in from transom windows along one wall. Maybe they could pile crates on top of each other and get out through a window.

Beatrice bent over and peered inside an open crate as long as a coffin, its lid leaning against the side. "I wonder what they're packing?"

She pushed aside the straw to reveal a mummy case, her eyes widening as large as those in the portrait staring back at her. "William," Beatrice hissed. "Take a look at this."

He joined her at the open crate.

"It's a mummy case. Like the Fayyum mummies from Egypt we saw at the British Museum, remember?"

An encaustic portrait of a young woman decorated the head of the case. She was youthful, with black hair and pearl drop earrings.

William ran his fingers over an edge of the portrait. "So smooth. Like it had been made yesterday and not almost two thousand years ago."

Beatrice examined the case. "And the condition of the coffin is unbelievable. Not a chip in the wood."

William stood back to survey the crates and the room. "I wonder if each of these holds some archaeological gem such as this."

His gaze stopped. He motioned to Beatrice to join him. There was an entryway to another room.

He opened the door and stepped through first. Beatrice hovered behind, then followed him when it was clear no danger was present.

Another storeroom, its transom windows partially shielded behind curtains. Unlike the other storeroom, this one seemed more organized. Shelves lined the walls, housing scrolls, portrait sculptures, tiny bronzes, mosaic emblemata. In the middle of the room, two tables were covered with artifacts. One was set up as a scribe's table with an ink pot and reed pens and an unrolled scroll.

Odd how the scroll was only half filled. As if someone had been in the middle of creating it before they left.

Beatrice drew her finger down the profile of a sculpted portrait head. "This marble is so pristine, so clean. If it were Roman, it would have stains and weathering. But it's whiter and smoother than anything we've seen in the museums."

William circled around the table with the scroll. "Beatrice, I don't think any of these artifacts are real. Or maybe only some of them are."

"How do you mean?"

"Take a look at this."

She joined him at the scribe's table. Underneath the half-filled scroll was another scroll, but its lettering was complete.

"Someone is copying this scroll," he said, pointing to the finished one. "Read it."

She studied the two scrolls. Both Latin texts. Ovid. "Why, they're the same words. And the script is exactly the same." She pointed to a word. "And 'mentiar' is even misspelled in both." She took in the space again. "William, do you think Durukan is making fake antiquities?"

William strolled around examining artifacts. "It does look like it, doesn't it?"

"But why?"

"To sell to unsuspecting collectors? Then Durukan would get to keep the real ones for himself?"

The top of the second table held two mosaic hunting scenes. William stepped forward to get a closer look at the tesserae. "There's something too perfect about these."

"Then I wonder if that Fayyum mummy in the other room is also a fake."

"Bea, don't—"

Beatrice ignored William's plea. "We need more evidence," she said, and took off for the other room.

MEHMET RESTRAINED HIS HORSE to a slow walk as the stone entrance gate of Durukan's palace came into view. Borysthenes complained about the pace with a twitch of his tail. But Mehmet needed a moment to collect his emotions and restrain his ire.

As they passed through the stone arch and the gilded iron gates, his anger was quickly replaced with confusion.

The normally well-regimented courtyard of the palace was instead completely abuzz with chaotic activity. Men—and, surprisingly, a few women—scurried about, each focused on their own path, not bothering with following the lines of the diagonal stone walkways, instead forging through bushes to cross over lawns.

And not concerned with his presence at all.

He dismounted, the usual boy servant ready to take his reins nowhere in sight. Well, Borysthenes would not leave as long as he was tethered to something—unless, of course, Durukan had a mind to kidnap a horse, as well.

But from how he was being ignored by the palace staff, Mehmet was fairly certain Durukan was preoccupied with plots and intrigues other than horse-napping.

Mehmet wrapped Borysthenes' reins around the iron gate. He grabbed a servant who made the mistake of slowing to go around him. "My good fellow—"

The servant bowed his head with a jerk. "My lord, apologies, but I must leave you in better hands." He wriggled free and went on his way.

Mehmet turned around and crashed into another servant. This one again acknowledged him only with a clipped apology and went on his way.

He stood in the courtyard a moment and simply observed before proceeding to the arched doorway of the entrance to the palace proper.

A servant walked briskly past him, brushing his arm.

"A million pardons, my lord," the servant said softly in elegant Ottoman Turkish and not the local rural dialect. The servant paused to bow.

Mehmet contained his surprise and relief when he recognized Zeki, the servant he had sent to spy on Durukan once they'd returned from the archaeological field.

"It is nothing to be concerned with," Mehmet said in the local dialect, loud enough for no one to suspect their conversation would be anything but normal. "I am here to see Durukan Pasha, but did not expect such activity as this."

"You have arrived at an interesting moment, my lord." Zeki continued to use the elegant Turkish. "There is great excitement because of Durukan Pasha's wedding day—"

Holy of holies. Was that what he was calling it?

"I see the disgust on your face," Zeki said quietly. "I can assure you the marriage was thwarted."

Mehmet sighed in relief.

"Hence, why there is so much activity in the yard. The young woman has disappeared."

"And Durukan, where is he?"

Zeki gestured to the entrance portal. "I will show you. Walk with me," he said in the local dialect. "While I do not know the specifics, there are also some concerns regarding a shipment."

"Coming into the palace or leaving the palace?"

"I'm not quite certain, Excellency, but perhaps both."

Which begged the question, what was so important that the entire staff was involved? "So Durukan has lost his bride and has to deal with shipping logistics all on the same day."

"He is not pleased."

"I reckon he would not be." At the entrance, Mehmet stopped and surreptitiously surveyed the courtyard. "Perhaps the loss of his bride has somehow interfered with this shipment."

"Perhaps." Zeki bowed as if to indicate he had been seen with Mehmet for too long. He waved over a guard, giving the man instructions to take Mehmet to the throne room or wherever Durukan might be.

The palace corridors were slightly calmer with fewer servants running to and fro. A few of the palace servants knew Mehmet by sight and bowed their heads in greeting as he passed.

The throne room doors were closed, guards posted on either side. Mehmet's guard spoke in low tones to one guard who went inside. He returned a few minutes later and ushered Mehmet through.

In the throne room Durukan held court at the short end of a long table of ancient oak. He stood, pointing to charts of some sort, while around him men nodded and scribes took notes. The subdued symposium was spiked with a tension as thick as a London fog.

Durukan stepped forward, an affected smile plastered on his face. "Mehmet Pasha, welcome to my home." He snapped for a servant to bring tea.

Mehmet held up his hand. "I will not be long."

"To what do I owe the pleasure, Mehmet Pasha?"

"Two of the Englishwomen from the expedition have disappeared. They were guests at my palace, and were missing as of late this morning. I fear they may have gotten lost in the woods on some outing adventure. You know the English."

Durukan chuckled. "I do not, but it sounds as if they are a rather foolhardy race."

"They do not speak Turkish, my lord. I was hoping you could alert your men to the possibility that they may be lost and might wander over here." Mehmet made a show of looking over Durukan's shoulder. "But I see you are involved in some activity that preoccupies you and involves much activity among your servants and staff."

There was that chuckle again, bland and suspicious. "I am certain that in the time it has taken you to look for them and to travel here they have returned to your palace by now."

"You are very correct, Excellency. And I see you are so very busy. I will be on my way."

Durukan waved to a harried servant to escort Mehmet out. The servant was young, really still a boy.

"There is so much activity in the palace today," Mehmet said in the local dialect. "Have you ever seen so much activity?"

"No, my lord."

"Is all well? I have concern for my neighbor."

"I am not certain, my lord. Something about a ship."

"A ship?"

"I do not understand myself. We lack a proper harbor. Beyond that, I do not know."

They had reached the entrance portal. Mehmet reached into his pocket and fished out a coin. "That is for your generosity, my boy."

A blush colored the look of disbelief. The boy would remain silent for so generous a patron.

Borysthenes snorted when Mehmet untied him. He would send a few men to scour the shoreline to see what Durukan was up to.

WILLIAM SCRUTINIZED THE MOSAIC emblemata. Both pieces were scenes framed by a guilloche pattern of twisted black and white tesserae. Each was smooth to the touch, as if time had ignored the artifacts. One depicted a man holding a bunch of grapes over his head. William took a step to get closer to the other.

And hit the tip of his boot on something hard and unmovable under the table.

He bent down. A large block of carved marble. He stretched forward to get a better look.

A chill furred up his spine to tighten his scalp.

Not just any block of marble. No. One with carved figures. Next to it was an equally huge block with an inscription in Greek, rough edge adjoined to rough edge in an attempt to fit the two together.

The inscription spelled out the name *Antinous*. Just like William had seen at the excavation site before Durukan had seized their artifacts.

Unlike the other marble artifacts in the storeroom, these blocks were stained and weathered. Were these the very same purloined fragments from Mehmet's temple? Was Durukan planning on copying them?

The whoosh of a door opening behind him compelled him to scramble under the table, behind the fragments, to hide in their shadows.

Someone, a man from the heft of footfalls, had entered the room through a door previously unseen.

The man grumbled something in Turkish and fussed with items on the scribe's table. He strode loudly but calmly to the other room.

Damn and blast. Beatrice!

The only place she could hide would be inside the crate with the mummy.

More grumbling in Turkish. Then the scrape of wood on wood. Was he placing a cover on a crate? The one with Beatrice inside?

Disgruntled muttering was followed by the clank of a bolt being thrown. Someone outside called and the Turkish man called back. A moment later he strode past William and exited out the door he had originally entered, locking it behind him.

William waited another moment, then crawled out from under the table.

Very carefully, but as swiftly as he could, he navigated around the tables and artifacts to get to Beatrice.

The lid *had* been placed on the crate with the Fayyum mummy. He knocked on the cover. "Bea?"

She sneezed. "I'm fine. It smells like…like paste and paint in here."

The lid had not been secured. He lifted it. Beatrice was tucked against the mummy case, covered in straw. He brushed aside the straw and helped her out. She shook out her clothes.

"Did you understand anything that man said?"

"Unfortunately, no. He left through the other room." He pointed behind him. "I think he locked the door. I don't expect he'll be back soon." He took her hand. "I have to show you something. Come."

He led her to the table with the mosaics then crouched down. "I'm pretty sure this is what I saw at the temple site before Durukan stole it."

Beatrice's mouth fell open. She stared a moment, then dared touch the sculpture. Her finger slid across the marble, and she moved in closer.

"William," she whispered, "this is real. Feel it."

He traced the figures and the inscription. The marble was rough to the touch.

"And look here. Dirt and mildew."

"Do you think the people who make these fake artifacts were going to copy these as well?"

"Perhaps," she said thoughtfully. He watched as her fingers deftly explored the contours of the scene, wishing she were exploring him instead.

"But why?" She stared at him. "The inscription has missing chunks. If Mehmet has the other parts, or finds the other parts, then Durukan's scheme would be exposed."

"Perhaps because they want to make changes and then present the changed version as the real one?"

A little crease formed between Beatrice's eyebrows. "But why?"

William studied the inscription. "Because it mentions Antinous?"

She traced the Greek letters and sounded the words out loud. "My Greek is not so good that I can completely understand this. With missing bits, the inscription just seems random."

"Besides the name, they're just words. I don't know the connection." There wasn't time to think about any of this. At the very least, they needed to preserve the text and a rough idea of the image for Mehmet. If he were then given a fake artifact he'd know what was being covered up.

William looked about the room. "We need to copy down the inscription."

"Perhaps there's an extra scroll we can use?"

"We'd have to search a bit more. There's only this one that's part done."

"What do we have to write with?"

"The ink in this pot." William picked up the glass jar. It was mostly full.

Beatrice took the pot and opened it. She sniffed. "Sort of smells like wine."

"There's a brush, and this pen." He studied the latter. "The forgers were striving for authenticity. This is a hand-cut reed."

"Oh bother," Beatrice said as she shuffled through objects on the scribe's table. She stopped suddenly, and turned to face him. "I have it," she exclaimed.

"Oh? What is it you have?"

"The solution." She began to remove her dressing gown. "On my back."

"On your back?" William struggled to keep his shock at a low volume.

"Like a tattoo. I've seen photos of skin decorations." Her dressing gown fell to the floor. "And women in Mehmet's harem use something called henna to paint on their skin."

She proceeded to lift the hem of her nightgown, each inch arousing him unwittingly. Her calves, her thighs, her buttocks—

"Beatrice." William grabbed her hand to stop her. "Darling, let's think this through a moment, shall we?"

She gave him a stern look. "Why? Are you going to steal the unfinished scroll? If we're caught with it, we'll lose all the information." She took his hand in hers and stroked it. "If the information is hidden on one of us, it will be concealed. No one will think to look on our flesh."

"What if it doesn't work? How do we know the ink will stick?"

"Haven't you ever written a letter? I get ink stains on my fingers all the time."

"I suppose so."

She batted her eyes at him. "I'm volunteering. If you would prefer I write on your back, we can do that."

"Well, you're practically naked already." And he'd get to look at her naked for a bit. Something he had regretted not being able to do when he'd deflowered her.

Deflowered. What a horrible way to phrase it. He'd make it up to her. He would. Actually he couldn't wait. But right now he had to concentrate on the task at hand.

Except Beatrice had already hiked her nightgown up over her shoulders. She knelt before the blocks and bent forward, curving her back as if in supplication.

The canvas she offered was perfect. Unmarred ivory flesh was disrupted only by the ridges and indentations of her vertebrae running through the center to her tail bone. Further down, the furrow of her buttocks was a temptation before him. She was long and lean. And vertical. But if the canvas was turned on its side—

"Beatrice, I need you to turn to the right. I'll have more length that way, and your spine will be like that ridge of dentil molding."

"Oh, yes, I see." She flashed him a smile. "You're brilliant, William."

And you're far too naked. "Thank you, darling."

He grabbed a pot of black ink and the reed pen. He dipped the pen in the ink and hovered his hand over her for a moment.

"Are you ready?"

"Yes, William."

He copied the first letter. The dark ink pooled a moment, then seemed to dry, giving him hope this might just work. He continued with the second letter. Beatrice squirmed with a giggle.

"Bea, don't move. I can't do this if you're moving."

"Sorry. But it tickles."

His cock sprung to life once more. "I'll press harder so it won't tickle so."

He continued, copying each letter, trying to mimic the script, although artistry was not his forte. The ink bled into her, the edges of the letters turning from crisp to blurred. One word used up all the ink.

"I need more ink. Give me a moment."

He grabbed another pot from the table. The sight of a delicate brush gave him an idea. He didn't have anywhere near the artistic skill as Miss Trent, but she wasn't there, so he would have to do his best.

"One last word, love."

"All right. Hurry. We don't know how much time we have."

She was right. He dipped the pen in the ink pot. Blue ink. Blue ink that stained instantly. He forged ahead. His writing was not as careful as before. He could spend more time with the letters or he could continue to fill the canvas before him.

He exchanged the reed pen for the delicate brush. He dipped the brush in the ink and, with a careful study of the carved image he began to draw.

Beatrice sucked in a breath. "What are you doing now?"

"I'm copying the image using a brush."

"But we can just describe the image."

"Or we can do both." He continued despite her protest.

"All right, but hurry."

Just a few brush strokes, that's all he needed. Just enough to show where the elements of the image were located in relation to each other.

"Finished," he said.

Beatrice uncurled her back and stood up, wobbling on her feet a moment. He caught her.

"How does it look?"

The letters and image were squished and distorted now she was standing. He licked a finger and swiped it over a corner of a letter in black, then licked a different finger and swiped it over a letter in blue.

The ink had fixed.

"I think we did it. Get dressed quickly."

Beatrice pulled down her nightgown and he pressed the fabric to her back. "This should work. I hope this works."

She slipped on her dressing gown. "If not, between the two of us, we'll be able to explain most of it. Enough for Mehmet to have an idea of what we saw."

"Now how to get out of here?"

William tried the door the Turkish fellow had come through. "Locked."

"What about the door we entered?"

"I'll check." The door was unlocked. William hesitated, getting his bearings.

Two doors, one of which had a corridor beyond it, a corridor that curved around the two storerooms. All of this traveling was taking them further away from the front of the palace, where he and Mehmet had entered.

He looked up.

The transom windows beckoned.

He pushed the table with the mosaics against the wall and climbed on top. The transom was just out of view, although he could reach the curtain. He pulled it back and daylight spilled forth. He gripped the ledge and pulled himself up.

Below was the corridor they had been in. To the left was the curve of the corner the running men had disappeared around. To the right was a bank of windows.

With a view of the bay. *Damn.*

"We're on the wrong side of the palace."

"How do you mean?"

He lowered himself. "The bay is outside." He climbed off the table. "I came over land on horseback with Mehmet. There are groomsmen with horses waiting for you and Miss Trent. That was on the other end of the palace."

"We can't just go back the way we came." She paled.

"No." He had to think of something other than wandering all the way back through the palace. "At the very least, we're probably near an exit to the outside."

"Leading us in the wrong direction."

He thought a moment. "Unless we find a boat and I can row us along the coast." He gave her a questioning look. "Or you can swim?"

"I've only ever swum in a pond. Never in open water."

"And it might wash away the ink." He pointed to her back.

"I'm certain something will remain. How long does it take to get ink stains off your fingers?"

"Right." He regarded her sympathetically. "Do you think you can walk along a beach?"

Beatrice regarded her thin slippers. "I'll have to, won't I?"

He pointed to the next room. "We'll have to leave the way we entered."

She smiled. "After you, Mr. Peel."

BEATRICE SAID A SILENT PRAYER to whatever gods were watching that the corridor they had previously occupied would be quiet and empty. Still, William insisted they wait in the tiled alcove listening to any and every noise surrounding them.

Luckily there was blissful silence, the only distraction the itching sensations on her back.

They left the alcove and rounded the corner, following the path of the men who had run down the corridor not too long before. They reached the bank of windows William had spied from the transom. Beatrice crouched down beneath the sill while William observed the view.

"I think it best we crawl along the wall so we're under the sill. There are a lot of men outside. Someone may see us if they decide to look at the windows."

So they crawled along the well-worn wooden floor, shiny and smooth from centuries of use. Which made it almost like gliding on one's knees.

They reached another staircase, a few steps leading to a vestibule with a door to the outside.

"So do we just leave?" Beatrice asked.

"Can you wait here while I check it out?" William's voice held concern. "I mean, will you be all right on your own?"

"William, it's five steps. I'll be fine."

He smiled thinly then went down the steps.

Beatrice took a moment to review her surroundings. To her right was a deep alcove with an inset wooden banquette. Opposite, hanging on the outer wall, were a random assortment of tools. The ax, shovel, poker, and bellows suddenly made more sense when she spied the small hearth below the tools.

So an area where one would have to wait for so long a period they would need to keep warm.

Down the steps William looked out the window in the door, bobbing his head up and down so as not to be seen, but to be able to catch glimpses of whatever was going on outside.

Beatrice crawled over to the banquette. As she suspected it was actually a chest. She opened it slowly, not wanting any squeaks to draw William's attention away from what he was doing and attempt something he might consider heroic.

A hook on the wall enabled her to prop the bench open. Inside were several pillows, one the same length of the bench. So someone might sleep there, which meant—

Ah, yes, blankets, and even better, a pair of dingy sheets. One might only need a light covering during summer nights.

She pulled them out of the bench, closed it, then turned around to see William's worried expression.

"Beatrice, darling, don't make me fret so."

"William, love, I found us disguises." She held up the sheets. "I don't know what is going on outside, but if a blond-haired English girl in her dressing gown and an exceptionally tall English boy with ginger hair were to be seen, then I think all activity would cease and all attention would be on us, impeding our escape."

The worried look turned to one of conspiratorial glee. "You're brilliant, Bea."

She tossed a sheet to him. "Quick, put this on in some Turkish fashion."

Beatrice folded the sheet as a triangle then covered her head and wrapped one end over the lower part of her face. She tucked her hair as far under the sheet as possible. "All right, I'm ready."

"Good," said William. He'd slashed the sheet in the middle and poked his head through. But first he'd taken off his waistcoat and done something clever with it to cover his conspicuous hair.

Beatrice tried not to giggle too much.

"So, from what I can tell, there's a ship near the beach, and it looks as if it has run aground. There's not a harbor, so I'm not quite sure why the ship is so close to shore."

"Because they're going to put the artifacts on it."

"Yes, I suppose. At the moment there are dozens of men dragging the ship from the sand toward the water. I expect that's where it was supposed to be—out in the water so it could weigh anchor."

"Do you think the men will take much notice of us? Or are they preoccupied with what they are doing?"

"I imagine they are preoccupied. But maybe you could pretend to be a bent-over old woman. They're looking for a young woman. I have no idea if they are looking for a young man as well. But at least we can make it look like I'm out with my aged relative."

"All right." It was a good plan.

"Too bad you don't have a cane."

A cane? "Oh but I think I do." Beatrice retrieved the poker from the hearth. "Do you know which direction we should go in?"

"Once we're outside, to the right. It will be quite a journey along the coast. Once we're clear of Durukan's estate, we'll cut inland."

They walked down the steps to the back door. As a final check, William peered out the window in the top half of the door. Then he grabbed her hand and led them outside.

A chilly breeze drifted off the water. Beatrice was glad for the poker as her slippers were not meant for negotiating grasses and rocks. They plodded forward, not wanting to draw attention to themselves, fighting the urge to run. Beatrice's eyes hurt from looking sidelong too often, and when she almost fell on her face, she decided she'd keep lookout duties to William.

Rocks turned to sand as they got further away. Still they maintained a nonchalant pace. And if it weren't for the horrid circumstances, Beatrice would want to hold William's hand.

"Bea." William had to bend close for her to hear over the wind. "Do you see that mound just ahead? We'll walk more quickly after that. But we are still the only people on the beach."

"So, we'll continue to stroll."

"Yes." William sighed. "God, this is going to take forever, isn't it?"

It did seem that way. But every step along the shore was a step closer to freedom.

CHAPTER FIFTEEN

Clarissa had never needed a bath, a change of clothes, and a filling meal more than when she'd returned to Mehmet's palace. But nothing would be enjoyed as long as Beatrice was still out there somewhere.

And Mehmet had not returned either.

"Mehmet will return whether you have bathed or not, Miss Trent," Beria said with a knowing smile. "But he will know that you have dismissed his hospitality if you are still covered in dust."

She was right. Hospitality was greatly esteemed in Turkish culture.

"I urge you to take care of yourself now, so you can help care for the others when they return."

Of course a mother would convey such wisdom. And she helped Clarissa with everything she needed.

As late afternoon was beginning to fade into early evening, a clean and properly fed Clarissa paced the silk carpet in the sitting room. Beria, Althea, and Cornelia all sat quietly while Clarissa was practically a hurricane in their calm presence.

"My dear Miss Trent, please have a seat and enjoy a cup of tea with me." A kind light shone in Beria's eyes that seemed exclusively for Clarissa.

Such tenderness was flustering. Her interest in Beria's son was far from scholarly and professional. Did the mother suspect something was between them?

A clatter and a gleeful yelp presaged the sitting room doors swinging open with vigor.

And in walked Mehmet with Beatrice and William.

Clarissa wanted to exclaim a gleeful yelp as well. She remained as calm as one could with one's heart pounding with joy and knees weakening with relief.

The professor's wives tended immediately to Beatrice and William, offering them tea and biscuits and fruit.

Beria stood and came forward, kissing her son's cheek. "I am glad you are returned."

"I was lucky to have discovered Beatrice and William walking in a field."

"And we were lucky Mehmet had his groomsman Cahit and two horses," said William.

"Mother, I see you have tea ready for us." Mehmet's gaze held great adoration.

And then he turned that gaze with a difference upon Clarissa. "Miss Trent," he said as he scanned her up and down. "I am delighted to know you took a moment to refresh yourself while you awaited our arrival."

Beria hid her smile of amusement behind her hand.

"I am afraid I've spent most of my time fretting for everyone's safety." Clarissa's head hurt behind her eyes from want of fully expressing her relief at seeing Mehmet.

"Now you can rest." He gestured to the sofa. "Miss Trent, please, have a seat and some tea while we regale you of our adventures." He murmured something to a servant who left after a bow of her head.

Beatrice and William settled into chairs near the tea table. The pair were bedraggled and disheveled. Beatrice's slippers were torn and wet, and there was a bit of hay in her hair. They really had been on an adventure of a sort.

The servant returned with a tray piled with food and placed it on the table between the two. William glanced about the room before delving into the repast with gusto. Beatrice was a bit more ladylike in her attack, carefully placing a savory pastry and stuffed vegetables on her plate.

Mehmet paced the same stretch of carpet as Clarissa had moments before and began his tale. "After I left Miss Trent, I returned to the entrance of Durukan's palace intending on inquiring if he knew the whereabouts of Miss Trent and Miss Smythe as they had not returned from a morning walk." He stopped for a sip of tea, replaced the cup on the table, and resumed pacing. "When my horse and I entered the palace courtyard, I knew there was something very, very wrong."

Clarissa accidentally rattled her teacup.

"Chaos reigned, servants—both men and women—running about in a rather haphazard fashion, as if no one knew what to do."

Mehmet glanced around the room, then dismissed the servants with a gesture. Only he, Beria, and the British remained, everyone now thoroughly attentive.

"I have a spy in Durukan's palace. He is there as a lowly servant, so he does not know information in great depth. This is for his protection, really. He knew Durukan had a bride but did not know who she was. And he knew the pasha had, as he put it, lost his bride."

"Beatrice and I had already escaped by then," said a smiling William.

"And were still skulking about the palace," said Mehmet. "I was able to meet with Durukan briefly in his throne room. He was examining charts with his staff. Later I heard there was some problem with a shipment—either to or from the palace, my spy could not say."

William made an excited peep.

"I returned to Cahit and the horses, but there was no sign of William and Beatrice. So we went looking for them. When we found them wandering along the shore, they told me the most curious story of their adventure."

"More curious than being a pasha's unwilling bride?" Clarissa sputtered.

"Oh, yes," said Beatrice with a mouthful of food.

"Miss Smythe is a lovely young woman," blurted William. "There's nothing curious about a pasha wanting her for his bride." His face turned a very bright shade of red after the last word.

Mehmet chuckled. "More curious than an old man wanting a beautiful young woman for a wife is the fact that the very same old man has a secret laboratory where he manufactures fake Greco-Roman artifacts."

Clarissa almost dropped her teacup this time. "My God."

"William and Miss Smythe told me a story about a very specific and special artifact and that they had evidence of its existence. But they would not tell me any details of this evidence. And now I await their explanation."

"We saw it, Clarissa," Beatrice said. "We saw part of the pediment of the Temple of Antinous."

"How do you mean?"

"There was this set of rooms in the palace. One room was filled with wooden crates, like what one might see being used for shipping at London docks. And in one of those crates was an Egyptian mummy case with an encaustic portrait of a young woman, like the ones found at Fayyum."

"But what would such a thing be doing here in Turkey?"

"Exactly what I had thought," said Beatrice excitedly. "And then we began to explore the other room. An ancient scroll was laid out, and someone had been copying it."

"The scroll wasn't finished," added William. "But what we saw was a perfect replica. There were also mosaics and portrait heads and little bronze sculptures. It was like being in the British Museum."

"Oh my," was all Clarissa could manage to say. It seemed too fantastic.

"And that's when I found two huge chunks of marble from the temple," said William.

"Pieces Durukan stole?" asked Clarissa.

"It seems so," said Beatrice. "They were on the floor, under a table, and dirty as if they'd been recently excavated. Everything else in the room was in pristine condition."

"I made a drawing of the inscription and the image, and we want to show it to you both." William cast a sheepish glance between Mehmet and Clarissa.

Beatrice took his hand in hers. "But I think we need to show it to Clarissa first."

"Clar—Miss Trent?" Mehmet seemed a tad miffed. "Why Miss Trent?"

"Yes, Beatrice," Clarissa said. "Please explain. Researching the temple has been Mehmet's avocation."

"I consider it my life's work, really." Mehmet's tone seemed a bit let down.

Beatrice looked at William, and he nodded. "Because the drawing is on my body."

All the women in the room gasped in unison. Mehmet gaped.

Beatrice lowered her gaze. "I apologize for shocking everyone."

Clarissa went to her, kneeling at her side. "No, dear, don't apologize. This is simply highly unusual."

"So you understand why I want to show it to just you, first?"

"I do."

"But William—" Mehmet stopped, his cheeks coloring above his beard.

Of course, the implication was that William had seen Beatrice's body. Good for him. Clarissa struggled to keep down a smile.

Beria stood. "Come, Althea, Cornelia. Let us take a walk." As they left, Beria offered Mehmet a stern look.

William clapped his hand on Mehmet's shoulder. "Let's leave the women alone, and I will explain everything to you."

Beatrice watched as the men left, not moving until the door closed behind them.

Only then did she begin to take off her dressing gown. She stood and slipped it off, then began to lift off her nightgown.

"Beatrice, what are you doing? You can just show me the part the drawing is on."

Beatrice continued disrobing. Once nude, she pressed her nightgown to her front. She sat on the divan, tucked her legs under her on the seat, then extended them and turned to lie facing the back of the divan.

Clarissa could not believe her eyes. There before her, drawn on Beatrice's back, was a Greek inscription written below her spinal column, and a crude drawing in the register above.

"Is that a horse? And a lion?" Clarissa touched Beatrice who flinched a little.

"Yes. I can't see what William drew, but I saw the fragment, and there was a horse and a lion in the scene."

"My God," Clarissa breathed. "Mehmet will need to see this."

"We thought maybe you could make a better drawing for him."

"Oh, my sweet." Clarissa grabbed Beatrice's dressing gown and handed it to her. "Put your clothes on."

Beatrice did so.

Clarissa sat on the sofa with Beatrice and took her hands. "I want you to consider giving him the opportunity to see what William drew firsthand. We can drape you with cloth, or even construct a sort of box around you, like a frame. And William and I will be at your side."

"Why is it so important he see me?"

"Because this is his life's work, as he said. You have the information right now. He should see it right now, so he can begin revising his research. I'll also make a drawing that he can refer to later."

Beatrice looked away, a tear forming on a lid.

"Darling, there's something else, isn't there?"

Beatrice wiped her eye.

Realization struck. "Beatrice, Mehmet would never want to look at you for his own prurient enjoyment."

"I know," she said with a sigh. "I'm just…I'm just… It's been a very unnerving day."

Clarissa wrapped her arms around Beatrice, hugging her tightly. "I can only imagine what you went through. But you're safe now." She kissed her hair. "And if we can gather evidence that Durukan has been raiding Mehmet's land for artifacts to sell, the Turkish and British authorities will want to know all about that."

"He's doing something illegal, isn't he?"

"If not illegal, then unethical. And he's an Englishman impersonating a Turkish governmental official, remember?"

"Yes, I do." Beatrice brightened. "When William and I were hiding in the bedroom, I heard Durukan speak English. He sounded like a London costermonger."

"Mehmet will need to know all of that. And I still need to tell him what I know."

Beatrice smiled, and a warm glow stirred in Clarissa's heart.

"You love him, don't you?"

"I'm afraid I do."

"I think he might love you back. He looks at you in the same way William looks at me sometimes."

Clarissa hoped Beatrice was right.

* * * * *

THE WAIT WAS INTERMINABLE. But Mehmet was a patient man. Especially to see something he had spent years searching for.

William poked his head out of the door to the public sitting room. "We're ready for you."

"Do I have to shield my eyes or anything?"

William chuckled. "No. We have her very well covered."

Mehmet followed William inside. There in the middle of the room on a couch was a very curious thing.

A drawing draped on all four sides by black cloth. Lines of Greek text were in the register below a scene involving—

"A horse? And a lion?"

Clarissa laughed softly. "Yes, that is what they are intended to be. When I make my version, I will involve William and Beatrice's memories of what they saw and try to make the image as true to the original as I can without myself seeing it. Until that time, you have this." She gestured in presentation at the drawing.

Mehmet knelt down and began to read the inscription out loud. "Antinous...hero...sacred...temple." He sat back on his heels, heart pounding with the excitement of possibilities. "I was correct." He reached out to trace the letters.

Clarissa grabbed his hand.

The drawing came into focus for what it really was. The palest, unmarred ivory flesh, with ridges and valleys of vertebrae between the two registers. A slight indent on the left suggested the lower back was on that side, the private area of a girl who suffered recent shock just beyond.

"Please accept my apology, I was overcome and forgot myself. This is a magnificent undertaking." He stood and nodded to William. "And so very clever."

"It was Beatrice's idea." William grinned with pride. "She's the clever one."

"William's clever too," came Beatrice's muffled voice from under the sheets.

Mehmet knelt once again to examine the wondrous canvas. "Just one more look." He stood and turned to Clarissa. "What happens next?"

"I will make copies of the inscription and the scene involving the horse and lion, and have William and Beatrice review them. Then each will have a bath and a good night's sleep."

"I've added guards to the harem. The public gardens, as well. And at all entry points."

"Thank you," Clarissa said with slight bow of her head. "Tomorrow, William, Beatrice, and I will once again review my drawings, and I'll create a final version to show you."

Mehmet regarded the inscription and picture. "Will the bath scrub everything away?"

"I don't think so," said Clarissa. "Well, yes, eventually, but one bath will not entirely erase the image. So if I need to refer to the original, Beatrice and I can arrange that."

So much joy pulsed through him. "Thank you for showing this to me. Thank you, Miss Smythe, for allowing me to see this. I understand it is uncomfortable for you. Please know that this opportunity has reinvigorated my heart and mind for my research."

He took Clarissa's hand and kissed the top, wanting to kiss every inch of her. "I eagerly await our meeting tomorrow, Miss Trent."

The glow in her eyes gave him hope that he would not have to wait so very long to see her again.

CHAPTER SIXTEEN

Mehmet strolled aimlessly through the garden, the sunset streaking orange and purple across the horizon. He'd barely seen Clarissa all day, and now pangs of unrequited lust plagued him. But she needed to create the drawing so poor Miss Smythe could resume a normal life.

Well, as normal as one could after Durukan did heavens only knew what to her. Mehmet vowed to ask Clarissa if Miss Smythe needed to see a doctor, and to keep watch to see if she was sleeping soundly at night or waking from fitful dreams of the horrors she had endured.

But Miss Smythe was an energetic and resilient girl. She would most likely turn any fear into action.

Like helping him uncover what appeared to be an antiquities smuggling conspiracy.

"Mehmet?"

Mother's serene voice was a balm to his worried soul. He smiled at her and she joined him, threading her arm in his. He relaxed in her presence and slowed his pace.

"I have just come from making sure our guests have all they need. The three of them are working diligently for your cause."

"Thank you, Mother." He patted her arm. "Did you get a look at the drawing?"

"Now, Mehmet, it is not for me to meddle in such things." She looked away as she smiled. "Besides, the easel and model were positioned away from where I was seated while serving tea."

He laughed.

"You seem agitated, son. Tell me."

"This last day has been rather full of commotion and surprises. I am trying to figure out what Durukan might be up to."

"Of course there is that. But there is something else."

The last thing Mother wanted to listen to was the confusion that was his love life. "I think what we have just been through is the measure of it."

"You cannot fool me, Mehmet. I have seen the love-sodden eyes of your sisters and their maidservants for handsome soldiers and well-muscled farmhands. I was surprised to see the same look in your eyes. And while I know the passions of a young girl are fleeting, they are not so fleeting in one such as you. You have the world on your shoulders. You have never given in to emotion. But now I see that you want to. And yet you hold back."

"Miss Trent is from a different world."

"Does it matter if your hearts are one?"

"Are they, though?" Mehmet turned to face Mother, her expression of understanding loosening his tongue. "How can I be sure?"

"Mehmet, I am not an innocent. I suspect there has already been intimacy between the two of you."

Mortification burned his cheeks. "How can you tell?" If Mother could tell, was the whole palace privy to his love life?

"Because I am a woman, and I understand the look another woman gives my son. It is a look of calm yearning, as if she has already had a taste, but would like a bit more."

So perhaps only a few had guessed about them.

"Son, I approve of your heart's choice. She is an intelligent woman, as well as a beautiful one. You are very deserving of happiness, but I wonder if you will follow through with pursuing your desire once their stay in this country is over."

A reminder that Clarissa was not to be his for very much longer if he did not act.

"Are there legal impediments to a marriage between a pasha and a foreigner?"

Mother contained her smile. "None that I know of."

"Religion?"

"You barely follow yours, and she seems to not be preoccupied with the matter. The imam will want to bless your children, though."

Children. Heavens above. Children.

Would Clarissa want children? Did he? He'd never even considered such a notion. Probably because he'd never been in love before.

"There are many things to think about, son." Mother patted his arm. "But I believe you will come to the right decision." She angled her cheek to him. "Kiss me good night."

He kissed her cheek. "Good night, Mother. And thank you."

BY THE TIME WILLIAM AND BEATRICE had eaten and bathed, night had fallen. Exhaustion had also descended, but nervous anxiety niggled at William.

He and Beatrice strolled through the terrace garden, a line of punched metal hanging lanterns lighting their way. Beside him Beatrice seemed to shiver, despite the air starting to have the warmth of summer.

"Will you be warm enough, Bea?"

"I think so." She glanced up at him. "Thank you."

They each carried extra blankets just in case.

The path of lanterns stopped before a roof-less pavilion with a large round divan covered in pillows and furs. "I thought maybe you'd like to see the stars."

She smiled, and he was sure she blushed as well. "Now what?'

He tossed their blankets on the divan. "The night is ours to do whatever we wish." He held out his hand. "We could dance."

Her laugh was all the music he needed.

She took his hand but pulled him to the divan instead of into a waltz. "I just want to lie down and look up at the stars with you."

William's heart pounded with elation as they stretched out on the divan, side by side, covering themselves with furs and silks and woolen blankets.

Earlier that evening, he'd had a serious conversation with Mehmet. Both were afraid for Beatrice's state of mind, that she might be experiencing mental and emotional shock. William especially did not want to leave her alone so soon after such a distressing incident. Mehmet said he would allow them being together one night on the public terrace, that he would discreetly post guards of both genders so as to dispel any notions of impropriety.

When William had proposed their spending the night together, Beatrice had been visibly elated, her expression almost returning to the joy he had seen before she'd been kidnapped.

She sidled against him now, gazing at the sky. "I don't think I've ever been in a prone state to look up at the stars." She grasped his hand under the covers. "I supposed you do this when you are camping out with your father."

He grinned. "We do. It's special just sleeping under the firmament. Although we always have a tent at the ready in case of rain."

Her giggle thrilled him.

"My father taught me the constellations, which I suppose made me curious about the Greeks and the Romans." He pointed.

"There's the North Star. Once you see that, you can ascertain the surrounding constellations."

"Yes," she said. "I know Ursa Major and Ursa Minor."

"Just below that, do you see a W shape? That's Cassiopeia."

"The queen of Ethiopia who boasted that her daughter was more beautiful than the sea nymphs."

"Which angered Poseidon." William drew his finger against the sky. "Next to Cassiopeia is her husband, King Cepheus. His stars are not as bright."

Beatrice snorted. "He's not as beautiful as his wife."

"Or his daughter, Andromeda. She's on the other side of Cassiopeia. Above her is Pegasus, and below her is Perseus."

"Her hero."

William gave her hand a squeeze. "Poseidon demanded Andromeda be bound to a rock as a sacrifice for the sea monster Cetus. Perseus rode his winged horse Pegasus and saved her from her undeserved punishment."

"And like the hero Perseus, you freed me from my unwarranted fate."

"I would do it again."

She turned halfway around, nestling her backside against him. "Hold me."

He did so, gently, restraining his true emotions of wanting to clutch her as tightly as possible to him. He'd bound his groin to contain his desire. He did not want to disturb her with reminders of male lustfulness.

She slowly melted against him, her trust softening his anxiety.

He'd been reluctant to bring up what needed to be spoken about. He had to say it now.

"Bea, I'm sorry it had to happen that way. You know… It wasn't what I had imagined for us."

She drew in a deep breath, then let it out slowly. He remained as still as possible.

"No," she finally said. "But I'm glad it was you. However it happened. I am so glad it was with you."

Despite the warmth of the blankets and their bodies, William chilled. Beatrice had been tied up and left as an offering to appease a monster. He couldn't possibly fathom the terror she must have felt.

She twisted to face him. "There will be another time for us. A better moment. The right moment." She kissed his lips, lightly, tenderly, then returned to snuggling against him. "Thank you for rescuing me, William. I love you."

The chill dissipated as a warm glow grew in his core. Tears dampened his lashes. Tears of joy, of hope. "I love you too, Bea." He loved her so damn much he was bursting.

As he held her, keeping her physically safe, keeping himself emotionally secure, he let his body and mind slide into slumber.

THE CLICK OF HER WOODEN HEELS against the travertine terrace seemed overly loud in the quiet night. Clarissa walked on tiptoe as she skirted the pavilion where she knew William and Beatrice were huddling.

After the flurry of activity that afternoon and evening, Clarissa had rested well. Energy and anticipation coursed through her now.

She knew Mehmet would be out on the terrace. Beria had said as much. As if she'd wanted Clarissa to go to her son.

Clarissa smiled as the lamps of Mehmet's pavilion came into view. She hastened her pace just a little.

"Pardon me, Excellency," she said, approaching the pavilion. "May I join you? Or would you prefer to be alone?"

His smile was enigmatic. "I fear I am not truly alone as I am quite distracted by thoughts. Although, I wonder if my thoughts are good company, with how they pester me so."

"And if I promise not to pester you?"

"Then you may have a seat beside me." He patted the pillow next to him. "I'll let your thoughts pester me for a while."

She mounted the steps to the gazebo. The curved space was filled with a wide banquette, big enough for sleeping, with a surfeit of pillows and fine wool blankets and furs draped along one edge in invitation to such activity. A low table was laid with food.

"Am I disturbing your supper?"

He chuckled. "No." He gestured she should sit. "My mother seems to think I need food at all moments of the day. She has the servants bring me trays of bread and cheese with olives and nuts on a regular basis. Please help yourself as you like."

Clarissa sat, tucking her legs under her. "Your mother is a very caring woman. She has been looking after Beatrice as if she were her own daughter." She grabbed a few almonds. "Beatrice will be sleeping with Emine in her room after tonight."

"I talked with William earlier. I will allow tonight's indulgence. He assures me nothing untoward will happen."

"I think they are both too exhausted and troubled for unchaste acts."

Mehmet sighed. "I fully comprehend being troubled about today's events."

His pain was palpable. "Mehmet, it is not your fault."

"And yet, I feel the weight of responsibility. Despite what Occidentals believe, the harem is not a place where women are kept separate from men. It is a place where women are kept safe. I have discovered weaknesses in my palace that I have already begun to rectify."

"But you did not expect such a determined enemy."

"No. I did not. I did not believe I had enemies at all. And to be sure, Durukan is not really *my* enemy, but an enemy of society, an enemy of history."

"Be assured your mother and sisters have been very concerned for my and Beatrice's well-being. They are looking after us."

"I am thankful they have taken on that task. As I am a man, there is little I can do in the women's quarters. I should have done more to begin with."

"Mehmet, I am exceedingly grateful you put so much effort into finding me and Beatrice."

He slowly drew in a breath. "When I discovered you missing…when you were taken from me, there was a pain in my heart I have never felt before. As if part of my heart was missing along with you."

Emotion swelled at his confession. "Mehmet, oh…" She turned from him, wiping a tear from the corner of her eye.

"Clarissa, I do not expect you to feel the same. But I do want you to know, while we still have this time left together, that you have been an inspiration to my heart and to my soul."

The stray tear became a flood.

Mehmet moved closer and wrap his arms around her. "My sweet, my love, why are you in pain?"

She sucked in a sob. "It's what you said. We've not much time left together."

Lights bobbed in the distance as servants walked through the garden illuminating lamps. Perhaps Beria making sure Clarissa's path back to the palace was lighted.

But what if she did not want to return to her room?

A servant approached the gazebo and, with bowed head, placed two oil lamps on the steps, then quickly left, obviously not wanting to disturb his master for too long.

Mehmet hung the lamps from the hooks on the gazebo posts. A golden glow spilled into the space.

"How romantic," said Clarissa.

Mehmet chuckled. "I swear I had nothing to do with this. My mother runs the household."

"Your mother seems to be playing the matchmaker." Clarissa wiped her wet cheeks with her sleeve. "After she told me Beatrice would be sleeping in Emine's room, she said nothing about my sleeping arrangements."

Mehmet chuckled. "It seems my mother would like to allow you privacy to come and go as you please." He took her hand, rubbing her palm with his thumb. "Sweet, I would like to continue our intimacy." He met her gaze. "Deepen it. But only if you wish it, as well."

"I do, believe me, I do." She gently shook her head. "I just don't know how one has a love affair in a Turkish palace."

"A much easier task than conducting an affair at an archaeological encampment."

Clarissa laughed, her mirth impelling her to throw her arms around him.

He drew back slightly, until his mouth was poised just above hers. She flicked her gaze to his, finding her desire reflected in his eyes. He pecked her lips, the simple touch flaring the passion smoldering within. She pressed her body closer, opening her mouth to let her tongue dance with his.

She tugged on the buttons of his kaftan, brazenly slipping them free. "I'd like to deepen our intimacy as well."

Her heart pounded as he remained still while she removed his kaftan and gömlek. Once he was nude on top, she began on the drawstring of his trousers. She pushed him back onto the pillows and straddled him in a flagrant act of wantonness.

Mehmet grinned. "I believe you have discovered the correct way to have a love affair in a Turkish palace."

She tugged on her lower lip with her teeth. "I cannot stop thinking about you."

"Nor I, you."

She glanced around. "Aren't we so very public here?"

"A servant or two will see us."

Clarissa cringed.

"You're not used to servants, are you?"

"Not when they watch one engage in intimate relations."

He lifted her off him and stood. He removed the hanging oil lamps from their hooks, blew out the flames, and set the lamps on the table.

He removed his shoes and pulled down his trousers, stepping free of them.

Clarissa was still fully dressed, his state of undress highlighting that fact.

He worked on the buttons at the front of her entari, pulling the garment off her shoulders when undone. He untied the waistband of her trousers. Silently, she stood and removed the garment standing before him clad only in her linen gömlek.

Mehmet stared, licking his lips. Then in one swift move, he grabbed the chemise by the hem and yanked it off over her head.

She immediately crossed her arms over her chest.

"Oh, no, my sweet. When one has a love affair in a Turkish palace, one must let the master see your charms."

She slid her arms to her side, displaying herself to him, her skin pimpled to gooseflesh in the night air.

He picked her up and lay her down on the cushions, then covered her body with his own.

"Are you warm enough, my sweet?" The heat of his skin permeated her.

"I have a feeling I will be very warm very soon." Indeed the chill of her flesh dissipated as their bodies melded together.

He took a nipple in his mouth, sucking, tasting, swirling his tongue around her hardened peak, thrilling her nether regions. Clarissa arched her back, murmuring his name, hoping for more. He continued licking and nipping her soft skin as his lips skipped down her body until he reached the thatch of curls at her mons.

But she wanted something different that night. She grabbed his hair and pulled. "Mehmet."

He lengthened over her once more, until they were face to face, his a little lined in concern. "Sweet, is something wrong?"

"No, not wrong. No, I..." She distracted herself from saying her desires aloud by stroking the hair on his chest.

"Clarissa, please know you may ask anything of me."

She met his gaze with a flash of excitement. "I've been desperate for you."

"And I, for you."

"I want something more than what a man and a woman might share."

Mehmet blinked. His lips parted. "Which is?"

"Make love to me as Hadrian would have Antinous. In my most intimate of places."

WITH JUST HER WORDS, Mehmet's body was a conflagration. Her desire was his dream come true. But an innocent would be surprised by the pain. "Sweet, have you ever done such an act?"

"No." Her breathlessness held a slight tremble.

"It is a most unusual pleasure. For you there will also be pain."

"Pleasure mixed with pain?"

"Yes, and at any moment you need to stop, you should tell me and I will do so." His cock would hate him for it, but he would do it for her.

"I will, Mehmet." Her gaze held pleading.

"Let's start with pleasure, shall we?"

Mehmet rolled off to lay by her side, a chill returning to her flesh. He grabbed a blanket and covered them both, then burrowed underneath and drew a taut nipple into his mouth.

She softly moaned her approval as she stroked his hair.

He wanted her in a state of supple relaxation, her body softening, growing receptive to his plans. He tickled her stomach, eliciting a jerk and a gasp, then continued until he reached the hair of her mons. He cupped the mound, the yearning heat radiating into his palm. He slid a finger through her sex. She was soaking wet, so slick it was difficult to find and keep a hold on her clit, but when she flinched he knew he had found his goal.

He rubbed gently at first, still tasting her nipple and kissing her soft breast. He wanted a slow build, and he measured her movements as her strokes on his hair turned to feeble tugs on the strands, to her digging nails into his shoulders, her body's undulations jerkier, her moans throatier.

And when he slid two fingers inside her cunt, she gripped him with a gasp and a thrust of her hips. His cock complained from want of attention. He draped a leg over hers and rubbed his erection against her soft thigh.

With his thumb on her clit, he slowly fucked her with two fingers, watching her face in the soft glow of distant lamplight as she tumbled into sensual oblivion, her eyes closed, her head rolling side to side.

"Yes, yes," she moaned. "More, just a little more."

He kept her on edge as long as he could. Another gasp and another tightening of her cunt signaled she was almost at her peak. He took his hand away.

She opened her eyes. "Mehmet?"

"I have a much better pleasure for you now."

She licked her lips.

"Believe me, your crisis will be greatly enhanced with the piquancy of pain."

He grabbed an oil lamp from the table. He opened her legs wider and knelt between them, her delicious cunt on display before him as temptation. He needed a modicum of relief. Relying on getting his satisfaction from her tighter hole might mean he would be too rough. He aimed his head at her feminine passage and pushed in.

His growl of satisfaction resounded in the intimate space between them. She smiled and flattened her hands on his chest, perhaps feeling the rapid beating of his heart.

"Darling," she said, rocking her hips to his languid rhythm, "I thought we were going to…do something else."

"We will," he assured her. "But my cock was overeager."

He pulled out, glistening with her juices, then reached for the oil lamp. He poured out a palmful of warm oil and massaged his iron-hard shaft as she watched in fascination.

"Am I not wet enough for you?"

"There is no natural lubrication in that particular orifice, my love." He poured a little more oil in his palm. "Lift up your hips."

Clarissa did so, holding her body in the air. He reached under her and touched her crinkled hole with oil-slicked fingers.

She winced, the expression fading as he very gently massaged more oil around the rim, pressing inside just barely an inch at first, holding her gaze as he pressed deeper still.

Her tremulous gasp meant she was still unprepared.

"Drop your hips. Breathe. Relax around my finger."

As her tension melted, he pressed in further until his knuckle reached the rim. Then slowly he pulled out. She whimpered at his withdrawal.

He added more oil to her cleft, then positioned himself. "Are you ready?"

"Yes," she said breathlessly.

He pushed in, fighting the urge to slam inside, instead reveling in the slow slide through glorious tightness. She paled momentarily, her face twisted.

"Clarissa, my sweet, breathe. Deep breaths. Let them out slowly. Remember to relax, let the sensuality overtake you."

Each exhalation eased his way deeper inside until he was embedded to the hilt.

As he began to pull out, he pressed his thumb to her clit.

She squealed in ecstasy, his sign to continue.

He slowly slid back in, then pulled out at an equal pace, all the while massaging her clit. Her eyes closed as she lolled her head, her mind lost in some fantastical rapture, her breaths in rapid puffs. He increased his pace a little bit.

"More, Mehmet," she said deliriously. "I want more. Faster—"

He obliged.

"Harder."

He complied, his body not his own anymore but controlled by her desires and by a dark carnality within.

His mind screamed *No!* He should not abuse her, a virgin in this regard, and yet, there she was, underneath him, moaning and rocking to the rhythm of his thrusts, egging him on with breathy exhortations, urging him to pleasure her in this new fashion.

"My God, Mehmet." Her voice was husky and hoarse. She grabbed a pillow and covered her face as she screamed her orgasm, her body tightening around him.

With a final thrust he came, emptying his seed into her depths, the much-craved-for release spreading relief and joy throughout him.

He held himself over her, heart pounding in his head, letting his cock soften before he shocked her with his exit. When he was certain he was pliable enough, he pulled out and sagged to her side.

Somehow the blanket had scrunched up in a ball. He pulled it over them, then kissed her hair.

Emotion welled within. They had shared something so intimate. "Sweetness, how are you feeling?"

"Oh, Mehmet. It was extraordinary. It was spectacular. I simply cannot put into words how fabulous it was." She snuggled against him. "I had my strongest crisis ever. It was glorious." She swirled her fingers through the hair of his chest. "I wish we could stay this way forever."

Forever. Yes, he certainly could take pleasure from her for forever…

Or a lifetime.

But asking her for such a commitment was too soon. There had been too much emotion that day for either of them to think clearly.

"Clarissa, spend the night with me. Here on the terrace."

She stiffened.

"Yes, there are servants around. They help protect us so we can sleep soundly. And you sleeping in my arms is really no different from young William and Beatrice being together."

"You forget, perhaps, my lord, that we are utterly naked. I suspect our charges are thoroughly dressed."

Mehmet chuckled.

She nuzzled against him. "Sleeping with you is a dream come true."

He pulled her into his arms as drowsiness descended.

CHAPTER SEVENTEEN

After almost an entire day finessing the drawing of the temple fragments with Beatrice and Miss Trent, William was eager to show off what they'd created to Mehmet.

The unveiling would be a private viewing like what the Royal Academy of Art had for the royal family before the Summer Exhibition.

It was all too exciting.

They'd set up the drawing in the palace library on a large easel draped with cloth so Mehmet would be held in suspense when he arrived. That was Miss Trent's idea, and she got a sort of gleam in her eye when she proposed it.

Probably because she and Mehmet were lovers.

William's face heated. He and Beatrice were officially lovers. Except they hadn't done anything since they'd returned. Well, they'd kissed a bit, and slept on the terrace together, but that was all.

He'd wait for her to be ready. He'd have to. She was so very precious to him.

"William," Beatrice half-whispered. She pointed to the carpet at her side.

He fell into place. Miss Trent opened the door to the library and ushered Mehmet inside.

"So much mystery," he said. A subtle happiness brightened his face when he gazed at Miss Trent. It was quite endearing.

Miss Trent blushed a little. "Mehmet, I want you to stand right here." She indicated a spot on the carpet.

He did her bidding with a pleasant smirk, standing precisely where she told him.

"Beatrice, will you do the honors?" Miss Trent remained next to Mehmet.

Beatrice stood before the easel and carefully rolled up the black cloth. She stepped aside.

Mehmet's face melted in gawking surprise.

"Yes," he said, approaching the drawing. "Yes. That's it." He traced his fingers around the image, then bent down to examine the inscription. "Heavens above. This is almost precisely what I had imagined once I saw the initial sketch." He shook his head and blinked his eyes. "And you say you saw these?" he said to Beatrice and William.

"We did," said William. "The fragments are actually larger than the drawing."

"How can you be certain they're real?" Mehmet straightened with a shake of his head. "I apologize for my suspicion. This scene is astonishing, and you said Durukan is creating fake artifacts. I am dubious."

"And rightfully so, my lord," said Miss Trent.

"I understand your suspicions, Mehmet. But from what Beatrice and I could tell, the artifacts are real. There was dirt—"

"And the marble was stained in the same way we've seen other marble finds from the site stained."

"Besides, the fake artifacts we saw were perfect and clean."

"Someone must make them appear old at some point," said Miss Trent. "Otherwise, no collector would buy such an object."

"There are such collectors who pride themselves in owning the only artifact that is in pristine condition," said Mehmet.

"The problem, then, would be there were too many objects in pristine condition," said William. "What if all those collectors decided to donate their objects to museums?"

Mehmet drew up a chair before the easel and sat. He steepled his hands under his chin as he leaned in and studied the drawing. "Magnificent." He glanced back at William and Beatrice. "Do you know what this scene represents? A man on horseback with a spear aimed at a snarling lion. Keeping in mind the other fragment we found with the woman, wreath, and lion skin."

"You thought it might be a leopard skin representing Dionysus," said Beatrice.

"With these few words of what must be a longer inscription we have more evidence as to what the scene might represent: 'Antinous, hero, sacred, temple'."

William glanced at Beatrice, who shook her head.

Mehmet chuckled. "If Albin were here he would know." He stood and went to a bookshelf, clicking his fingernail against the spines. "Ah-ha. Here." He pulled a worn leatherbound volume off the shelf. "*The Deipnosophistae* by Athenaeus of Naucratis. Book fifteen." He glanced up at William and Beatrice.

"I've never heard of it," admitted Beatrice.

"Nor I," said William.

"It sounds obscure," added Miss Trent.

Mehmet grinned. "Not to a scholar of Hadrian and Antinous." He flipped through the pages, pressed his finger against a passage, and began to read. "'I have mentioned Alexandria…in that beautiful city there is a garland called the garland of Antinous, which is made of the lotus—'"

Miss Trent gasped. Mehmet winked at her.

He tapped his finger against the page. "This story tells of an Alexandrian poet by the name of Pancrates. He suggested to

Emperor Hadrian that this particular red lotus be called the Flower of Antinous, as the lotus is grown where the ground was stained red from the blood of the Mauritanian lion, a beast killed by Hadrian when he was hunting near Alexandria."

Beatrice studied the drawing. "Then is that supposed to be Hadrian?" She pointed to the man on the horse. "He has no beard."

Mehmet guffawed. "Absolutely brilliant, Miss Smythe. Why women are not allowed at Cambridge and Oxford, I'll never understand." He raised a brow in her direction. "So who is it?"

She smiled. "Antinous. The lion is about to attack him. That's why Hadrian slew the lion."

"And when we find the rest of the pedimental sculpture, we'll know if this is indeed what is depicted. Athenaeus the author"— Mehmet tapped the page again—"implies Pancrates wrote a poem about this hunt. Unfortunately, we no longer have that poem."

"But one day we'll have the pediment, an illustration of the poem."

Mehmet put the book down and placed his hand on William's shoulder. "Let's hope we get everything back."

"But why would Durukan have these among all the other objects?" Beatrice pointed at the drawing. "These are so much more unique than a scroll of Ovid. A scroll could have come from anywhere. But this sculpture with a scene that matches all the other fragments could only have come from one place."

"He did it to blackmail you."

All eyes turned to Miss Trent. Mehmet paled, his mouth falling open.

"He could destroy them, alter them, do God only knows what." Miss Trent waved her hands as she spoke. She turned to Mehmet, her brow furrowed. "And that would change your research and your thesis. You would pay him almost any amount to get the original fragments back."

Mehmet stood. "That's it, Clarissa." A slight blush appeared on the flesh above his beard. "And unfortunately he would be correct. I have your evidence, and if I ever publish, I can include this drawing and say the original was destroyed. Which would work until Durukan comes forth with his altered version."

"So you would pay anything?" asked Miss Trent.

"I suppose I would. I mean, within possibility."

"And we have Beatrice."

All eyes were on William now.

"If he thinks you would pay anything, he might think you would give him Beatrice."

Beatrice emitted a choking noise. William was at her side instantly.

"That is too high a price." Mehmet was stern.

"But we have something against him," Miss Trent said. She raised an eyebrow at Beatrice. "Don't we, Miss Smythe?"

Beatrice nodded. "He's British."

Mehmet looked between the two women. "Who's British?"

"Durukan," said Miss Trent.

Mehmet gazed at her with incredulity. "What are you saying?"

"That Durukan speaks Turkish with an East London accent," said Miss Trent.

"And when William and I were hiding under the bed," added Beatrice, "we heard him swear in English with a lower-class accent."

"Durukan is an Englishman impersonating a pasha?" Mehmet's incredulity persisted.

"To gain access to government bureaus to facilitate his exports of forgeries and fakes, no doubt." Miss Trent looked sheepish. "I've been giving it some thought."

Mehmet sat down. "I'm not sure what to do with this information. I do not want those fragments to be destroyed, but the authorities need to be alerted."

"Well," William began, "Durukan does not know you know he has the fragments. Yet."

"There is that," said Miss Trent.

"We could rescue them," suggested Beatrice with enthusiasm.

"No." It was said by everyone but Beatrice.

"Thank you, Miss Smythe," said Mehmet. "That is a very good idea, but I must object to your use of the word 'we'."

"Beatrice, darling, you are not to go anywhere," said William.

"So I am to be stuck here like a jewel in a treasure chest?"

William tried to calm himself. He would lock her up in his own room if he had to. "Have you forgotten what just happened to you not a day ago?"

"Have you forgotten, William, Durukan would not want me? I'm no longer a virgin."

William was certain his face looked at least as red as Mehmet's. Miss Trent, however, was ghostly pale. She took Beatrice's hands in hers.

"Darling," Miss Trent began shakily, "you're among friends. Did he violate you?"

"What?" Beatrice drew back, shocked. "No!"

"No, no, Miss Trent." William sucked in courage. "I did. I mean, I didn't. I mean, I did not violate her, but I...I..."

Mehmet held up his hands and chuckled. "I think we understand, Mr. Peel."

Good God. He'd have to marry her now everyone knew what they'd done.

"However," Mehmet began soberly, "Durukan has no knowledge of this. We have to assume he still seeks Miss Smythe for her...charms."

"I'm not so sure about that," said Beatrice. "We left, er, evidence."

Mehmet glanced at Miss Trent while hiding a smile. "That was courageous."

She *was* courageous. And she was William's.

"But we should wait to see if Durukan acts." Mehmet addressed the two women. "I know you are both eager to return to your work in the field, but I must insist that you stay within the palace walls for the time being. Until we see what he does next."

"Yes, of course," said Miss Trent. "I think Beatrice and I can enjoy the offerings of the palace for a while. What say you, Beatrice?"

Beatrice flashed a worried look in William's direction. "I suppose."

"I don't mean for you to be cloistered, Miss Smythe," Mehmet assured her. "You may still visit with Mr. Peel and everyone else."

Inwardly, William let out a sigh of relief.

A soft knock resounded on the wooden library door.

"Enter." Mehmet rubbed his temples. "*Girmek,*" he repeated the command in Turkish.

The door clicked open, and a servant with bowed head walked softly to Mehmet, presenting a note on a silver salver.

Mehmet took the missive and read it, then dismissed the servant.

"Sinan has returned," he said, his demeanor suddenly impassive. "With a government official from Istanbul." He glanced at the drawing, then at William and Beatrice. "Hide that."

Beatrice perked up. "I'll put it in the room I'm sharing with Emine."

"Yes. Good." Mehmet turned to leave, then caught Miss Trent's eye. "Please join me in my office." He leaned in and whispered in her ear. She nodded and watched him leave.

William met Beatrice's worried gaze. Something very serious was happening.

As Mehmet had suggested in his whisper, Clarissa had dressed to appear more modest. With Beria's help she added a hirka—a sort of waistcoat—under her entari, and a generous headscarf to cover her hair and neck.

At his office door, she rapped softly before entering and taking a seat on a bench along the wall. Besides Mehmet and

Sinan, there was another man, middle aged, short and round. He stared at her with a touch of dubiousness.

Mehmet cleared his throat. "Excellency," he said in Turkish to the short man. "May I present Miss Clarissa Trent, a valuable member of my archaeological expedition team."

Sinan bobbed his head in her direction. "Miss Trent is the artist of the temple sketches I showed you."

The other man turned to Mehmet. "She is English?"

"She is."

"I do not speak English."

Mehmet nodded. "Miss Trent is fluent in Turkish." He turned to her with a smile. "Miss Trent, may I present Yusuf Ibrahim Pasha." He indicated the short, middle-aged man. "He is a vizier from the antiquities department of the sultan."

Clarissa kept her head bowed. "Excellency."

"You may speak openly in front of Miss Trent, vizier. She is a trusted scholar."

"Yes, well..." Yusuf studied her for a moment until resignation softened his features. "I'll get right to the point. The man who is calling himself Durukan Fakir Pasha is not who he seems. He is not Turkish, and he is not a pasha."

"Thank you, Yusuf, for the confirmation," said Mehmet. "We actually know he is not Turkish. We have ascertained that he is English."

Yusuf raised his eyebrows in surprise. "How do you know this?"

"Miss Trent," said Mehmet. There was a hint of pride in his answer.

"Does Miss Trent know the man?"

Mehmet gestured in her direction. "Please explain."

Clarissa drew in a deep breath steadying her nerves. "I have a skill with accents. I could tell his Turkish was tinged with an English accent. Once I figured this out, I concentrated when I heard him talk again. I believed him to be a Londoner."

Yusuf's surprise was renewed.

Mehmet was clearly subduing a grin. "The English students who are part of our expedition actually heard the man speak English. He is indeed a lower-class Londoner."

The vizier combed his fingers through his beard. "This is good information," he said thoughtfully. He straightened and addressed the room. "Durukan's real name is Ivor Bunsby." He studied Clarissa. "You don't by any chance know him?"

"I do not. I have never heard that name."

"Ah." The vizier nodded as he paced. "Eski Saray fell into disuse after the owner died. And then the district in which the palace was located changed. The whole area is now under a new vilayet—"

Turkish geographical and political designations were confusing at times to the British, but Clarissa knew a vilayet was a sort of viceroyalty.

"I suppose Durukan's taking over Eski Saray went unnoticed with all the political changes."

"A new viceroyal would not know if he had rightful claim," commented Mehmet.

"Yes, I think that is precisely what happened," said Yusuf. "But your man Sinan came to the Department of Antiquities with a particular complaint. Durukan's taking of your artifacts is worrisome. Do you know what his intentions are?"

Mehmet gestured to Clarissa. "Miss Trent and I have recently been alerted to a forgery scheme being undertaken at his palace."

"I see. And did you witness this, Miss Trent?"

"Not I. But the English students who are part of our expedition saw a room in the palace where such forgeries are being made."

Yusuf knitted his brow. "These students were in Durukan's palace? How did this happen?"

"I and the female student were kidnapped by Durukan—or Bunsby, rather. Mehmet and the male student helped us escape." Clarissa left it at that. If the official wanted more information, he could ask for it.

"Ah. Were the items taken from Sevilen Tapinak also in this room?"

"Two were seen," said Mehmet. "Miss Trent interviewed the two students and has created a drawing of what they had seen. One was a fragment of the pedimental sculpture, and the other an inscription. I had not had a chance to see either when they were taken from the ground the day Durukan came to our site. The image and text fit with what I had theorized about the purpose and dedication of the temple."

Yusuf remained silent, his hand combing his beard once again, as if thinking. He paced a spell, before addressing Mehmet. "I would like for you to return to your site. Continue to dig and collect artifacts as if nothing has happened."

"To what end?"

"We need to catch this Bunsby in the act of pilfering your finds. I will install a team of my men in your camp. When Bunsby as Durukan comes to collect what he claims is his, we will arrest him. It will be easier to seize his palace if he is not there. I will have my men search for your artifacts at that time."

A bold plan.

Mehmet nodded. "I can give you a list of items we know were stolen, although I am certain there was so much more than what I thought. I have a man embedded at Eski Saray. Perhaps he can help you get one of your own men inside. He might have to be a servant, though."

Yusuf waved his hand. "That will not be a problem. My men are trained to act in many capacities. Let us arrange for that. In the meantime, may we use your palace so as not to draw attention to ourselves?"

"Certainly."

The vizier turned to Clarissa. "We will need you to help us with the British authorities."

"Yes, of course. I will do anything I can."

"There are two Cambridge academics with the expedition," added Mehmet. "They are still at the camp. They have been keeping watch for any unusual activity."

"Very good," said Yusuf. "I would like you to call them back for a few days and have them write letters and telegrams to their government and any official contacts they may have." He glanced at Clarissa. "Along with Miss Trent. Any and all leads will be beneficial for our investigation. One of you might know someone who knows this Bunsby." He now turned a smile to Clarissa. "We both know our shared Roman heritage is very important to our national identities. I look forward to having our governments work together to capture a criminal."

She bowed her head concealing her smile. "Yes, vizier."

CHAPTER EIGHTEEN

Mehmet tilted his wide brimmed hat against the sun and surveyed Sevilen Tapinak from atop the knoll overlooking the temple excavation. The site bustled with activity once again. Satisfaction stretched his lips into a wide smile. With the help of the Department of Antiquities, they would continue making progress.

Yusuf had insisted all artifacts taken to Mavi Saray for safekeeping be returned to the site. No more hiding, no more keeping of secret catalogs. As a scholar himself, the vizier had wanted to see what had been uncovered. Earlier that week, he had met with Mehmet, Albin, and Spencer, walking the landscape, surveying the topography, discussing where the temple was probably situated. Albin and Spencer had made a bit of progress while everyone was at the palace. They'd dug a small test hole, finding a block of marble where they'd surmised steps leading to the portico of the temple were.

Yusuf's men were not mere bodyguards, but trained archaeological specialists. Some were showing Mehmet's men the best practices to dig based on what was expected underneath the ground. Others were explaining how to stack broken columns based on crack assessments.

Others were bodyguards with knowledge of how to comport themselves in an active archaeological excavation. They kept to the perimeter of the site, using bird calls to signal each other.

Mehmet turned his attention to the center of the site. There William walked alongside Albin and one of the workmen trying to ascertain where precisely the steps to the temple might be. Once the steps were uncovered, they would start their search for the mosaic floor.

To their left, a man was surveying the landscape. One benefit of having the government on one's side was gaining access to that which was in short supply. Yusuf had included a photographer with his staff. The man was now diligently taking photos of all areas of the site.

Which meant Clarissa could spend her time doing other tasks.

In the shade of the artifact tent, Clarissa and Beatrice worked on reconstructing the pediment from the fragments they still had, as well as Clarissa's wonderful drawings.

At the other end of the long tent, Mrs. Acker and Mrs. Stanfield sorted other types of fragments using their precise notes to guide them.

Eager expectancy pulsed through the entire camp. The academics had sent letters and telegrams to every governmental official and antiquities scholar they knew. Albin was especially keen to hear from a former student who had some sort of official capacity in Greece.

Everything was falling into place. With hands on hips, Mehmet breathed in the dusty air, then scrambled down the hill to join his team.

* * * * *

WILLIAM DRANK A GLASS of lemon water a little too swiftly. Water splashed down his open shirt, cooling his skin. A gentle breeze added a welcoming chill. The day had been long and hot, but the work had been invigorating.

Thanks to Professor Stanfield and Mr. Acker's exploration of the site while everyone was having their own adventures, they now were fairly certain where the front steps to the temple were. William had spent hours digging alongside Mehmet's trusted laborer Yazid, and they had uncovered a flat marble surface. The professor thought it might be the top step. Which meant they knew roughly where the main floor of the temple should be. Mehmet was eager to find a mosaic floor.

Not too far from the refreshment tent was the new pediment tent with a worktable for processing pieces and a low platform for laying them out alongside Miss Trent's drawings. There Beatrice and Miss Trent continued to work. Surely they were overheated as well?

William poured two glasses of water and walked them over to the two women.

"Why, thank you, William," Miss Trent said with happy surprise.

Beatrice gulped her water down. "I always forget how thirsty I really am until I've had a glass of water." She beamed at him. "Thank you."

Wisps of blond hair stuck to her sweaty cheeks, and her nose had smudges of dirt. But she was still so utterly beautiful. A sparkle shone in her gray-green eyes.

"Well," Miss Trent began as she closed her leatherbound notebook and tied the leather strings to keep it closed. "I think we have done enough for today, Beatrice. Could you please wrap up the drawings? Then get cleaned up for supper, I should think."

"Yes, Clarissa."

Miss Trent glanced around until she found what she was seeking. Mehmet chatted with the academic men, gesturing, his intensity probably very attractive to one such as Miss Trent. She smiled and bade them good afternoon before joining Mehmet.

William watched her until she was far enough away. He turned to his beloved. "How are you, Bea? How has your day been?"

"It feels good—rewarding even—to get back to working with artifacts, to thinking about history." She glanced around. "To thinking about what this place once looked like."

He agreed.

She sought his eyes. "I can say this to you, but others would not understand. Well, except for Clarissa."

"What, Bea?"

"I feel I have a purpose in the field." She huffed a breath. "Here, I'm not a man's secret desire, nor a young woman to be protected. I'm a budding scholar with a talent for piecing blocks of marble together to tell the story of people long ago."

"You are."

"And when I'm here, everyone respects me for this. I just felt that when I was at the palace, well, really because of what happened, I was nothing but a young woman who needed protection."

There was a melancholy in her voice. He wanted to pull her into his arms and comfort her.

She sighed. "I am grateful that being out in the open air has given me a bit of freedom."

"How so?"

"No dark corridors or doors concealing danger. We are surrounded by guards, and I see them. I know they are there. So I feel safe. But more than that, others feel safe for me. I think the presence of the guards alleviates the apprehension others feel for me."

Was that true for him, as well? At the palace, William had felt compelled to protect her. But here, in the camp? Perhaps not as much. Beatrice was exceptionally perceptive.

"However," she began as she dusted off her work apron, "there's the wondrous bath at the palace. If only we could somehow transport the bath house out here in the field."

William laughed. "You know, Mehmet can probably figure out a way to do just that."

She met his gaze. "Next year. When we return."

The warmth of desire flooded over him. "Right. Yes. Next year." They would be together again, as scholars.

And lovers.

"I can give a paper at Girton. And you, at Cambridge." Her excitement was palpable. "Everyone will want us to continue our work." She looked off into the distance.

"Beatrice?"

She turned to him, her eyes glazed. She shook her head. "Oh, sorry. I was dreaming."

"Of our future."

She blushed. "Yes." She smiled, this time without the stars in her eyes, as if remembering where she was. "And what have you discovered today?"

He drew up a chair. "I've discovered that as much as I love to work in an excavation pit with Mehmet and Professor Stanfield, I miss having adventures with you."

Her smile shot a dart of lust to his groin. "And what shall we do about this?'

He grinned and leaned forward, his elbows on his knees. "I thought we might try to arrange to be together alone tonight. What say you?"

She blushed. "I would love that, darling." She looked about, but no one was really very close and everyone was preoccupied with their work and not the machinations of a young man and woman.

"Well," William also briefly looked side to side, "Miss Trent has been sleeping in your tent since we arrived back at camp, has she not?"

A knowing smile crossed Beatrice's lips. "She has."

"And Mehmet seemed uncharacteristically distracted today. I have a feeling the two of them will try to arrange a midnight tryst."

"And how will we know they do?"

"Because you will be up at midnight."

"And what will we do about it if they do indeed have an assignation at midnight?"

"I will be waiting for you. But not where they will look for you. I will be in the temple ruins."

"And what if they choose to also make love in the temple ruins?"

William chuckled. "I suppose I hadn't thought of that." He took her hand. "Still, you should expect me to be waiting for you. I will wait until dawn, if I have to."

She smiled a smile that indicated he would not be waiting until dawn to see her.

His heart pounded. He could not wait.

THAT NIGHT, IN HER COT, Beatrice could not sleep. Thoughts of being with William—and wondering when Clarissa would leave—kept her awake.

She tried not to toss and turn too much. Tried to make her breathing seem like the regularity of sleeping.

And then it happened. The susurration of blankets in the dark meant Clarissa was getting up. There was a quiet moment where she was probably putting on her dressing gown and boots. Then a shadow slipped through the tent door.

And Beatrice was alone.

She scrambled out of her bed quickly, donning her own dressing gown and boots, throwing a dark cloak around her shoulders, then peered out the tent flap into the night.

The moon was bright, illuminating the landscape. Their guard was absent, probably still escorting Clarissa to Mehmet's tent.

Once Beatrice's eyes had adjusted, she could see enough light to find her way, and enough shadow in which to hide.

She slid along the tent, keeping an eye on the temple ruins.

A lamp bobbled, held by a lanky figure.

William.

He waved at a guard who waved back. *Good.* The guards knew it was he, so they would not investigate whatever it was he was doing. Perhaps he was analyzing the aspect of the temple at night.

She grinned. William was so very clever.

Now it was up to her to get to him. Luckily, the dark cloak shielded her as a shadow. She wended her way toward where he was near a partially reconstructed column. The lamp went out. He must have seen her.

She rushed forward, trying not to stumble, finding him in the dark, reaching out her hand.

Wordlessly, he pulled her to him, taking her in a deep kiss.

When they parted, he pressed a finger to his lips. He took her by the hand and led her up the hill to the top of the knoll.

They each glanced around, before their gazes met.

William chuckled softly. "I suppose I half expected to see Miss Trent and Mehmet up here," he whispered as he leaned against a boulder and drew her to him, the shadow obscuring them from any guards below.

"Me too," Beatrice said with a laugh. "But I think they are in his tent." She wrapped her arms around him and drew in a long breath. She exhaled into the shelter of his arms.

She could stay like this forever.

"Love," William said, pressing his lips to her hair. "I asked to be alone with you for a reason." He paused, nuzzling her. "I had wanted our first time to be special."

"It's not your fault, William."

"I know. I know." His fingers skittered across her upper arm, his delicate touch radiating to her sex. "I want to make it right. I want us to have a first time again."

Her heart swelled with love and joy.

"When we recall our experiences during this expedition, I want us to remember tonight as our first time together." He kissed her hair again. "Your first time."

"Oh, William." She stretched to touch her lips to his.

He answered her with a kiss full of tender emotion.

"And," he said after drawing back, "as it is your first time, you get to choose what we do."

She hardly knew what one could do besides what they had already done together. "I suppose I would like to do what any conventional man and woman might do."

He leaned his forehead against hers. "Of course." He kissed her again, this time with a bit more passion and urgency. Holding her in his arms, he turned them half around until it was she who was leaning on the boulder, her cloak a cushion against the hard surface.

She planted her palms on his chest, the waistcoat and shirt barriers to what she truly wanted to feel. One by one, she freed the buttons of his waistcoat, then the placket of his shirt. She leaned in and kissed his bare chest before pressing her ear to hear his heartbeat.

It pounded in a frantic rhythm, as if he were running a race.

"Darling, I suspect a conventional man would not necessarily be compelled to please a woman before he took his satisfaction. But I am not a conventional man."

William lifted her nightgown to her waist, tucking it behind her. His fingers tickled as they danced across her stomach, down her hip to the top of her thigh.

"May I touch you?"

"Yes." *Oh, God, yes.*

His fingers continued their waltz, this time to her sex. One finger explored, finding her pleasure spot on its slippery quest.

"You are so deliciously wet," he murmured. "I wish I could drink you."

Heat flared in her belly. She cupped his crotch, his cock huge in her palm. When they had been together in the hamam, he had let loose his seed. "I could drink you, too."

"Oh, darling…that would be divine." He collapsed a bit, leaning on the rock. "Just not tonight."

Another time, then. Something to look forward to.

William stroked her slowly, deftly, his steadfast fingers at odds with his erratic respiration, his uneven breath warming her temple, her cheekbone, her neck as he slumped into her.

She should help him. He needed release.

Beatrice unbuttoned the fly of his trousers, surprised to find his cock under just the thin layer of linen, and not behind an additional barrier of drawers. She wrapped her hand around his shaft. William jerked forward, losing his rhythm.

Confidence made her smile. She stroked him as he stroked her. He seemed lost in insensibility while she continued, more determined.

Until a moment later, when he regained his composure and became more determined himself.

"Bea, I want to make love to you."

"Yes, William, yes." She was more than ready. Especially since now she knew what to expect.

He took over, grabbing his cock, nudging her legs apart with his knee, lifting up her thigh. She gripped his shoulders as he aimed his cock at her entrance, clinging to him as he entered, stretching her. Her body gripped him, as if wanting more despite the slight discomfort as he slid in his length.

"Breathe, love."

In her nervousness, she had stilled her breath. But now with the reality, she calmed.

This is what the two of them were meant to do.

As William slowly plunged and withdrew, perception heightened, dizzying her. The glow of the moon and stars, the heat of her lover's skin, his rhythmic moans, her own desire coiling within sent her reeling.

"Touch yourself," he murmured. "Touch your clitoris."

She slipped her hand between them to press on the erect nubbin, flinching from the exquisiteness of it all, clenching William again.

He held her steady. "Don't stop, Bea. Bring yourself to climax. Trust me."

As she rubbed furiously, her body reveled in the hardness within. Concupiscence weakened her, her body no match for the onslaught of sensations. She sagged against the rock, her hand falling to her side, as William plowed into her.

"Bea," he murmured into her ear. "Stay with me. Let's climax together."

She revived, planting one hand on William's chest, while the other snaked to her clitoris. She resumed her self-pleasuring, gripping him, trying to find a rhythm, their rhythm.

"Grip me when I pull out, release me when I push in."

She would do anything for him at that moment. He slowed his movements as she discovered how to match his rhythm, how to grip and release him, how two became one.

"God, yes, Bea," he said through gritted teeth.

The build to rapture began undaunted, rising, swelling within until she was hovering at the peak, her body and William's perfectly attuned, his breathy murmuring revealing he was there too.

She let go and plummeted into the abyss of delight, covering her mouth, silencing her cry of ecstasy. William pulled out, grabbing his shaft and spewing his emission onto the ground.

He collapsed at her side with a sigh, sweaty, breathing heavily.

"I hope no one discovers your seed in the morning."

William chuckled and pulled her more closely against him. "How was your first time, my love?"

"More amazing than I could have imagined."

"It was, wasn't it?"

"William, thank you for making it right."

"Darling, you're my best friend and lover, and I care deeply for you." He lifted her chin and kissed her tenderly on the lips. "And I love you."

"I love you so much."

"However, I regret to say we only have a few moments left tonight, my love."

They shared one last lingering kiss before he pressed his forehead against hers.

She sighed. "I suppose I need to return to my cot before Clarissa discovers me absent."

"That would be prudent."

Together they retraced their steps along the rocky path in the dark, until Beatrice scampered off to her own tent.

She could not wait for a time when they would make love in a proper bed and spend the whole night together in each other's arms, naked.

CHAPTER NINETEEN

"Something just isn't right." Clarissa bent over the worktable in the pediment tent.

Beside her Beatrice rummaged through a box of orphaned marble chunks. "I'm not sure any of these fit with the larger blocks we already have."

"Hmm." Beatrice was probably correct. Clarissa stared at her drawings filling the spaces between the larger fragments on the low platform. There must have been a decorative element or a figure she hadn't imagined that should have been included in her preliminary drawings.

She moved down the worktable, perusing the smaller fragments, looking for clues—

"Clarissa? Er, Miss Trent?"

At the sound of a familiar voice, a pleasant tenor she never thought she'd ever hear again, Clarissa looked up.

And met the sapphire-blue gaze of a man she never thought she'd see again.

"Nigel?"

He beamed. "It *is* you."

Clarissa wiped her hands on her apron and stepped around the table. Before her was the man she once thought the epitome of men—a scholar, a gentleman, and a friend who also just happened to be exceptionally handsome. His linen suit was rumpled from travel, his leather bag at his feet covered in dust. She took his hands, the touch livening nostalgia within.

"Oh, dash it." She threw her arms around his neck. "Nigel Babbage, how wonderful to see you."

His chuckle rumbled through her as he hugged her close. "I'm rather astonished to see you, myself."

She extracted herself from the embrace, trying to staunch the flood of fond memories. "Whatever are you doing here? I heard you were stationed somewhere in the Mediterranean?"

"The Aegean, actually. Athens. Albin, er, Professor Stanfield wrote me." He glanced around. "I did not expect to see such a magnificent organization as this." He noticed Beatrice and smiled.

"Oh, where are my manners? Nigel, this is Miss Beatrice Smythe. She is currently working as my assistant as we try to reconstruct a temple pediment." She turned to Beatrice. "Beatrice, this is Mr. Nigel Babbage, an old friend from Cambridge who has suddenly appeared in our midst."

Nigel laughed. "A pleasure, Miss Smythe."

"Likewise, Mr. Babbage." Beatrice's wide eyes revealed her curiosity, as her blush revealed her appreciation of Nigel's good looks.

"But where is Albin? I simply thought to approach you because you looked to be the only ones who spoke English. I fear my Turkish does not go beyond 'good day', 'please', and 'thank you'."

Beatrice cleared her throat. "The academics—I mean, Professor Stanfield, Mr. Acker, and William Peel are in the professor's study tent. And Mehmet is coming our way." She indicated with a toss of her head.

Indeed, Mehmet was walking toward them at a clip, probably motivated by a need to protect her and Beatrice.

A motivation that became patently clear when he came up alongside Clarissa. "Good day." He did not mask his suspicion.

"Mehmet," Clarissa began, "this is Nigel Babbage, an old friend from Cambridge. Nigel, this is Mehmet Pasha, the owner of this land and the director of this archaeological expedition."

Nigel reached out his hand. "Oh, a pleasure, Excellency. I have heard wondrous stories about you and your site."

"You have?" Mehmet was nonplussed as he slowly shook Nigel's hand.

"From Albin, I mean Professor Stanfield. We were colleagues at Cambridge. We've continued a casual correspondence. But the other day he sent me a most cryptic letter. And then there was a telegram." Nigel pulled out a folded piece of stationery from his inside breast pocket. "He wanted to me to come at once. So here I am."

Mehmet smiled. "And so you are. Are you stationed in Istanbul?"

"No, sir. Athens. I'm an archaeological consultant for the the British envoy there. I took a boat and then merely had to mention your name to a man with a cart." He turned to Clarissa. "I had no idea Miss Trent was part of the expedition." He smiled sheepishly. "Oh, of course, I presume you are still Miss Trent?"

Mehmet seemed to move a bit closer to her.

A flush of abashment crept up Clarissa's nape to burn her cheeks. "I am."

"Miss Smythe," Mehmet said to Beatrice, "would you please escort Mr. Babbage to Professor Stanfield's study tent? I am certain Albin is eager to see his friend."

"Of course, sir." Beatrice gestured Nigel should follow her. He doffed his hat at Clarissa and Mehmet, then picked up his bag and walked with Beatrice to the professor's tent.

"As Babbage is Albin's friend, I expect we can trust whatever it is he will be helping us with," Mehmet said quietly.

"Oh, absolutely."

"And also because he is your former lover."

Clarissa turned to him, agape. "How on earth did you know?"

"The way you look at him." He shrugged. "How you look at each other. But he is the one who prefers the company of men, is he not?"

Her cheeks burned more hotly. "And how do you know that?"

"The way he looks at me."

Clarissa laughed and looped her arm in Mehmet's. "Let us see what he has to say to Albin."

WILLIAM DID NOT KNOW if he enjoyed his new task as secretary. Truth be told, he'd rather be digging in the ground, but organizing governmental correspondence regarding a villain was rather intriguing.

"Spencer, did any of your contacts respond to your correspondence?" asked Professor Stanfield.

"Only one," Mr. Acker replied. "He knows a man in Corfu. But that's a bit far afield, don't you think?"

"Professor?" Beatrice's lovely soprano floated through the tent doors.

"Yes, Miss Smythe, come in."

The goddess of his dreams entered, lifting William's spirits. She found his gaze and offered a smile.

And then an exceptionally handsome man followed her inside the tent. She turned her smile to the stranger.

William's spirits deflated instantly.

"Nigel!"

Professor Stanfield jumped from his desk and ran to the stranger, embracing him vigorously.

"Albin," the stranger said. "I came as quickly as I could."

"Oh, my boy, thank you." The professor stepped back. "It is good to see you. You are doing well?"

"I am." Somehow the stranger's smile made him even more handsome, despite his bedraggled appearance.

Professor Stanfield addressed everyone in the tent. "I would like to introduce Nigel Babbage, my former student." He turned to Mr. Acker. "Nigel's with our diplomatic legation in Athens, so a little closer than Corfu."

Mr. Acker approached Mr. Babbage. "A pleasure," he said, shaking his hand. "I am Spencer Acker, lecturer in antiquities."

"William?" Professor Stanfield said.

"Yes? Oh." William stood and gave a nod of his head. "I'm William Peel. A student of classics at St. John's."

"A pleasure to meet you all," said Mr. Babbage.

At that moment Miss Trent and Mehmet entered. William took the opportunity to move closer to Beatrice.

"I see you have met our visitor," said Mehmet.

"Albin," said Mr. Babbage, "your correspondence was vague, but clearly urgent." He glanced around the tent. "Would now be a good time to tell me what is going on?"

"Yes." Professor Stanfield gestured to an empty chair. "Tea?"

"Please." There was an enervated lilt to Mr. Babbage's voice.

Miss Trent jumped to get the tea. Mehmet looked amused.

"I've already written about our progress with the archaeological exploration," said Professor Stanfield. "But there is another layer of complications. A neighboring pasha, Durukan, claimed he held the government right to take one-third of what we excavated. He took many of our artifacts. And now we have discovered what he did was illegal. More than that, we have discovered Durukan is not a pasha, and not Turkish. He is an Englishman."

Mr. Babbage gaped.

"This Durukan is in fact a man named Ivor Bunsby. I had hoped, given your work with the Fitzwilliam and British Museum you might have heard of him by either of those names?"

"Certainly not Durukan. I've never heard that name." He took a sip of tea. "But Bunsby? That name does sound rather familiar.

Nothing recent, though. Perhaps when I was at the Fitzwilliam?" He took another sip of tea, then set down his cup with a *clunk*. "I don't recall much more than that right now, I'm afraid."

"Nigel, you've just arrived." Professor Stanfield offered a sympathetic mien. "You must be tired and hungry."

"I suppose I am."

"Mrs. Stanfield and Mrs. Acker will find you accommodation and some dinner. We can continue our discussions in the morning."

"Thank you, Albin. I do think I should rest."

"William," the professor began, "please fetch my wife and Mrs. Acker."

"Yes, sir." As William left the tent, what Mr. Babbage had said echoed in his brain. Bunsby and the Fitzwilliam. Why did that seem so familiar?

WHILE BEATRICE DID ENJOY working with artifacts covered in dirt, she was not so disinclined to assist Professor Stanfield and Mr. Babbage in their quest to find information about a man named Bunsby.

Especially when that quest involved her sitting at a table next to William, their knees sometimes rubbing together, and their hands sometimes accidentally brushing, while they paged through catalogs and notebooks.

Well, it was Professor Stanfield's study tent, so perhaps not as private as she would like. But it was shaded and out of the dust and William was next to her, which made everything just fine.

The professor, Mr. Acker, and Mr. Babbage held their own conference on the other side of the tent. They discussed correspondence and telegrams and raised their voices at times about aspects they disliked about the Turkish government, then Mr. Babbage would remind them of certain aspects of their own government.

Trying to keep track of their conversation while also paying attention to the catalogs and notebooks from the professor's library was all rather daunting. Beatrice knew that paying mind to the written pages before her was far more important at that moment than trying to decipher archaeological politics.

William's fingers brushed against hers as he turned a page. Moments like this were few and far between for them now. A cot for Mr. Babbage had been ensconced in William's tent. So, there were no more late-night trysts as William had been reticent to leave in the middle of the night in case his absence was discovered.

But it seemed Mr. Babbage's appearance had put a damper on Clarissa's late-night trysts with Mehmet, anyway. So Beatrice was not free to leave her own tent at night.

Which meant she and William had to make the most of it during the day. And if perusing books while sitting next to him was all she could get, then so be it. She was happy at his side.

A Turkish guard entered the tent. "Message. Professor."

His heavily accented dispatch sent the professor and messieurs Acker and Babbage scurrying out the tent door.

Beatrice glanced sidelong at William. "I think we're alone now," she said.

"Oh?" He was engrossed in a catalog for the Fitzwilliam Museum at Cambridge.

She sighed and returned to the British Museum catalog opened in front of her.

Still, she rubbed her knee against his. He smiled but did not lose his concentration on the task at hand.

They were looking for any mention of the name Bunsby. It seemed a futile effort, really.

"Eureka!" exclaimed William.

She turned to him. "What do you mean?"

"I found it! More precisely, I've found the name. I knew I'd seen it before, I just couldn't remember where." He tapped the page of a catalog.

Beatrice leaned over. His finger pointed to an engraved image of an urn.

"I remember seeing the urn and noticing the name on a donor plaque at the Fitzwilliam when I was—"

He stopped. He glanced at her and blushed a dark crimson.

"William?"

"I… I can't tell you."

"Yes, you can."

He chewed on his lower lip for a moment. "I'd been thinking of you, and I needed to find a private place."

Her scalp prickled.

"I had been walking, and the museum was right there. So I went downstairs." He met her gaze, his expression forlorn. "I found a dark corner. I remember seeing the name Bunsby on a donor plaque for a Grecian urn before I…" He stared at her, utterly flustered.

"Before you what?"

He heaved a breath, then another. "Before I tossed myself off to a fantasy of you."

A flush overcame her. She had not been expecting that.

Beatrice angled forward. "You pleasure yourself to fantasies of me?"

William's breath teased her lips. "I do."

"I think of you, as well, when I touch myself."

He smiled, then cradled her head in his hands and pressed his lips to hers.

Sensations exploded all around her. As kindling on a fire, their kiss burned bright. His lips devoured hers, his tongue delved deeply. She gave back what she was given.

It had been too long. They'd barely had any moments alone to even hold hands. Now they had this precious moment to reconnect physically.

His touch was frantic, as if he wanted to touch all of her, but did not know how long they had. She just wanted to feel him close, feel the heat of his body imbuing hers—

"Oh my stars." Mr. Babbage's squawk broke the moment.

Beatrice shot up to standing, tipping over her chair in the process. "Mr. Babbage."

William remained seated, probably to hide his arousal.

Mr. Babbage had flushed the same color of red she was sure stained her face.

And then he smiled, the color fading from his cheeks. "Of course. I should have guessed. You two make an endearing couple."

They did?

"We do?" said William.

"Thank you, Mr. Babbage." It was really all one could say in such a situation.

Mr. Babbage cleared his throat. "I only returned for my notebook. Now I have it"—he tapped the leather binding—"I'll be on my way."

"Wait," said William. "I've found evidence of Bunsby in the Fitzwilliam catalog."

"Oh?" Mr. Babbage approached their worktable.

"Yes," said William. "I saw the listing in the catalog and suddenly remembered why I knew the name." He pointed to an engraving of a Grecian urn. "I saw this urn and had read the card when I was at the museum." He drew his hand along the margin, then turned the page and did the same. "Someone has written in the name of Bunsby for certain items in the catalog."

"Yes, I see." Mr. Babbage picked up the catalog and examined it. "Yes...I remember. Bunsby donated some artifacts of middling quality." He looked at the back cover, then turned to the first few pages. "It seems Albin purchased this catalog secondhand," he surmised. "Whoever owned it first made an effort to inscribe Bunsby's name alongside his donations." He placed the catalog on the table. "William, you have made quite an interesting discovery."

"Thank you, sir."

"I shall fetch Albin to see what he has to say about the matter."

Mr. Babbage exited.

"Bea," William whispered. "I'm so sorry. I was indiscreet."

"I am equally at fault for any indiscretion."

William smiled and leaned forward as if he were about to kiss her again. She leaned forward as well, but the entrance of Mr. Babbage and the professor thwarted William's amorous intentions.

"What's this I hear?" said Professor Stanfield. "You've found something interesting about Bunsby?"

"I have." William handed the open catalog to the professor.

"Hmm… yes… of course." Professor Stanfield made various grunting noises as he turned the pages. "I purchased this catalog at an estate sale for a curator of the Fitzwilliam who had died. This marginalia must be his."

Mr. Babbage looked over the professor's shoulder at the catalog. "How old a man is this Durukan?"

"I don't rightly know, really," said the professor. He glanced at Beatrice. "Miss Smythe? What is your assessment?"

Older than Mehmet. Maybe the same age as the professor? "I think he's around my father's age. Or older."

"Well, that would not fit at all," said Mr. Babbage. "Perhaps a relative."

"Do you want to tell us what you are thinking, Nigel?"

"Yes, of course. I suppose you cannot read my thoughts," he said with a dark chuckle. "I did know of an old man when I worked at the Fitzwilliam Museum for a spell. His name was Bunsby. He had been involved in the Greek War of Independence."

"Yes," said Professor Stanfield, "that would make your Bunsby quite a bit older."

Mr. Babbage nodded. "He would offer rather aggressive advice about how best to display our Greek artifacts."

Professor Stanfield pressed a finger to his lips, then regarded William and Beatrice. "So we conclude the elder Bunsby was a collector of Greek antiquities."

"And the younger Bunsby is a fabricator of antiquities," said Beatrice.

The professor nodded with a grin. "Very right." He tapped the finger against his lips. "What can we make of this knowledge?"

Mr. Acker poked his head into the tent. "Albin, it seems we have visitors heading in our direction."

"Ah, let us hope there is some news to buttress any speculation we might have about the Bunsbys." Professor Stanfield nodded before exiting.

"Now I have my notebook," said Mr. Babbage, "I shall take my leave." He smiled knowingly at William and Beatrice. "You may stay here as you like. Wherever you choose to have your adventure." With a wink, he left.

And, once again, they were alone. "William?"

"Yes, love?"

"I think perhaps we should see what's going on outside."

William kissed her full on the lips then grabbed her hand. "Let's go."

MEHMET WATCHED AS HIS workmen dug into the dirt while others carted the dirt away. It had to be there. The mosaic floor *had* to be there. They'd already dug a hole a few feet away and had found nothing. Which was, of course, unfortunate and unexpected. But over a thousand years of earthquakes and weather could move a floor, or simply change what one expected a site to look like. So they were trying again.

The laborers worked as swiftly as prudence would allow. Mehmet was transfixed by their rhythm, the strength of their bodies, the delicacy of their movements. After the shovels had removed several feet of dirt, the men were on their knees using trowels and small picks, goading each other to be cautious and successful.

A shout from one of the workmen drew everyone's attention. He'd found something, he thought. He conferred with another man. Then they both turned to Mehmet and waved him over.

Mehmet knelt on the ground and stared into the hole. A glimpse of dirty white marble tesserae sent a chill down his spine. This was the very moment he had dreamed of for far too long. His overly excited heart threatened to expand to the point of incapacitation.

He stood and instructed the men with shovels to continue digging, but to angle the cut of the earth in the event the mosaic floor had buckled during an earthquake. He directed Yazid to find the photographer to document what he hoped was uncovering more than just a few dirty white tesserae.

Then he proceeded to the tent where Clarissa worked tirelessly on solving the mysteries of marble fragments. She was seated at an easel, drawing. She looked up and smiled at him.

Their eyes met, his gaze perhaps a bit too intense. The blush on her cheeks reflected the heat he felt rising in his own face. He smiled back. He could spend the rest of his life with this woman.

She put down her pencil. "I see there is a bit of excitement at the temple site."

"They found the mosaic. Well, a bit of it, anyway."

"Oh, my." Her eyes widened as her mouth fell open. She stood. "May I see?"

"Of course."

He wanted to take her by the hand and run to show her the dig, but he refrained. Instead they walked side by side, casually, as if this were not the most thrilling discovery of his life.

At the sight of Clarissa, the workmen paused and stepped aside, doffing their caps deferentially. She looked at the hole, then got on her hands and knees for a closer examination. Her gasp was captured by the earth. She stood and looked at the hole then surveyed the site.

"Do you think this is the south-east corner?"

Excitement once again thrummed in Mehmet's body, excitement for their find and for this very astute woman. "I was thinking precisely that, yes."

She beamed at him. "Since you now have government protections, I presume the digging will proceed?"

"Without delay." Mehmet waved at his men to continue their work. He turned his attention to Clarissa. "Shall I escort you back to your easel, Miss Trent?"

"Please."

A commotion near Professor Stanfield's tent drew their attention. A group of men on horseback had arrived at the camp, met by Sinan and Yusuf.

Clarissa wrapped her arm around Mehmet's. "Perhaps we should see what is happening over at the professor's tent."

"Yes, I think we should."

CHAPTER TWENTY

Beatrice squeezed William's hand as they exited Professor Stanfield's study tent, then let go before anyone saw. In the clearing before the tent the British academics mingled with Turkish officials. Sinan was there, as was Yusuf wearing a fez hat. The other Turkish men were unknown to her, but all wore military uniforms. Mehmet and Clarissa approached, unlinking their arms as they drew closer. Clarissa took her place at Beatrice's side.

Sinan and Yusuf greeted Mehmet, then began polite introductions. The language was Turkish, with Sinan translating quietly for Professor Stanfield and the other academics.

Clarissa leaned in. "Yusuf knows some of these men from his work with the sultan's antiquities department." She listened intently to the discussion.

Beatrice could only catch a word here and there. But the gestures indicated they were moving to the covered porch of the dining tent, a much larger shaded place to hold what looked like an important conversation.

Mrs. Stanfield and Mrs. Acker were at the ready with lemon water, tea, and coffee, whichever their guests preferred. Hospitality was valued by the Turks, and the academic wives had adopted the customs of their hosts.

William handed Beatrice and Clarissa glasses of lemon water then took his place at Beatrice's side as her private sentinel. Two uniformed Turkish men began to talk, as if telling a story. One man was lean and graying. The other was muscular with a dark mustache.

"The men are officers with the Ottoman navy," Clarissa translated in sotto voce. "Several months ago, they had been alerted to unusual shipping activity from the mainland to the island of Samothrace."

"Unusual? How so?" William said behind his glass.

"Unscheduled, at night." Clarissa glanced up at him. "They have their ways of knowing."

"Ah."

"One night they watched men offload crates from the ship, then followed the carts carrying the crates to a warehouse where the crates were unloaded." Clarissa listened more intently. "They assumed the men were pirates, so closed in."

The mustachioed officer chuckled and shook his head before continuing.

"He was so surprised by what he found."

Realization hit Beatrice. "The fake antiquities."

"Yes," said Clarissa. "But upon further investigation they discovered the warehouse was the place where they made the fake antiquities look old."

"Like with dirt?" asked William.

"Yes, clay, paint, other means." Now it was Clarissa's turn to shake her head in disbelief. "How strange."

The gray-haired officer addressed her with a question.

Clarissa nodded. "Beatrice, William, can you tell the man what you saw at Durukan's palace? I will translate."

Beatrice drew in a breath. "There was a room in the basement…"

Between her and William they related their experience, the officers at times asking questions, while Clarissa facilitated and translated their conversation.

At the end, both officers bowed and thanked them. "*Çok teşekkür ederim.*"

"*Rica ederim, efendi.*" Beatrice hoped she had said "You're welcome, sir" properly. Smiles from the officials let her know her attempt was appreciated and understood.

The officers resumed their report, this time including William and Beatrice in their conversation with glances and nods.

"Because of what Sinan and Yusuf had reported," Clarissa continued her translation, "the naval officers want to connect the activity on Samothrace with Durukan, but they do not have enough evidence."

Mehmet asked a question.

"Why don't they simply raid one of Durukan's ships?" Clarissa listened, nodding. "They do not want to raid a ship because that might set into action any plans he might have to destroy his workshop—"

At this point the officials gestured to Beatrice and William.

"That these brave young people discovered."

Beatrice was certain she blushed. William grinned.

Mehmet began to speak again, pointing to the temple.

"He says despite our renewed activities, we have not had a visit by Durukan. Perhaps we should entice Durukan to the site—"

Beatrice shuddered.

Clarissa wrapped an arm around her shoulder and leaned in more closely. "The workmen have just found a corner of the temple's mosaic floor."

"Truly?"

"Yes. Be assured you will be kept safe."

"Thank you."

Mehmet continued. Beatrice caught the word *mosaik* in his speech. As his discovery was related and translated, signs of surprise and jubilation passed through all present.

"Magnificent!" said Professor Stanfield.

The gray-haired officer grinned while he spoke.

"The plan now is to entice Durukan to the site by spreading the news of the finding of the mosaic. Once he is here, his ships will be seized, and his palace will be raided. While he is here, he will be arrested for impersonating a pasha." Clarissa's voice held triumph. "They will be able to detain him on that charge while they continue their investigation."

Beatrice never wanted to see the man ever again. But seeing him in shackles would be gratifying.

FOR THE FIRST TIME in what seemed like an endless stream of days, William finally felt a sense of calm, even as he sat next to Beatrice, her subtle fragrance teasing his nostrils every time he leaned in a little too closely.

Last night he'd been at bursting from need to pleasure himself. Finally, in the darkest hours, Mr. Babbage had turned onto his stomach and began to snore loudly. William had scrambled out of bed and scampered to the knoll above the site, dodging guards. Once alone and far away, he frigged himself, not once but twice. Only then did he feel that particular relief he had not felt for far too long.

And now Beatrice was here, at his side, culling through old catalogs. Across from them, the three British academics wrote correspondence, consulted catalogs, and chatted. It seemed pointless as they already knew who Bunsby was. Well, perhaps they would find evidence that Bunsby had donated artifacts to other museums.

Besides, paging through catalogs meant he got to be next to his lover and best friend, sometimes even touching her.

"Professor," Sinan bellowed as he entered the tent. "We have just had a delivery of telegrams and some correspondence. Your British Museum has quite a bit of information for you."

Sinan handed the stack of accumulated missives to the professor.

"Oh, my, yes. Thank you."

"The messages are in order by time. The earliest on the top."

"By time?" queried Mr. Babbage.

"The telegrams began coming in yesterday. The telegraph secretary was transcribing all night."

"Please extend our sincere gratitude to the man," said the professor.

Sinan grinned. "Now I must address my own stack from our government." With a slight bow of his head he left.

Professor Stanfield looked a bit stunned and overwhelmed. He sat in his leather chair and read while Mr. Babbage and Mr. Acker watched, a bit stunned themselves.

Even Beatrice stopped paging through catalogs. They were all eager for some news.

"The telegrams are all from Sir Kenneth Lloyd-Jones, an under-secretary for the Principal Librarian at the British Museum. He is in contact with the Fitzwilliam Museum as well as agents who work for private collectors. It seems the man whose name is scribbled in the Fitzwilliam catalog is one Rawdon Bunsby, an Englishman who fought alongside the Greeks in their war for independence." Professor Stanfield stopped and glanced at the tent doorway.

Decades ago, the Greeks had fought against Ottoman rule. There were still animosities. "It's just us British here, professor," said William.

Professor Stanfield nodded. "Right."

"That would fit the age of the man I encountered at the Fitzwilliam," offered Mr. Babbage.

"The Fitzwilliam and the British Museum both believe the works purchased from or donated by Bunsby forty years ago to be authentic. They became suspicious when, in the last few years, Bunsby began to offer items of middling quality and wanting hefty payments. He claimed the objects were from his original collection." Professor Stanfield looked up. "They've dismissed the man, but he's persistent."

"The artifacts in Durukan's basement," murmured Beatrice.

"Later found on Samothrace," added William.

"So it seems," agreed the professor. "Lloyd-Jones is unclear on whether the elder Bunsby is trying to sell artifacts for personal gain or is raising money to finance some new rebellion." Professor Stanfield raised a brow in Mr. Babbage's direction. "Nigel? Is revolution brewing?"

Mr. Babbage cleared his throat. "The opposite, really," he said quietly. "There are negotiations at this moment for the Ottomans to cede territory to Greece. The Greeks demanded more, of course, but I think that dispute has been resolved."

"That would be confidential information, correct?"

"Most definitely." Mr. Babbage glanced around the room.

"We won't spread it around, Babbage," said Mr. Acker.

"Well, the British government will certainly want to know if one of their own citizens is attempting to incite rebellion at the very same moment the government is in negotiations to resolve the matter."

All eyes turned to Beatrice, shocked faces conveying they were not expecting such a conclusion from a mere student. Or perhaps a woman.

"You are very correct, Miss Smythe," said Professor Stanfield. He put down his stack of telegrams. "However, we do not have sufficient evidence to ascertain whether the elder Bunsby is attempting to incite rebellion."

"But the Turks should have something with which to charge Durukan—or Ivor Bunsby, whatever he's called," said Mr. Acker with a shake of his head.

"They'll have to have evidence that the fake artifacts were destined to deceive someone other than mere tourists," said the professor.

"British museums should be able to confirm attempts to sell fake artifacts," said Mr. Babbage.

"Is selling fake artifacts illegal?" asked Mr. Acker. "Smuggling real ones would seem to be more of a crime."

Beatrice stood abruptly. "What about Durukan's crimes against me and Miss Trent? What about kidnapping charges? I am the daughter of an English peer. Surely the British government will want to try Durukan for the injury he has caused me and another of its citizens?"

William brushed the back of her trembling hand with his. She grasped his hand and exhaled before sitting down again, her breath unsteady. Another man would feel pride for her courage. But pride implied ownership. Beatrice was no man's woman. Instead of pride, he felt awe.

"Miss Smythe?" Mr. Babbage stared at her in shock. "You were kidnapped?"

"Yes. Miss Trent as well."

"Clarissa?" Mr. Babbage paled. "Oh my stars."

"Mehmet and I rescued them," explained William.

"I see." Mr. Babbage turned to Beatrice. "And you say you are the daughter of a peer?"

"The Earl of Ryburgh," said Professor Stanfield.

"Then should you not be styled Lady Beatrice?" Confusion lined Mr. Babbage's expression.

"I choose not to use that honorific."

"Oh." Such a notion seemed strange to Mr. Babbage. He looked askance briefly before meeting her gaze. "Your government will protect you, Lady Beatrice. You have my word."

* * * * *

"He's here."

At the sound of William's voice, Beatrice looked up from taking notes in the artifact tent. Clarissa had been dictating the progress of digging out the mosaic. "He?"

"Durukan."

Clarissa tensed at her side. "We should not be conspicuous, Beatrice."

She was right. No woman should be seen by that monster. Their tent was open on all sides. "Where are Mrs. Stanfield and Mrs. Acker?"

William looked around. "I think they're in the professor's study tent."

A place that was enclosed and shielded. Beatrice grabbed her notebook and glanced at Clarissa who nodded. They scurried to the study tent.

The academic wives were indeed inside.

"Clarissa? Beatrice?" said Mrs. Stanfield. "You both look as if you have seen a ghost."

"Just Durukan," said Clarissa. "He's here."

Mrs. Stanfield offered a crooked grin. "As are the arresting Turkish officials, if my husband is correct."

Relief washed through Beatrice. Justice would be served.

Mrs. Acker shifted in her cushioned chair, holding her belly. "Spencer says Mr. Babbage has contacted the British authorities. Whatever the sultan can't charge him with, I'm certain we can."

More relief. Still, an irksome sense of dread prevailed. What if Durukan had garnered support for his side?

The thunder of horse hooves dispelled all thoughts and speculations. Beatrice peered between the tent flaps to see Durukan arriving with an entourage.

A rather scraggly entourage who seemed more unwillingly pressed into service than ardently supportive of their pasha.

Gathered and waiting on the dusty plain were Mehmet with his legion of workmen ganged up behind. To the right were Sinan and Yusuf and what appeared to be Ottoman officials.

The academics hovered off to the left. Mr. Babbage paced slowly, like a caged animal. William flicked his gaze to the study tent. He said something to Professor Stanfield and Mr. Acker, both of whom glanced over at the tent. They knew where their wives were.

No refreshments or other ceremonial accoutrements had been provided. Nothing implied welcome. But dozens of men at the ready implied challenge.

Durukan dismounted, straightened his turban, then strode deliberately toward Mehmet, his embroidered robe dragging in the dirt. That he wore traditional costume stood in stark contrast to the true Turks who wore fezzes and frock coats as their sultan had ordained for official matters.

The fake pasha exuded a confidence he should not have. Everyone present knew who he really was. Why didn't the authorities swoop down on him at once?

"Bea, breathe," Clarissa said gently. "You're turning an unpleasant shade of red."

Anger was making her feel a bit lightheaded.

Mrs. Acker handed Beatrice a glass. "Drink this, dear."

"Thank you." Beatrice gulped down the cool water.

Clarissa placed a stool near the tent opening. "Sit. I will stand and translate."

Beatrice sat while Mrs. Stanfield and Mrs. Acker gathered close by.

"Durukan is surveying all present, but does not appear shaken. He's speaking." Clarissa turned her ear to the outside. "'I hear you have a treasure for me,' he says. 'I hear you have discovered a mosaic. I would like to see it. I believe one-third belongs to me.'" Clarissa conveyed the last bit with unabashed contempt.

They all knew fraudulently acquiring artifacts was Durukan's scheme.

"Mehmet is unmoved. He's not saying anything at all. Durukan looks flustered." Clarissa studied her view. "Yusuf has stepped forward. 'You have no right to demand antiquities from Mehmet Pasha,' he says. Durukan has taken on a haughty, arrogant air. 'The state has a right to one-third of any antiquities discovered on private land,' he says."

"That is somewhat true," Mrs. Stanfield muttered. "But this Durukan has no right to any finds."

"Oh my," Clarissa murmured. "Yusuf is now directly in front of Durukan. He's signaling to someone, maybe near the entrance to the site. I can't see over there." She listened. "'Ivor Bunsby, you are hereby seized and charged with impersonating an Ottoman government official.'" Clarissa stared with wide eyes at the scene.

Beatrice enlivened and turned to watch the unfolding events.

From behind Durukan and his gang came a troop of Turkish men wearing military uniforms. A melee ensued, the soldiers grabbing Durukan's men, restraining them, dragging them to a wooden cart.

Surprise mixed with anger marred Durukan's expression before panic set in. Two men in uniform grabbed him. He struggled, squawking his discontent as he flailed futilely against the determined soldiers.

"Unhand me! I am an English citizen," he bellowed.

Mehmet and the academics stared at him, perhaps registering how utterly discordant his true accent was from attire and circumstance.

Durukan continued to struggle. "My government will contest this outrage."

Suddenly, Mr. Babbage ran to face Durukan. "Your government will sentence a criminal like you to the harshest penalties." He swung his fist and landed it perfectly against Durukan's jaw, the sound of flesh hitting flesh alarming.

All the women in the tent gasped.

As Durukan's now listless figure was hauled to the cart, Professor Stanfield and William calmed Mr. Babbage. Mehmet conferred with Yusuf and Sinan.

The women glanced at each other, too stunned to speak and unsure what to do next. Sitting seemed like a good idea and each seemed to have that idea at the very same moment.

The tent flaps were opened with great force, and Mr. Acker ran inside, scanning the space, his expression distressed. His gaze landed on his wife, and he went to her, pulling her into his arms, kissing her full on the mouth.

Beatrice had never before seen the couple interact so lovingly.

"Cornelia," he said, drawing back, then pressing his hand to her belly. "How are you? How is the baby?"

"I'm fine, Spencer." She blushed like a newlywed bride. "We're fine."

He kissed her forehead. "This business was positively dreadful."

Beatrice agreed. The business had been dreadful. And now it was over.

From the shade of the pediment tent, Clarissa looked up from her temple sketch to survey the busy archaeological site before her. She stood and stretched, breathing in a long inhalation and exhaling satisfaction. Now unhindered by anxiety regarding the fate of the mosaic floor—and indeed the temple itself, Mehmet had instructed his men to continue their exploration. They had a certain rhythm of digging, hauling the dirt away, then inspecting.

Mehmet had been overjoyed to see a glimpse of a mosaic border with a crested wave design.

On the very same day Durukan had been carted away, artifacts from Mehmet's excavations had started to be returned. Oddly, all crates save for two had remained closed and undisturbed. The two crates that had been opened were those containing the large blocks Beatrice and William had seen.

Clarissa went to the low platform to study the pediment and the frieze with the inscription below it. Every fragment they'd uncovered had now been fit into place. There was still much to be uncovered or cleaned to reconstruct the entire pediment, but what was before her made her heart swell with pride. Her finished drawings based on William's sketch on Beatrice's back were very close to the real thing.

Mehmet joined her at her side, his expression shifting from wonder to joy. "It really was a horse and lion in William's rendering," he said with a laugh.

She squeezed his hand briefly. His own theory as to what the scene depicted had proved to be true, even from just the fragments they had.

The lion was at the center of the pediment, his body angled to the left while his head whipped around to the hunter at the right. To the left they only had a fragment of a horse's hoof, but that detail implied another hunter on horseback— probably the emperor Hadrian, according to Mehmet and Albin. To the right was Antinous on horseback, his left hand crossed in front holding the bridle rein, his right hand held high. A wood-and-metal spear would have been in the chipped marble hand. Further to the right was the lion skin draped over the tree, and a woman holding a wreath. They'd found the fragment with her head. She wore a crown made of city walls revealing her to be the Tyche of Alexandria, the personification of that city.

Beneath the pediment was dentil molding separating the sculpture from the frieze with the inscription. A bit more of the frieze had been uncovered, naming Antinous as "hero of the hunt."

The scene, the inscription—everything pointed to a temple dedicated to the emperor Hadrian's lover Antinous.

While Clarissa was satisfied kand delighted with all the work she had done, Mehmet was elated that his hypotheses had been vindicated. He had renewed energy for exploring the site, planning to continue excavations year-round as weather permitted.

He watched the workers excavating dirt at the site of the mosaic floor. "I really will need a manager for such an undertaking."

"Wouldn't that be you?"

"I suppose." He chuckled. "What I really mean is that I will need a team, such as what we have here now. I know Albin and Spencer can't be here all year. Nor our students. Even if I had several other academics involved, there would possibly be a lack of consistency. So I will need someone to manage the academical matters."

"You still want to maintain connections to English universities?"

"Such connections garner wealthy English patrons. Albin was quite successful in securing financial support, including William's father's business associates who were rather generous." He scrubbed a hand across his beard. "There's so much to do now that I've discovered what I'd wanted to discover."

She placed a hand on his shoulder. "And with no more threats, you have all the time in the world to do the job carefully."

"I suppose." Mehmet gazed at her, a touch of longing in his green eyes. "Regardless, I will need a plan." He took her hand in his. "And you, what is your plan for the future?"

Heat rose in Clarissa's face. "I… I'll go home and resume my duties at Girton, I suppose." She tried to keep the disappointment out of her voice.

"But will you return here?" He rubbed her palm with his thumb, the intimate touch radiating heat to her sex.

"If you will have me back, Mehmet."

He smiled. "I want—"

"Mehmet?"

At the sound of Nigel's voice, Mehmet dropped her hand and turned. "Yes?"

"I've just been informed that Ivor Bunsby has arrived in Istanbul."

Mehmet gave a slow nod of acknowledgment. "Thank you."

"Will you be giving testimony against him in the capital?"

"No. Sinan and Yusuf will handle our case in Istanbul."

"What about London?"

Clarissa narrowed her eyes at Nigel. "London?"

"If our government presses charges against the Bunsby father and son."

A corner of Mehmet's mouth quirked upwards. "I had not considered such a notion. It has been a few years since I've been to England. There are many attractions." His smile widened as he glanced at Clarissa.

"Brilliant," said Nigel. "I'll let my contacts in the government know. By the by, I would like to stay on to help Albin and Spencer pack up, if that is acceptable to you?"

"Of course, Nigel. Stay as long as you like."

"Thank you." After a quick bow of his head, Nigel headed off to Professor Stanfield's study tent.

Mehmet looked around before taking up Clarissa's hand once again. "Tonight, after dinner, will you join me for an evening stroll? I would like to talk to you about your future."

Her future? "I would love to, Mehmet."

"Excellent." He kissed her hand. "I will see you tonight, then."

Clarissa's heart pounded in anticipation as she watched him walk away.

CHAPTER TWENTY-ONE

Mehmet had to contain his eagerness and subdue his apprehension for Clarissa's consenting to join him for a late evening stroll. He'd been preparing for this moment for longer than just that afternoon.

He'd been preparing for such a moment for years. His entire life, really.

They walked with the aid of lamplight and moonlight to a spot inside the temple site, above the excavation of the mosaic floor. Pillows and blankets awaited them. Mehmet knelt down, then helped Clarissa onto the makeshift divan.

She snuggled against him. "This is lovely, Mehmet."

His servants had done a fine job of making a lover's nest.

"It is a fine night for a romantic tryst."

He chuckled. "Truly, I simply wanted to talk to you."

"Oh?"

"About the future."

She tensed at his side. "You mean what lies ahead for the excavation?"

He nuzzled her hair. "I mean your future. Our future together." He drew back so he could see her face. "Clarissa, I must confess I'm in love with you."

She drew in a sharp breath. A beat of silence followed before she murmured, "Mehmet?"

"Share my life with me." He cupped her cheek. "Marry me." As he said the words, tears blurred his vision.

A tiny mewl escaped her throat. "Oh, love. You cannot imagine how much I want to."

"I think I can." He pecked her lips, tasting the salt of her tears. "However, there are certain conditions for such a union, and I need to make certain you are aware of them."

"Conditions?" She drew back a little. "Such as?"

"I am expected to have children, most importantly, a son. Would you be amenable to having my children?"

"Truthfully, I do not know if I am capable of bearing children, but I am happy to find out." She playfully rubbed the tip of her nose against his cheek. "Trying to become with child will be enjoyable."

He chuckled. "Indeed." He sobered. The next condition was more worrisome for him. "Our society is more segregated than British society. As the wife of a pasha, you will be expected to be deferential to men, to be present when needed, but silent." He turned to her. "You are a scholar and an independent woman. I would never expect you to act otherwise in my palace—in *our* palace. I need your expertise with this excavation, so you will have a preeminent position here. But in the larger community, away from this site, away from the palace, you will encounter men—and women—who will expect you to act a certain way."

"I understand, Mehmet. I will ask for guidance from your mother and your sisters as I navigate this new life."

His heart expanded. She was truly magnificent.

"What else?" she asked.

"Ah, yes. We are Muslim, and you come from a Christian society. You will be expected to convert to our religion."

"Your God is the same as the Christian God, is he not?"

"Yes. And Jesus is revered as a prophet in Islam."

"I am not a religious woman, Mehmet. I only go to chapel when it is expected of me and not of my own volition. I confess that I would view converting to Islam as more of a cultural experience."

He heaved a sigh. "I am not a religious man myself. I suppose I only perform the rituals when they are expected of me, as well."

"When we visit my parents during Christmastime, you will be expected to participate in our rituals."

He chuckled. "I will look forward to that."

"Are there any other impediments to consider?"

"Those were the major concerns I had. If you marry me, your life will be vastly different than what it is now."

"You mean, *when* I marry you."

"Then your answer—"

She pressed her lips to his. "Is yes. I love you, Mehmet, and want to be your wife."

Tears of joy flooded forth as he pulled her more tightly into his arms, taking her in a deep kiss. She shook with emotion as she kissed him back.

He reached into his pocket. "I have something for you." He brought the lamp more closely to them then held out a ring in his palm. "It was an anniversary gift from my father to my mother after twenty-five years of marriage. She prays it will bring us as much joy and harmony as she shared with my father." He took Clarissa's left hand, and hoped the ring fit at least one of her fingers.

It fit her fourth finger perfectly.

Clarissa held out her hand admiring the ring. "Mehmet, this is beautiful. What are the stones?"

"Turquoise and lapis lazuli set in gold. You will see their colors better in the daylight."

She giggled. "As will everyone else."

Heat spread across his face. "Ah." He chuckled. "I suppose we should make a formal announcement at breakfast?"

"Yes, we should." She snuggled against him once more. "In the meantime, let's enjoy this moment we have together alone."

He turned down the lamp then wrapped his arms around her. There would be many more moments like this in their future. He'd make certain of that.

CLARISSA PLACED A STACK OF BOOKS in her trunk. It did seem silly packing for England if she were simply going to return to Turkey with all of her belongings.

Giddy happiness tugged at the corners of her mouth. She really had to keep her emotions in check.

Well, she did have two trunks. She could put what she really needed for England in one, and put the rest in the other.

"You're getting married in England?" Beatrice had already finished packing and sat on her cot watching Clarissa.

"Yes. We will have a ceremony in England, then one here in Turkey."

"If Mehmet is not a British citizen, how will that work?"

"Mehmet will take up residency in Cambridge by living with Professor Stanfield. We'll publish the banns, and be married in the parish church. We'll have a separate ceremony here according to Turkish laws and customs."

"It seems so complicated."

"When you love someone, you will do what you need to do to be with them."

"You can love someone and not marry them."

Clarissa suppressed a grin. "I suppose you can. But society does frown upon women who live with men without marrying them. Such women are called harsh names."

"Oh, pshaw."

The reaction was vexing. "Beatrice, your wealth and position allow you certain privileges. I am middle class and would be thought a harlot or worse if I did not marry Mehmet."

"Because you share his bed?"

Clarissa stopped folding clothes. "In any society on this globe, an unmarried woman sharing the bed of a man would be ostracized." She sat next to Beatrice on her cot. "I chose to be with Mehmet in that way because I love him and I know he loves me. What I did was bold. I do not endorse such actions on the part of any other unmarried woman."

Beatrice stared at her with wide eyes. "I would never tell anyone. I am also guilty of such an offense."

"Oh, dear, it is not an offense." She took Beatrice's hands in hers and gave a little squeeze. "One day, perhaps, there will be a time when women can be as free as men with their affections."

"That's what my father fights for in Parliament."

Clarissa laughed softly. "Yes, yes, he does."

Beatrice traced the band on Clarissa's fourth finger. "It's beautiful."

"It is." She rose and resumed packing.

"If you marry, you won't be able to own property or vote."

"Spoken like a true Radical's daughter." Clarissa suppressed a grin.

"Because I am."

"Beatrice, I would never be able to own much property given my earnings, and I could only ever vote in local elections. Once I marry Mehmet, I will live in a palace, and I will help manage this archaeological site. I am willing to make that trade."

"Will you be safe here?"

The question was reasonable. "Physically, yes. I trust Mehmet will keep all the women in his household safe now that there has been a threat. Legally, we will have a proper marriage settlement in place, so if something happens to him, I will be protected."

Beatrice sighed. "I reiterate: marriage sounds complicated." She got off her cot. "I think I'll help William pack books in

Professor Stanfield's tent." She tilted her head. "Will you be all right?"

"Yes, thank you. Go be with William."

Beatrice beamed then left.

The trunk for her life in Turkey was filling up. Really all she needed was a carpet bag for her trip back to England.

"Clarissa?"

Nigel stood at the door.

"Please come in."

He entered and took in the scene, glancing between the two trunks. "Are you leaving or staying?"

She laughed. "There's no point in dragging my things back to England only to have to bring them back."

"I want to offer my congratulations. Mehmet is a good man."

"He is."

Nigel glanced away, as if he wanted to say something.

"You needn't be worried for me, if that's what you're thinking."

"I'm not. This is a wonderful future for you. Trust me, I think you'll enjoy living abroad."

"There's something else, though."

He seemed to calm himself with a slow breath. "Clarissa, I wanted to apologize. About us. I broke things off badly. I hurt you."

His confession shot an arrow to her heart. "Nigel, there's no need to apologize. It was a long time ago."

"Please, I need to hear you've forgiven me. That I was so dismissive of your feelings ate at me for years. Then when I saw you again…" He huffed. "I was reminded of both the fondness we had for each other and how I ruined it." He took her left hand in his and stroked her ring with his thumb. "But I am glad you have found your happiness."

"And you, have you found happiness?"

A blush colored his cheeks. "I've met someone, yes. Gavin." His eyes sparkled when he said his lover's name. "He's a consultant with the Archaeological Society of Athens. We share bachelor quarters. It's all very marvelous, really."

Clarissa gave his lips a tender peck. "Then I will give you my forgiveness so you can forge ahead without impediment."

Nigel drew her in to his arms. "My friend, let's not be strangers."

"My life will be here. I am only a boat ride away."

He grinned. "Gavin and I would love to join your archaeological team." He gestured broadly. "I don't think I've done such a thing since I was William's age. And Mehmet's undertaking is spectacularly well-run."

"You will be welcome any time. The excavation of a temple to Antinous is profoundly meaningful to men such as you and Gavin."

"Yes, it is. Thank you, Clarissa." He kissed her hand, then left.

Tears of joy and relief poured forth. Everything was changing, and for the better.

CHAPTER TWENTY-TWO

London, England, July 1881

The buzz of voices in the Earl of Ryburgh's drawing room was a comfort to William. All around him were people he considered family. Some, such as Mama and Papa, were actually family, but he'd become close to so many of the others they all just felt like family.

And a breakfast to wish Clarissa and Mehmet *bon voyage* before they embarked on their honeymoon to Hadrian's Wall was a perfect occasion for this new, extended family.

The breakfast part of the event was long over, with everyone now casually chatting away in the drawing room. Doors and windows had been opened to let in as much breeze as possible on the unusually warm summer day. Women fanned themselves, creating a symphony of scent in the air. The effect was pleasing to the senses, bordering on…

Erotic.

William had to stop thinking about such a thing immediately. It was bad enough that Helena and Lavinia were on the other side of the room laughing and talking. He'd kissed one of them, and had bedded the other and now was not the time to remember those moments.

Instead he turned his attention to Mehmet and Uncle Arthur deep in conversation, probably about the archaeological site as Uncle Arthur was a financier of the excavation. Nearby, Clarissa spoke with Beatrice's older sister Olivia, who had wed just a month ago. Something enveloped the two as they conversed, an energy, a glow perhaps, which probably reflected their excitement for their newly married states.

A few days ago, Clarissa and Mehmet had been married in Cambridge with all the academics in attendance, plus her family and Girton friends. Mehmet's family were expected after the honeymoon to accompany the couple to Paris. His sisters were, apparently, excited to go shopping for the latest fashions.

Today's occasion showed marriage was a celebration of love, a beginning of a new life together.

But such a notion was anathema to Beatrice. William sighed. Perhaps two could share a life without marriage?

Where was she anyway? She had to be somewhere. It was her London home, for goodness sake. He hadn't seen her since the breakfast.

A passing footman offered relief from anxiety. William grabbed a glass of punch from his tray and downed it just in time to return the empty glass to the salver.

"William?"

The familiar voice of Nicholas was calming. He'd been generous offering advice about university, and generous in allowing his wife Helena to maintain a friendship with William. Well, perhaps that was how things were done? One maintained relationships with people one had kissed?

Good God. Nicholas had slept with Lavinia. William had slept with Lavinia. William had kissed Helena, and now Helena was Nicholas's wife.

He needed another punch.

Nicholas patted him on the back. "How was your first year at Cambridge?"

"Wonderful, thank you. Top tier."

Nicholas chuckled. "Is that what the students are saying these days? In my day it was 'terrific' or 'spiffing'."

"I've heard both from the upperclassmen."

Another footman with another tray paused before them. William grabbed a glass.

"You had quite the adventure in Turkey, I hear." Nicholas also took a glass of punch.

"Yes." William met his kind brown eyes. "Oh, I'd almost forgotten. You spent time in Anatolia."

"I did. Had a terrific experience. Except I was escaping England. You went there with purpose."

"We found a temple with a mosaic floor," William said, perhaps a bit too excitedly. "It's rather spectacular. I hope to return next spring."

"Wonderful." Nicholas seemed to hide a knowing smirk behind his glass.

William glanced at a clearly pregnant Helena across the room. "I should congratulate you on the addition to your family."

"Thank you," said Nicholas. "Helena and I are looking forward to our Robert having a brother or a sister."

A flickering movement near the far door drew his attention. *Beatrice.* She was an absolute vision in a pale yellow. Like a glimpse of sunlight on an overcast day.

She caught his gaze and tilted her head with a smile, then hid her mirth behind her unfurled fan.

Nicholas cleared his throat. "I see you're a bit distracted."

"What?"

"William, go to her. Looks like she's beckoning."

She pouted at him then left the room.

William handed his punch glass to Nicholas. "Will you be my alibi?"

"Of course."

With the deftness of a hunter stalking his prey, William moved stealthily through the drawing room so as not to bring attention to himself.

He exited into a corridor with a staircase in the center. But she was not at the bottom of the stairs. She stood at a door and motioned for him to follow just before opening the door and slipping inside.

The door was plain undecorated oak. The servants' door. He went inside.

Beatrice was in the cramped space at the foot of the stairs, clinging to a wall, her mewling sigh the only sound. Surprise stunned him into immobility only for one moment. He reached for her, and she fell into his embrace, lifting her face to accept his kiss.

"William, come to my room with me." She teased his lips with hers. "I want to be with you. Naked."

His body responded instantly in the affirmative. "But what if someone wonders where we are? I only told Nicholas."

"I also have an ally who will provide distraction for anyone looking for us."

"Who?"

"The Countess of Petersham."

"Lavinia?" William squawked. He was certain he'd just turned beet-red.

Beatrice gave him the queerest look, studying him before her mouth fell open. "It was she, wasn't it?"

"Er, what do you mean?" William hoped Beatrice did not mean what he thought she meant.

Beatrice stared at him. "Lavinia was your first. She taught you about women."

William sighed. "Yes. I mean, well, not just her."

"Who else then?"

"Helena. We grew up together. She taught me how to kiss once she'd learned how."

Beatrice hid her laugh behind her hand. "That's positively endearing."

He pecked her forehead. "And you."

"Me?"

"Helena may have taught me how to kiss, and Lavinia may have instructed me in how to have sexual relations, but you showed me how those acts of intimacy are so much better when one is in love."

She beamed up at him.

"I love you, Beatrice."

"And I love you, William." She took his hand. "Come with me to my room."

"With pleasure."

BEATRICE GRABBED WILLIAM'S hand and practically ran up the servants' stairs until she reached the second floor, then scurried down the corridor to her bedroom. She hauled a befuddled William inside, locked her bedroom door, and pushed him up against it.

She flattened her hands atop his chest, the rapid rise and fall invigorating her own breathlessness. His expression exhibited both wonderment and apprehension.

"William, I've been wanting to be with you in a real bed, enjoying our time at a leisurely pace, without any anxiety that we're expected somewhere else."

"There's a party downstairs, Bea."

"We have our allies to make our excuses. Besides, the party is about Clarissa and Mehmet, not us."

He sighed then pulled her into an embrace, his deep kiss full of promise and desire. "I've wanted this moment as well."

Good. Beatrice unbuttoned his jacket and started on his waistcoat. "First I want you completely naked."

William held up his hands as she did her work. "At your service, Miss Smythe."

Undressing William herself seemed rather perfunctory. She leaned against her bed. "I think I would like to watch you complete the task."

He grinned too widely. William took his time, neatly folding each item as he disrobed, making a fastidious pile on the bench at the foot of her bed.

She stared, thrilling in the revelation of his body. Undressing was something lovers did. She could watch him undress for a lifetime.

A chill spread across her scalp. A lifetime did not need to imply marriage, did it?

Now completely nude, William slowly turned around to show off his tall, lean, athletic body, his arms well-muscled from punting, shoveling dirt, and hauling marble. Meeting her gaze with a lift of one eyebrow, he smacked his shapely buttocks, the sharp sound enlivening her as if from a dream.

She bit her lower lip. *Goodness.* She was aroused from just looking at him.

"Darling, I want to undress you now," he said.

The request shot a shiver of desire up her spine. "Yes, please."

Beatrice turned her back to him, and William proceeded to unbutton and unhook her bodice, then the waistband of her skirt. He came round to the front and pulled off her bodice, revealing her form-fitting camisole.

He gaped. "You're not wearing a corset."

She stepped out of her skirt. "Mama's part of a new society that thinks corsets are unhealthy." She grinned. "You never knew I rarely wore corsets in Turkey, did you?"

"No. Well, I often had to distract myself from any thought of you other than as my colleague." He untied her petticoat. "That was the most challenging part of the whole expedition." He pulled the garment down, followed by her drawers.

She toed off her pumps before he stripped the stockings from her legs.

He stared at the pearl buttons of the camisole, licking his lips as he unbuttoned the cotton garment. He pulled it over her shoulders and tugged it off revealing her shear chemise.

"You're not wearing anything else under this?"

Beatrice giggled and shook her head.

His quickening breaths fanned her lips as he stripped off the chemise. Wrapping an arm around her waist, he bent his head and took a nipple in his mouth, the warm wetness melting her.

"William," she said, grabbing his hand. "Get into bed."

She clambered onto the mattress and under the covers. He slid in next to her, his skin warm.

"I have a confession," she said, pressing close to his body.

"Oh?" There was a touch of worry in his voice.

"I had a conversation with Lavinia—"

William gulped.

Beatrice ignored his qualms. "She gave me something called a pessary. A woman puts it inside her so that her lover can be free to spend when he's having his crisis."

His alarmed expression softened. "You did this for me?"

"For us."

She rolled on top of him, his erection between their bellies, then slid up until they were face to face, her legs draping across his hips. And had a realization.

"So this is what it would be like for a woman to be on top."

His heart pounded against her chest. "Yes."

She kissed him and maneuvered until his manhood was in the furrow of her naked sex, thick against her entrance.

William pulled back his shaft letting it bounce against the cleft of her buttocks, then placed his hands on both her shoulders.

"Sit up."

Beatrice tucked her legs under her to sit up, straddling him, his cock now rubbing against her tail bone.

"Raise yourself on your knees."

She did so. His cock bounced toward his belly.

William drew a finger through her sex. His lips curled into a crooked grin before he sucked his finger clean.

Oh my. Her body responded as if he had licked her.

"Now grab my cock and slowly lower yourself onto me."

She wrapped her hand around his shaft and aimed it at her entrance, then held him steady as she took him inside her, groaning at the gloriously gratifying sensation.

With a deep inhalation and exhalation, she continued her slide down his shaft until he was embedded to the root.

William let out a moaning sigh with half-closed eyes. "Perfect."

Beatrice lifted and lowered her hips in a slow rhythm, savoring every sensation. A fluttering deep inside enticed her to pick up her pace.

"Yes, oh, yes," William murmured.

A new stirring goaded her to change her angle. With hands on either side of William's head, she leaned forward, rocking her hips—

"Oh God." She clenched around his thickness and fell on top of him. William lifted her back up, his hands on her shoulders.

"Your first crisis, my love."

"First?"

William gripped her by the waist and held her fast as he plunged into her. "How about another?"

"Yes, please."

William took control, holding her while he pumped slowly, increasing his speed with each thrust. She bent over, hands on his shoulders, gripping while another wave of pleasure swept over her.

She shouldn't make a sound, she really shouldn't, but *oh, God,* she wanted to scream his name, confess her love.

Could it get any better than this?

His left hand propping her up, his right hand snaked between their bodies to touch her clitoris. A yelp of surprise escaped her lips.

She bent her head and watched their joining, his fingering, seeing the euphoria she was feeling, his breathy sighs enhancing the experience.

Bracing herself, she let him lead their intimate dance, hoping to find a rhythm so they would reach their crises together.

And then another wave of ecstasy crested and crashed.

She kept her position, his shaft rubbing her in one particularly sensitive spot while his fingers fumbled in their ministrations.

Oh, this was absolute bliss.

She gazed down upon him, his face awash with sensual intoxication, a mirror to her own abandonment.

His finger no longer quested for her pleasure, but no matter. She had found another spot within provoked by every slide of his cock. From the dissolute glassiness of his eyes, she would have to take control.

She grabbed his hands and stretched his arms over his head, pinning him down. His momentary shock melted into excited surprise as his body relaxed, letting her command him. His acquiescence added to the thrill of the clandestine encounter.

Beatrice was determined. She needed release. Pounding her hips against his, focusing on that one spot, that glorious, newly discovered spot, letting the friction take her to the precipice of climax where she wallowed only momentarily until orgiastic joy overcame her. She gulped down her cry of release as William jerked upwards, groaning as he came inside her.

With a sigh of satiation, she slumped to his side, sweaty and blissfully exhausted.

William cuddled her close. "Oh, Bea, that was wonderful."

She snuggled against him. "I can't wait until we're free to make love and spend the night together all the time."

"I often think about the terrace, in the pavilion, sleeping all night in each other's arms."

"Yes. That was lovely." She raised herself on an elbow. "William, I talked to Mama, and she and Papa will allow you to be a house guest when your family is not staying in town."

"Oh?"

"And then Mama said it would be all right for you to spend the night in my bed."

He blinked. "I dare say that is most unconventional."

"As are my parents."

"As are you." He kissed her forehead then slid out of bed. He rummaged in his jacket on the bench, then returned to her side. He held out a small blue silk bag with a satin drawstring. "For you."

She sat against the headboard and opened the bag, spilling the contents into her palm. A ring with stones of green turquoise shot with veins of gold was slung through a gold chain. She stared at him. "This is beautiful."

"A promise ring." He opened the clasp and placed the chain around her neck. "The stones are the same color as your eyes."

She fingered the cool ring. "Are we engaged?"

He shrugged. "You eschew marriage." He wrapped his arm around her. "I'm not sure I want to get married either. I want an academic career, and marriage might limit my opportunities for fellowships." He kissed the top of her head. "Whatever our futures may hold, I promise I'll always be there for you."

"When I come into my legacy, I'll buy a house in Cambridge. You can be my lodger. No one will know."

"People will probably figure out our relationship if we live under the same roof."

"I'll have other lodgers. Men like Mr. Babbage."

He chuckled. "In the meantime, we'll see each other while at university."

"And every spring at Mehmet's temple." She grinned. "After university, I'll finance my own archaeological expeditions."

"To where?"

"Wherever."

"I would like to accompany you on all your adventures, Bea."

She burrowed against his chest, finding comfort there. "And I would love to go on more adventures with you, William." For the rest of their lives.

The Harwell Heirs

Victorian aristocracy has very strict rules concerning marital connections and familial obligations. But the Harwell heirs—Helena, Sophia, and Arthur—discover love doesn't always follow the rules. Scandalous affairs force these scions of society to choose between duty and desire, deference and destiny.

Book 1: *The Pleasure Device*
Helena and Nicholas's story

Book 2: *Disobedience By Design*
Sophia and Joseph's – and Arthur and Joseph's – story

Book 3: *Where Destiny Plays*
Arthur and Lavinia's story

Book 4: *A Delicate Seduction*
Percival and Bertram's story

Book 5: *Discovering Her Delight*
William and Beatrice's story

Book 6: *Their Noble Deceit*
Percival, Bertram, Penelope, and Viola's story

More historical romance by Regina

Victorian
The Westerman Affair (*Art & Discipline* Book 1)
The Invitation (*Art & Discipline* Book 1.5)
Disputed Boundaries (*Stories from the San Juan Islands*)

American Revolution
The General's Wife: An American Revolutionary Tale
Winter Interlude: An American Revolutionary Novelette

About the Author

Regina Kammer is a librarian, an art historian, and an award-winning, international best-selling, multi-published writer of provocative historical romance and contemporary romance with a touch of history. Her short stories and novels make history sexier, whether the era is Roman, Byzantine, Viking, American Revolution, or Victorian. She's even sexed up contemporary settings, Steampunk, and Greco-Roman mythology. She has been published by Cleis Press, Go Deeper Press, Ellora's Cave, House of Erotica, Story Ink, Loose Id, The Naughty Literati, and her own imprint, Viridium Press. She began writing historical fiction with romantic elements during National Novel Writing Month 2006, switching to erotica when all her characters suddenly demanded to have sex.

Keep up with Regina
Check out her website: https://reginakammer.com/
Never miss a new release! Subscribe to *Kammerotica News*:
    https://reginakammer.com/newsletter/